TEARS OF INNOCENCE

TEARS OF INNOCENCE

BILL RAPP

FIVE STAR
A part of Gale, Cengage Learning

GALE
CENGAGE Learning·

Farmington Hills, Mich • San Francisco • New York • Waterville, Maine
Meriden, Conn • Mason, Ohio • Chicago

GALE
CENGAGE Learning·

LIBRARY OF CONGRESS CATALOGING-IN-PUBLICATION DATA

Rapp, Bill.
    Tears of innocence / Bill Rapp. — First edition.
      pages ; cm
    ISBN 978-1-4328-3011-3 (hardcover) — ISBN 1-4328-3011-2
(hardcover) — ISBN 978-1-4328-3006-9 (ebook) — ISBN 1-4328-
3006-6 (ebook)
      1. Americans—Germany—Berlin—Fiction. 2. World War, 1939–
1945—Germany—Berlin—Fiction. 3. Germany—History—1933–
1945—Fiction. I. Title.
    PS3618.A728T43 2015
    813'.6—dc23   2014038269

First Edition. First Printing: February 2015
Find us on Facebook– https://www.facebook.com/FiveStarCengage
Visit our website– http://www.gale.cengage.com/fivestar/
Contact Five Star™ Publishing at FiveStar@cengage.com

Printed in the United States of America
1 2 3 4 5 6 7 19 18 17 16 15

ACKNOWLEDGMENTS

As with any book, there are many acknowledgments the author must make. First of all, I owe much to my wife and daughters for their patience and tolerance as I worked to tell the story of Karl Baier. When I told my wife that I was thinking of another novel set in Berlin but earlier in the immediate postwar years, she suggested I use the situation her late father found himself in when he first arrived there shortly after the end of the war as part of Operation Paperclip. Like Karl Baier, Karl Weber found himself living in a house in the neighborhood of Dahlem that had once belonged to a man with the exact same name, Karl Weber, also a German officer but one who never did return to Berlin. At least not that my father-in-law ever knew. After that, however, their stories diverge, and Karl Baier found himself facing challenges that Karl Weber, thankfully, did not. But I do owe him a debt of gratitude for sharing a part of his postwar history and helping launch Karl Baier on his own career.

CHAPTER ONE

It was the women he would remember best. *Trummerfrauen,* they were called. Rubble women. They provided his first distinct impression of Berlin in the immediate aftermath of the war, the once mighty capital of a thousand-year Reich now shrunken to a ruin of a skeletal remain, more dust and dirt than architecture after just twelve years of Nazi rule. Poverty and privation lingered in every street the jeep passed, as the residents struggled to build a new life and a new city. They also struggled to survive.

Captain Karl Baier had arrived at Tempelhof airport just hours earlier, a warm September sun splashing the long patched runways with a bright flash of yellow and lining the gray rubble-strewn streets with pillars of light and warmth. The shredded remains from a handful of German Focke-Wulf fighters lay huddled to the side of an open field, outlined by the broad semi-circle of Tempelhof's main terminal built in the pseudo-classical style so beloved by Nazi architects like Albert Speer. Now it was a bombed-out relic that stretched for over a kilometer, a source of pride for the Nazi regime while it lasted. A scent that first reminded him of smoldering charcoal from cookouts back home but then more like burnt wood from a damp fireplace drifted by every few blocks, a smell that seemed out of place in the large city on a sunny afternoon. Then he noticed all the women.

"Why are the women wearing their overcoats on such a beautiful day?" Baier asked his driver.

The jeep alternated between a breath-robbing speed impossible in American cities and a crawl through piles of debris, burnt-out vehicles, and Germans who seemed to drift aimlessly among the streets and sidewalks. Except for the rubble women. They had a purpose, working without pause sorting bricks from the bombed-out buildings, chipping off the old mortar, then passing them down along a line of more shapeless female forms in tattered overcoats and dusty, discolored headscarves. At the end, the bricks found themselves stacked carefully at curbside, presumably for future use.

"A couple of reasons, sir, but mostly I think to hide." The corporal shrugged. His name tag said Perkins. He had informed Baier right off that he, Perkins, had been assigned as Baier's driver during his assignment in Berlin. "Also, they don't have a whole lot of much else to wear."

"What are they hiding from?"

"The Russians mostly," Perkins replied. "There's some pretty horrid tales going around, sir, about what the Russkies have done to the German women, especially here in Berlin. I think the gals here don't want their shapes, you know, to give the Russian boys any ideas."

Baier had heard the tales, too. Rapes by the thousands, as the Soviet army exacted its revenge for all that the Germans had done in that country. It had given a fearsome edge and gone well beyond what many had originally expected of the Red Army as it exploited the fruits of victory. There had been tales of other atrocities, too, including brutal, cold-blooded murders, and not just against Nazi criminals and political opponents. The expulsions of Germans from their homes in the east had also led to many deaths. No one was sure just how many, perhaps thousands more. But mostly you heard about the rapes.

Baier pressed on. "Where have you been hearing these tales, Corporal?"

"Oh, all over, sir. But also from the gals themselves. We've gotten to know quite a few here."

"Oh, have you? And have they been telling you how much nicer and stronger and more handsome the American G.I.s are?" And probably how much less of a scandal it would be for the locals if they connected with an American, since the G.I.s would not seem to bring the same kind of shame, nor did they represent the embodiment of the Bolshevik hordes and Asiatic *Untermenschen*. Or so Baier would expect from the residents of the former capital of Hitler's empire. But they wouldn't say that now, not to the G.I.s.

"Not really, sir. Mostly they're just happy to have someone treat 'em nice. They're mostly scared and hungry. And it's amazing what some chocolates and cigarettes will do."

I can just imagine, Baier thought to himself, a smile creeping across his tired face. The jeep picked up speed as it approached an open stretch of road on *Hohenzollerndamm*, just past *Fehrbellin Platz*, named for one of the victories of the Great Elector, Frederick Wilhelm, the first ruler to begin building Prussian military power in Europe. Baier remembered at least that much from his minor undergraduate readings in history at Notre Dame, studies he had continued to pursue independently after graduation to understand better what had driven the Germans and the rest of Europe toward this quest for power and racial purity. Fat lot it had gotten them now.

A first generation American, Baier was returning to the land of his parents' birth, bitterly disappointed that its people could have given themselves over to such a hideous and criminal enterprise. He thanked the heavens above that the stork had seen fit to drop him down an American chimney, and now he hoped to have the chance to bring some of his New World insight and outlook to this vestige of Old World ignorance and self-destruction. He smiled as they drove through the square, a sense of condescension and triumph infusing his spirit. The streets and sidewalks of Berlin were filled with the defeated Germans who appeared to drift with little purpose through the piles of rubble and debris that had spilled from fallen or shattered buildings over the pathways below. He wondered if they would ever clean up the mess the Nazis had left behind. It was a parade of defeat.

"Thinking of finding your own *Fraulein,* sir?" Perkins matched Baier's smile with a grin of his own.

Baier glanced briefly at his driver, his smile gone. "That's enough, Corporal. Let's remember to show some respect, both to the uniform and the locals." Baier pivoted sideways again as the jeep sped through *Fehrbellinplatz.* He studied a crowd of several dozen civilians gathered around a large wooden billboard with patches of paper covering its entire front, some even spilling beyond the thin wooden border along the sides. "Just what is it that those people are looking at?"

Perkins glanced to Baier's right. "That, sir, is where the Germans look to see if they have any family left and, if so, where they might find them."

"Come again?"

"Well, sir," Perkins continued, "because of all the bombings and expulsions and stuff, families often got torn apart. And then there's some of the soldiers starting to get let out as well. So if someone passes through a town, they'll put a notice up addressed to a family member to tell them they're still alive and where they're headed."

Baier was incredulous. He spun to address Perkins. "Does it work? Does anyone ever find his family?"

Perkins nodded. "Yes, sir. I think so. You hear of a case every so often."

The jeep swung left onto *Kronprinzenallee.* Perkins's face settled into an impassioned, stoical mask. Baier wasn't sure if it was because he had given him a brief reprimand minutes earlier, or if he was bothered by the thought of all those German families ripped apart by a devastating war they had brought upon themselves. They raced past the *Gruenewald,* the urban forest that spread off to the right. Baier decided to reach out to Perkins to make sure he hadn't done any harm to the man's pride. If he was going to be Baier's driver for the duration, then they had to find ways to get along. Besides, Perkins's remarks hadn't seemed all that impertinent. Perhaps Baier had even encouraged him with that talk about the *Trummerfrauen.* He examined Perkins as the driver stared straight ahead, wondering where he had come from, what sort of military record the corporal had achieved, whether he had seen any combat. The man looked disciplined, with his closely cropped blond hair, smooth shaven cheeks, cleaned and starched khaki shirt under a pressed brown jacket that rested comfortably on broad shoulders and a flat stomach. He clearly worked on his appearance, which was a good sign.

His question about finding a woman had not been all that far off the mark. Baier thought back to his own limited experience in the world of love, or sex, since he really wouldn't classify his brief affairs as matters of the heart. Attending an all-boys high school at Loyola in Chicago and then four years of male bonding at Notre Dame had hardly prepared him for that sort of thing. The few women in his life, two to be exact, had not left much of an impression on him or his life. He suspected they could say the same. Maybe there would be more opportunities here, but Baier wondered what sort of restrictions he should follow in setting an example as an officer. Time would tell. Rules against fraternization appeared to have already been left by the proverbial wayside. His colleagues would hopefully be of some help in explaining what behavior was allowed or encouraged.

"Have you seen much of these woods, Corporal?" Baier inclined his head to the right.

"Not yet, sir." Perkins appeared to brighten a bit. "They say there's still some wild animals in there. Boars even. I hear they make good eating."

"I wouldn't be surprised. It was the hunting preserve of the Hohenzollerns."

"The who?" Perkins looked puzzled. He glanced at Baier but then shot his gaze back toward the road.

"The Hohenzollerns. They were the Prussian and later the German rulers. At least until World War I. The Germans lost that one, too."

"Then came the Nazis, right?"

"Well, there was an interlude, of sorts," Baier replied. "The Germans did have a republic for about a decade. Not a very successful one, obviously."

Perkins paused a moment, then spoke up again. "Well, you may get the chance to bag one, sir. You won't be living all that far away. Just over here on this nice side street named *Im Dol.*"

"Yes, perhaps so. But for now I'll stick to canteen food. And I'm pretty sure we're not allowed to do any hunting." He paused for thought. "Not animals, anyway."

"Excuse me, sir?"

Baier smiled and waved at nothing in particular. "Just thinking of my job."

"Hunting Nazis, sir?"

Baier smiled again and glanced at the *Gruenewald.* "Not exactly. But close enough."

The jeep pulled up with a brief squeal of its tires as Perkins halted in front of a sedate, modest, two-story home of red brick, set off from the street by a brown, waist-high wooden fence set in a crisscrossing pattern with a steel gate at its center. A stone path led from there to the front door, a massive wooden structure, oak, Baier guessed, painted black. Shrubbery slightly taller than a man ran along either side of the property, and Baier could see a host of large pines in the backyard, each one peering over the rooftop as though in anticipation of the new owner. Or the new occupant, at least.

"There's a lot that's not allowed here, sir," Perkins stated as he stepped out of the jeep. He marched to the rear and lifted Baier's two bags from the back. "But a lot of folks do them anyway." He glanced at the Captain's suitcases in either hand. "Is this it, sir?"

Baier shook his head, then smiled again. "For now. My trunk will follow in a few days." He studied the driver for a moment. "What sort of thing happens anyway, Corporal? Are we back to the boars . . . or the women? The latter would appear to have their work cut out for them rebuilding this city. At least until the men return. Those who survive and are still fit for physical labor, that is."

Perkins shrugged and looked at the street. He set the bags down. "Oh, all kinds of things. And not necessarily just with the women, sir. It wouldn't be right for me to say, though. I'm sure you can learn more from the other officers in the Command." He hoisted the bags once more and started toward the house. "And I guess you'll find out for yourself soon enough." He paused at the gate and looked back towards the captain. "This Berlin is a strange and fascinating place, sir. Not at all what I expected."

Just what had you expected, Baier wondered. And just what was he expecting, Baier asked himself, and what could he hope to find? It was then that Baier's first impression of the city he had just entered took shape as he glanced down the tree-lined residential street and thought of the drive to his new home. Back in the city center there was no skyline to speak of, no distinguishing architectural markers that make a city unique. Berlin represented little more than a collection of rubble, like some cubist painting. He thought of Picasso's famous painting of Guernica, the Spanish town ironically destroyed by German bombing during that country's civil war. It had all come home to roost here in the Third Reich's capital, and with a vengeance. Baier wondered if the city's moment in history had passed, if all the glamour and global impact had departed and passed him by in the process. He asked himself if there was any excitement left in this city, any adventures to be found.

CHAPTER TWO

It began with a laundry ticket. Not his own, at least not the American named Karl Baier. He had been living in his modest three-bedroom house for nearly a week, and it was the first opportunity Baier had found to poke about and become more familiar with his new home, the place where he'd be living for the next year or two. He couldn't be sure, because his deployment in Berlin really depended on the work. Baier had been sent to Berlin shortly after the Americans had first arrived in the city back in July, ordered to get his hands on the German industrial and scientific records and the people behind them as soon as possible. Which meant before the Soviets—and possibly the British and French as well—shipped everything back home. The Soviets were already dismantling entire factories for transportation back to Mother Russia, and Baier was there to find what records and experts he could and grab them for the good guys or, at the very least, obtain copies and depositions.

Baier had started his mission back in Frankfurt, working with the Enemy Personnel Exploitation Section, a program established to pick the minds and explore the backgrounds of the German scientific and industrial leaders. His wartime service had actually begun with the Office of Strategic Services, or OSS in more popular parlance, but Baier had never felt at home either in the analytic side of the business or during his training for the operations behind enemy lines for which the OSS was better known. Fortunately, he had never qualified for an air drop during the fighting and had found himself working with US Army intelligence as the war drew to a close, reporting to the Office of the Military Government, United States, through its Office of the Director of Intelligence. He had transferred over as soon as the future of the OSS became apparent. Despite "Wild Bill" Donovan's insistent recommendations that the OSS be converted to a peacetime intelligence agency, President Truman had demurred and abolished the organization shortly after the Japanese surrender.

Baier had begun working through the documentation at I. G. Farben in Frankfurt, the chemical giant that was turning out to have been not only supportive of the Nazi regime but also intimately involved in the extermination campaigns that came to light once the Allies had moved in. His task had been made much easier by the building having survived the war intact, and Baier uncovered boxes of scientific and historical treasure. During his research, however, he marveled at how many of these people were still at large, and he worried about the loss of their expertise should they never be found. At least, lost insofar as the Americans were concerned. And there was always the nagging issue of retribution and punishment for the crimes many had committed. But their culpability and guilt were another matter, and not one for which he was responsible. Frankfurt and its environs, in any case, were also crawling with Americans, and no Soviets. "Get your ass to Berlin, son," his superiors in Army intelligence had barked after reading an order signed by none other than General Lucius Clay, the US Military Governor for Germany. Major Frank Delvecchio, a hardscrabble and twice-wounded OSS officer from Brooklyn, had arranged everything after shouting that order in Baier's ear just before Delvecchio's organization had been disbanded. The man carried a great deal of personal authority thanks to his service with the Jedburgh units in Normandy, and Baier had marveled at the man's ability to get the Army's bureaucracy to work in such a short and efficient time span. Within a month, Baier was stepping off his plane at Tempelhof.

In Berlin, Baier's office was a modest room on the second floor of the two-story building that had formerly served as *Luftwaffe* headquarters but now housed the American command. His workspace contained just enough room for his desk, two shelves along the wall to his right, two chairs in front for visitors, and just enough space to walk from the door to the window at his back without having to suck in your stomach after a prolonged exposure to German beer and dumplings. Although part of a six-man team overseen by Major Frank Younger, Baier enjoyed a fair amount of autonomy in his pursuit of the former Reich's scientific and industrial refugees, thanks in no small part to his near-fluent German and a chemistry degree from Notre Dame, a subject his boss claimed was akin to alchemy.

Baier had already spent the better part of three days wandering around the Siemans compound just down the stretch of local Autobahn known as the *Avus*. That little bit of highway had supposedly been used as a runway for planes loaded with people—most of them high-ranking regime figures—fleeing the city as the Soviets closed in. Now it was a rare piece of open road bisecting burnt-out forest and bombed-out buildings. But Perkins told Baier that he enjoyed opening up his jeep whenever he could, so he had been happy for the assignment. It impressed the Germans, he claimed, since they enjoyed speeding on their highways more than most, maybe even more than invading Poland or France. Or maybe it was a temporary substitute, he joked.

In any case, Baier took the opportunity of an early evening at home to roam the first floor, peeking in closets and pulling out drawers, wondering if he'd find any clues about the family that

17

had lived there before him. Down at his office, the branch secretary claimed that the Allies had dispossessed only the worst Nazis, or families who had seized the properties of the disenfranchised and disappeared Jews, all of which would be returned when the rightful owners or their heirs were located. Baier doubted that the worst of the Nazis had lived so unostentatiously, but then again, he never knew what he might discover in these old cabinets. One OSS warrior had shown him boxes of machine guns, all loaded, that he had discovered in the basement of one high-ranking general back in Wiesbaden.

Baier did not find anything that exotic. A colorful collection of landscapes adorned the walls, none of which appealed to Baier. Most of the paintings were of the Bavarian Alps, but the Baltic coastline was also represented. The previous owner's taste in literature appeared to be confined to German authors from the previous century, with a heavy dose of the German Romantics. Baier came across one well-preserved first edition of Novalis's *Hymns to the Night* that he considered worthy of confiscation as war booty. Also represented were authors that must have been considered safe in the Third Reich, like Fontane and Sturm. All in all, the house, with its solid furniture and typical middle-class taste in art, reflected what the Germans would call "Biedermaier," pointing to someone who may not have been an ardent Nazi but certainly played it safe. Still, there was that copy of *The Buddenbrooks* by Thomas Mann on the shelf. The story was innocent enough, but the author had been disapproved of enough to have most of his work land on some of Goebbels's piles of burning books.

When Baier pulled the copy to study it, a worn paperback version of Heinrich Mann's *Der Untertan,* or *Man of Straw,* fell to the floor. Now this was more like it. A brother of the more famous Thomas, his book had definitely been banned, and the author had fled to France after the Nazi seizure of power. And there, tucked behind the row of Fontane's novels, was *Der Zauberberg*, or *The Magic Mountain*, Thomas Mann's allegory of Europe between the wars set in a Swiss tubercular clinic. Now the previous occupant was beginning to take shape as a real and even interesting person. Baier suddenly found himself imagining what the man had been like, if it would be possible to find him. Baier saw the two of them sitting together late into the night over a schnapps or brandy, discussing the events that had propelled Germany to its fateful end. Baier even imagined himself convincing this German of the superiority of the New World over the Old. Of course, this fantasy assumed the man was not a war criminal. If he was, though, would he have owned books like these?

First he needed a name, at least, and some information that might help him locate the individual would be even better. The best he could find right now, though, was an old laundry claim ticket he came across one evening that had been resting at the back of a drawer in a table set at the far corner of his living room. The first floor possessed an L-shaped design for the living and dining room, with an alcove that provided a vista out onto the backyard. Like the rest of the furniture, the table looked to be a solid piece of oak, a work table or desk of some sort with a single drawer in the middle and crafted well enough to survive several wars. There was an assortment of pens and pencils, as well as a postcard and some photographs of several German officers in Athens during the war. Baier wondered if one of them had been the previous occupant of the house.

But there was something truly odd about the laundry ticket. Baier stared at the slip of paper for several minutes wondering if this was some sort of joke. It had his name on it. Karl Baier. He certainly didn't remember dropping anything off to be cleaned at the Hoffmann *Reinigungsgeschaeft* on *Koenigin Louise Strasse*. And it absolutely could not have happened on the date stamped on the ticket: March 5, 1945.

Baier held the ticket pressed between his thumb and forefinger long enough to leave an imprint. Shadows danced across the backyard as a smooth breeze rippled the pines and the sun sank lower on the horizon. A half-dozen of those European crows hopped from lawn to branch or back, their gray bodies and black wings giving an American the impression that the birds had somehow changed their feathers after a long transatlantic flight. Baier's glance shifted from the ticket to the photograph from Athens, while his mind tried to sort through a puzzle that as yet had only two pieces.

Overcome by curiosity, he jumped up, ran to his bedroom upstairs, and changed into some civilian clothes: gray slacks, and a blue v-neck sweater over his khaki military shirt. Nothing fancy, but still a cut well above the war refugee look so common in Berlin these days. His main goal was to make a positive impression but also avoid having the proprietor retreat into a shell the moment he walked into the shop. That would happen soon enough, probably when he spoke and the owner and other customers were able to identify him as an American, which his clothes would probably do in any case. But at least he would not come across as Russian, or even French. Baier's German was pretty good. He had spoken it occasionally at home, whenever his grandparents visited his parents' house. It was their first language, clearly the one they felt most comfortable with after their emigration to America at the turn of the century with his father in tow as a young child. His mother had also emigrated with her family, and they both considered it fortuitous to have met each other in their new homeland. But they had also agreed to speak primarily English at home so their children would not be looked down upon as outsiders. Baier had begun with conversational patches, built on that at school, and his stint in Frankfurt had obviously helped further. But he was still not going to pass for a native, especially in Berlin.

After changing, Baier took the ten-minute walk along *Kronprinzenallee* to reach the American compound. In the main foyer Baier found Perkins lounging with a half-dozen other enlisted men, several of whom were sharing a pack of Lucky Strikes. Baier told him to grab the jeep for a short ride.

"How short, sir?"

"We're not going far," Baier explained. "I'd walk, but I'm not sure exactly how far it is." He stopped to let Perkins catch up. "Why? Did you have something planned with one of the locals?" Baier shot the driver a quick smile to let him know he meant this to be a friendly comment.

Perkins shrugged, tossing his cigarette onto the driveway when they got outside. "It can wait, sir."

As it turned out, the trip was not very far at all. The drive took less than ten minutes, down along *Koenigin Louise Strasse* to *Koenigin Louisen Platz*. The laundry shop was a small establishment nestled into a comfortable spot just around the corner from *Podbielski Allee*. Comfortable because the building seemed to have escaped major damage, unlike most of the rest of the block. The masonry out front was pockmarked from bullets and shrapnel, a fairly common sight in Berlin, but the structure itself looked pretty solid. Half the second floor windows were gone, and from what Baier could see there did not appear to be much left inside on that floor. He couldn't speak for the floor above, however, and Baier wondered if anyone lived above the shop. Probably, since housing was at a premium in the city. Beggars can't be choosers and all that. And Berlin did not have many choosers these days, certainly not among the Germans. Baier instructed Perkins to wait in the jeep.

A small bell jingled as Baier opened the door. A middle-aged German, somewhere in his mid- to late forties, Baier guessed, emerged from a back room separated from the rest of the shop by a row of beaded strings. They gave what was almost an exotic feel to the divide, as though a non-European or non-German world waited just beyond the opening. A small circle of light reached out from the back room, spreading a mild glow through the shop's gloomy interior and stretching the shadows poking out from the shelves as dusk spread along the walls from the sky outside. A damp smell hung in the air, as though the moisture from past rains had seeped through a broken roof and saturated the walls. The owner parked himself at a spot behind the counter with his legs spread, as though daring Baier to try to take even a single step closer.

The exotic feeling evaporated as soon as the proprietor spoke. The man had closely cropped light brown hair, something that reminded Baier of a military style, although many German soldiers seemed to have worn their hair pretty long, at least by American standards. Baier wondered if this individual had served in the *Wehrmacht* despite his more advanced age. Few in this country had been spared military service of some sort, especially in the later years of the war. From what he had seen in the POW camps, it was mostly the too young and the too old who had been conscripted at the end, but this German's solid build and broad shoulders would have made him fit for front-line service, even if they were hidden under a worn brown sweater that was becoming unwound at the edges. At least in Baier's humble opinion. He asked himself just how the man had spent the war years, the same question so many Americans, and the other Allies, were posing about most of the German males they encountered.

"Can I help you?" the man asked in heavy guttural German. He sounded as though he came from the country, speaking as he did a form of the *Plattdeutsch* one often found in Germany's rural areas. But this did save Baier from the nearly impenetrable

Berlin dialect, where the *g*'s and *ch*'s just seemed to disappear. Baier worked to keep the dialogue going in the finest High German he could muster.

"Yes, I was hoping these clothes might still be here." Baier extended the ticket.

The German took the slip and inspected it. His face showed no expression, not even curiosity, which Baier found odd. After all, the clothes would have been sitting on a shelf for about seven or eight months now. He realized at that moment that if the clothes were indeed still there, they might be carrying a hefty fee if they were claimed.

But the German only stared. He glanced once at Baier, then back at the ticket, chewing his lower lip. "We are closed now. Perhaps you could come back tomorrow." He paused, pursing his lips to give them some relief while he studied the ticket. Then he looked up at Baier again. "Who are you? And how did you get this?" he asked. There was an informal touch, maybe even a hint of politeness in the inquiry, but it was also clear he was challenging Baier's right to the clothes.

"Well, I believe I'm living in the man's house, and I found this in a drawer. I thought it was the least I could do to retrieve the gentleman's clothes, in case he comes back." He paused. "I gather you are Herr Hoffmann."

The owner nodded absentmindedly while he considered Baier's explanation for twenty or thirty seconds. Then he shook his head. "No, I'm sorry. There's nothing here anymore."

"Are you sure?" Baier pressed. "You haven't even looked."

"Yes, I'm quite sure. But I'll ask my wife." He barked a name over his shoulder that Baier could not pick out from the garbled rural dialect. It sounded almost like "Susan" or "Sandra."

A thin woman with light brown, almost blond, hair and piercing hazel eyes strolled forward and peered through the beads. She carried a worn, woolen shawl of green and yellow with

23

geometric patterns around her shoulders. Her stare burned through Baier as though he was personally responsible for the wanton destruction the Allied air raids had inflicted on this city and all the others in Germany. Beyond her face, Baier could see little more than a shadow, but he was struck by how much younger she looked than her husband. Somewhere in her early thirties, he guessed.

Without pulling his gaze from Baier, the proprietor switched and rattled off a string of Berliner dialect, from which Baier could discern only his own or his German antecedent's name, the reference to the house, the clothes, and an occasional *"immer noch."* It was as though he was challenging Baier to follow the conversation. When she answered her gaze, too, hung on Baier like the talons from the Imperial German eagle that could occasionally still be found about town. *"Of course not"* and *"Don't be ridiculous"* were two phrases that had come in High German, presumably for Baier's benefit.

"No, of course, I understand," Baier said. "It would be quite improbable. I was just curious. You never know, so much has happened here."

"Yes, certainly understandable." The proprietor had returned to a mixture of *Platt* and proper German as well.

Baier held out his hand for the ticket. "I'll just take that with me then."

The German's hand shot back out of Baier's reach. "But you have no need of it anymore."

"Still, it belongs to Herr Baier. So I think I should keep it in case he returns."

The shop owner's hand did not move. Neither did his eyes, which remained fixed on Baier. "Perhaps you could give us your name, and we can contact you if we find anything." His hand swept the air behind him. "Things are still quite confused here."

"Well," Baier explained, "this may sound a bit odd, but my

24

name is also Karl Baier."

The German's jaw literally dropped. Not quite to the floor, or the counter even, but an inch or two nonetheless. Yellow teeth peered out at the world beyond. Baier noticed that two were broken. War wounds perhaps. "Are you a relative? From America?"

Baier shook his head and smiled. "No, nothing that close. It's really pure coincidence. We just happen to have the same name. That's another reason I thought I'd do him this favor."

The German and the American visitor stared at each other, as though daring the other to make the first move.

It was the wife who broke the stalemate. She stepped forward and brushed aside the strings of beads in the middle of the doorway and maneuvered between them. Her eyes narrowed further as she studied Baier's face, but now the hostility had gone, replaced by a deep curiosity. After about a minute's silence, she strolled to the door, took in the jeep parked out front, then ambled past Baier in a more relaxed manner. She even wore a smile, which she beamed at Baier when she stopped and stood before him. Her gaze roamed his face, as though she was memorizing the details. Then she continued her retreat back into her sanctuary. "Oh, give it back, Ernst." Her voice seemed to escape from the back of her head as she sauntered away and the words drifted through the beads. "Perhaps Herr Baier will return someday, and then he will ask what became of his clothes. And other things."

A slight grin, or at least that's what Baier assumed it was, crossed Ernst Hoffmann's face. "Sure. I suppose you might as well keep it."

His hand moved slowly forward, and Baier grabbed the ticket before it was halfway across the counter. "Thank you. I'm sure Herr Baier will appreciate this."

Baier turned and started toward the door. Just before he

pulled it open, Baier turned. "And do you have any idea where this Herr Baier might be? I would like to meet him."

Ernst stared past the visitor, his gaze drifting to the door and the street beyond. He shrugged. "It's difficult to say. He could be anywhere. Why do you wish to meet him?"

It was Baier's turn to shrug. "No particular reason. I'm just curious, seeing as how I'm living in his house."

The woman's eyes stayed focused on Baier with a look that reflected a blend of mischief and a curiosity of her own. "We do know that he isn't here, though. We really can't say any more than that." Her smile broadened. "That's the way it is in Germany these days."

Baier nodded in appreciation and agreement, strode through the door, and walked back to the jeep waiting at the curb.

"How'd it go, sir?" Perkins inquired. "Did you get what you needed?" He was leaning forward, apparently eager to get a glimpse inside. Baier wondered if he had ever had the occasion or the need to visit a German shop.

"Not really, Corporal. It was all rather odd, actually."

"What was it all about? You don't have any clothes there, do you?"

"No, I don't."

"Then what was it, sir?"

"I wish I knew. I thought I was tying up a loose end, but I have the funny feeling I may have untied a knot instead."

"How so, sir?" Perkins gave up trying to peer inside the laundry shop and started the engine.

"I'm not sure," Baier replied. "But I had the funny feeling that they were uncomfortable with my being there. It was almost like they knew more than they were letting on."

26

CHAPTER THREE

A week later, Berlin sat under a dim gray blanket after two days of intermittent rain. Baier thought of the *Trummerfrauen,* wondering if they had to continue their task of dismantling and cleaning the city in such wretched weather. His thoughts drifted with the clouds that hovered far enough in the distance as they merged into a ceiling of depression, even gloom, while they hid the sun and turned the city into a darker shade of gray. Maybe this sort of mood was what brought so many Germans to vote for the Nazis and then accept their seemingly anointed fate, first as pliant subjects, then as conquering warriors, and finally as merchants of death, often their own.

"Jesus, but you look bleak. The weather got you down?"

Baier wheeled in his chair to find Dick Savage, one of the civilian political advisors shipped in by the State Department, leaning against the door frame to Baier's office. Savage was like-able enough, even sympathetic at times. Unlike Baier, he had arrived in Europe in the fall of 1944, although he had never served in the military. Savage had been one of the first gradu-ates of the School for Military Government run at the University of Virginia campus in Charlottesville and then shipped to Paris, where he waited impatiently for the US Army to liberate Germany so he could receive his first assignment. Not that Paris hadn't been enjoyable, especially for an epicurean man-of-the-world that Savage liked to make himself out to be. But he was ambitious and dedicated. So the bars and nightlife of the

French capital had proven to be only a temporary and not wholly satisfactory diversion. His break came in late November when Savage was assigned as an administrative and political advisor to Mayor Oppendorf in Aachen after the liberation of that city in October, an assignment that came to an abrupt and brutal end with Oppendorf's assassination in March, 1945. After that, Savage spent several more months fermenting in Paris before General Lucius Clay sent him to Berlin to assist in the revitalization of German political life, which was allowed to revive once again after the victorious Allies agreed to it at the conference at Potsdam. In August, party reorganization was permitted, and Savage spent the bulk of his time shuffling between the well-established Social Democrats and the newly formed Christian Democratic Union.

Through it all, Savage never lost his sense of bureaucratic competence and good humor. His impeccable dress—always in a suit and tie and never without his jacket—certainly gave him the air of proper intent and appearance. Today's edition was a smart gray herringbone number set off with a white shirt and a blue tie worthy of a Frank Lloyd Wright design. But Savage's demeanor and confidence were also a welcome aid as Baier and so many others sought to navigate the administrative morass that emerged when the US Army, three other Allied forces, and the chaos of a destroyed capital were thrown together in the space of a single city.

"So what's got you so bothered?" Savage pressed.

Baier smiled. "Well, the weather for sure. But I was also asking myself how useful it's going to be to try to run down any scientific work the Germans had been pursuing here."

"Ah, you mean the nuclear stuff?"

"Principally, but there's some other stuff as well," Baier replied. "Especially on the chemical and industrial front. People in Washington are stunned at some of the advances the Germans made there. The major brains on the nuclear program, at least in the field of physics, are still holed up over in England."

"Fat lot of good it'll do the Limeys. The Brits were never really in that game," Savage chuckled. "Then again, if anyone can pull those guys into the major leagues it will be the Krauts they've squirreled away."

"I thought Heisenberg and his cronies never made much progress in that area."

Savage shook his head. "Depends on whom you ask. There are those who believe that the lack of progress was intentional."

"Well," Baier conceded, "it'll be up to the British to find out, I guess."

"Or the Soviets. You know they were able to send several nuclear experts from the *Kaiser Wilhelm Gesellschaft* home before we even got here."

Baier nodded with a grimace. "Yeah, I know. They had the run of this place for way too long. I'm surprised there's anything left at all. Lord knows what else they made off with."

Savage straightened while his hand trawled in the right pocket of his suit jacket. He stepped towards Baier's desk and held out a slip of notebook paper. "Perkins was looking for you earlier. He wanted you to have this."

Baier reached for the note. "This morning?" Savage nodded. "Thanks. He must have come by while I was over at the Physics Institute here in Dahlem. Either that or while I was out at lunch."

"You mean the place where Heisenberg worked? Is that what put you to wondering?"

Baier nodded, reading the note.

"Well, I've got to run to a meeting at the *Rathaus.*"

"And how's that going?" Baier smiled. "Are elections looming on the horizon? Have you converted them to a Teutonic version of Democrats and Republicans yet?"

Savage gave him a disappointed look. "Hardly. We can't seem to get the Russians to agree to anything." He shrugged. "But it's still early. And I can guess why they're so suspicious of anything we want to do to revive political life here so soon. Besides, the Germans don't exactly have a lot of recent experience to build on. In any case, I'm sure you're making a lot more progress, especially during your afternoons at Siemans." His eyes rolled. "And I'm dying to hear all about it."

Savage slipped away, but Baier barely noticed. His mind had become completely absorbed in the odd slip of paper wedged between his fingers. Written in German, the slip held a bewildering, yet fascinating message: "If you would like to learn more about Karl Baier, you can meet me at the Hohenzollern *Jagdschloss* in the *Gruenewald*. I will wait there every afternoon from 2 to 3 for the next week. I will recognize you."

There was no date and no name. Baier wanted to know not only who had written and passed the note to Perkins, but also how his driver had come by it. That last point, however important, was also academic just now. Although he had barely finished reading the note, Baier knew one thing already. He would go. He had been thinking about that visit to the *Reinigungsgeschaeft* on and off for the last week, and, if anything, his interest in his German namesake had grown. There was just too much coincidence here. It was just too damn intriguing.

He waited through a decent interval of about thirty minutes after Savage had strolled off before hustling over to the motor pool in search of his driver. Baier found him toweling off the side of the jeep, obviously having given it a thorough washing. If Perkins was anything, he was proud of the vehicle and treated it as though it were his own. Which it was, in a way, Baier conceded. A bucket with suds brimming at mid-level or scattered over the concrete surrounding the jeep testified to his devotion.

"Perkins, can you come here a sec?"

Perkins tossed the damp towel onto the driver's seat. "What's up, sir? I'm finished here if you need to go somewhere."

Baier shook his head. "No, that's all right." He held up the note. "I wanted some information on this. Like why, when, and where."

Perkins's gaze took in the slip of paper, but then his glance dropped to the ground before climbing back up and settling on Baier. "Well, sir, it was kind of strange. It was a local about my size, but pretty thin. I'd never seen him before. He was wearing a gray suit that looked pretty worn, kind of like he didn't own any other clothes. And he had a hat, too, one of those *Wehrmacht* things that are round, you know, with a bill at the front. Like a baseball cap."

"His age? Any distinguishing features?"

Perkins grimaced. "Geez, sir, it's hard to say. It looked like he'd been through a lot. But then most of them do. This one didn't appear to have any major wounds, though. He did keep his one hand in his coat pocket most of the time, and when he brought it out with that note, I noticed that he had a couple fingers missing. Two, I think. On the end."

"And how old would you say he was?" Baier pressed.

"Maybe forty, or a few years older. Then again, they've all aged pretty fast in the past year or two."

"I see." Baier studied the slip of paper. "And how did you come by it?"

"Well, that was kind of funny, sir. A couple of us noticed him hanging around by Berliner Street. So I walked over to check the guy out. Once he saw me, his eyes lit up like I was a long-lost relative or something. Then he got this sly kind of grin and asked me to give that to you, sir."

"He didn't give a name, or mention who it was from?"

Perkins shook his head. "Sorry, sir. He took off right after.

31

It was like he was in a real hurry."

Baier thought for a moment. "Have you read this?"

Perkins's eyes studied the ground again as though he was counting the cracks in the cement, almost certainly, Baiers determined, to avoid his Captain's stare. When he answered, Perkins's gaze stayed riveted to the ground at his feet. "Well, yes, sir, I did. I wanted to make sure it wasn't something bad, sir, like a threat."

At least he's honest, Baier thought. "That's all right, this time. But I expect you to respect my privacy at all times in the future, Corporal."

"Yes, sir." Perkins apologized with a salute, which Baier returned haphazardly. "Do you want me to take you there to that hunting castle? That's what *Jagdschloss* means, doesn't it?" Perkins gestured towards the jeep. "It's all clean and ready."

Baier shook his head and looked off in the direction of the *Gruenewald*. "No, that's all right. I'll take it from here." He turned to go. "Besides, it's too late for this afternoon."

Baier gave a last glance at his driver before returning to his office, hoping Perkins might reveal something more in his face, a shifting of the eyes, a slight grin, or even a wrinkled forehead. Something to suggest foreknowledge, concern, suspicion, envy even. But the corporal's face remain passive, inert, more like a Sphinx than a G.I. Baier remembered how interested Perkins had been in his visit to the laundry shop and decided he'd do some checking later on his own to find out what role, if any, Perkins had to play in this unfolding mystery. The man was becoming an enigma of his own, given his talk about the black market, all the German women, and the mysteries of Berlin in general. Baier had the distinct feeling that there was more to Perkins than a military chauffeur.

CHAPTER FOUR

In the end, Baier waited two full days before heading off to his encounter at the *Jagdschloss*. Going the very next day was out of the question, he decided. After all, he did not want to appear desperate or over eager. Baier thought it would be necessary to skip the day after as well. And then, there was the weather. It cleared the day after he had received the note, but Baier wanted to give the ground some extra time to dry out if he was going to hike through the forest.

It took Baier about half an hour to reach the castle, twenty minutes if he hadn't lost his way. But he found the path back to the main road, *Huettenweg*, again easily enough. There were numerous other hikers out for an afternoon stroll, probably to escape their shattered homes and lives. Baier also saw some French and British soldiers, and even a few Americans. But no Soviets. Baier assumed they were kept on a much tighter leash.

Just as he was thinking about those Soviet allies, Baier stumbled upon an opening in the forest that led first to the edge of a large lake that backed up against a compound of white stucco and was bordered by an overgrowth of what appeared to be marsh grasses of some sort. Baier had yet to familiarize himself with the local fauna, but he figured about the only things alive in that water were carp and bacteria. He wondered if the lake had looked so poorly tended back in the days when Prussia's former royal family had visited for their little hunting excursions.

Just beyond the water's edge the footpath that Baier had been following curled around and opened onto a broad walkway that was fronted by a low, single-story white stucco building under a red-tiled roof. Baier guessed this would have been the stables. When he walked into the courtyard, Baier discovered that this particular building formed one side of an enclosure that surrounded much of the compound but left the side facing the lake uncovered. Probably so the noble visitors could have a better view, he concluded. The enclosure looked as though it had also contained a kitchen, probably a storehouse, and at least some of the servants' quarters. At the end of one side stood a three-story structure, more a villa than a castle by Baier's estimation, also built with white stucco and the same red-tiled roof. In the middle of the side facing the courtyard stood a turret that looked as though it had served primarily as a stairwell. No medieval fortress here, he noted, just a weekend hunting lodge for some European royalty.

In front of the turret stood a thin man about the same height as Perkins. He was wearing a threadbare gray suit, holding a cap in his right hand, with his left stuffed inside his coat pocket. He smiled in Baier's direction and marched over.

"Herr Hauptmann," he began in German. *"Melde gehorsamst."* "Reporting most obediently for duty," or something similar, and Baier half expected him to click his heels but then realized he didn't have the boots for it. Instead, his shoes appeared to be coming apart at the seams.

"You can forget that stuff," Baier replied in German. He suddenly found himself irritated that he had run out to this meeting, beckoned by a local, about whom he knew nothing. But he was also finding himself increasingly intrigued by the prospect of learning not just more about his German namesake, but also the world he had occupied before it all came crashing down around him and everyone else in this stricken country. Still, he would have to put this Kraut in his place. "Your *Wehrmacht,* or whatever you served in, is no more. Dropped in the dustbin of history where it belongs."

The German was immediately obsequious. He even bowed. "Yes, of course. I agree. Now we can build a new Germany. Will your country be staying to help?" the stranger queried.

"That's not up to me. But what does any of that have to do with your note? I did not come here to discuss world politics, least of all with you. It *was* your note, correct?"

"Oh, yes. Most certainly."

"Let's start with a name," Baier pressed. "And then tell me how you know about me."

The stranger swallowed and surveyed the other visitors before continuing. "You wouldn't perhaps have a cigarette, would you?"

Baier pulled a pack of Lucky Strikes from the inside pocket of his jacket, shook one loose, and offered it to his companion. Baier did not smoke, but he had taken to carrying a pack or two with him because, for whatever reason, these cigarettes had emerged as a sort of second currency in town.

The man's eyebrows arched. "An entire pack of Luckies can be quite valuable. Easily worth a day's food for several people, possibly more."

Baier held out the pack. The stranger grabbed for it, but Baier held tight. "Your name?"

"Joachim is my given name. Joachim Kleinwisser."

"Don't be clever, Mr. Know-Nothing," Baier admonished. He held tight to the cigarettes.

"But it's true. I know very little. All of what I do know, however, I'm prepared to pass along to you."

Baier released the Luckies. "So get started. How did you come to know of me and where to find my driver?"

Pocketing his loot, Joachim smiled, then raised one of the cigarettes to his lips. He lit it with a small wooden match that he struck against the sole of his shoe with a small shower of sparks, then blew a lungful of smoke into the air around them both as his smile widened.

"Ah, thank you very much. You Americans are truly a generous people. It only makes sense to fight you if one is certain to lose. But you I know because I was at the cleaners the other day when you came by. I was in the back room. That's how I knew your driver as well. I watched you leave."

"What were you doing there?"

"Visiting my sister. She's the woman with whom you spoke."

"The wife of the owner?"

Joachim smiled again and drew another mouthful from the cigarette. It sparked and crackled, then Joachim held it out from his face for several moments, savoring the taste and rush of nicotine. "Not his wife, not legally. Yes, she lives with him and has for almost three months now."

"I'm glad for her," Baier said. "And him. She's very attractive."

The smile returned, and Joachim's head shook as he glanced at the ground. "You shouldn't be." He looked back up into Baier's eyes. "She was Karl Baier's wife before he disappeared."

"Come again?" Baier took a step back, glancing at the other visitors in the courtyard in an effort to gather his thoughts. "Why didn't she say anything at the shop?" The German shrugged and smiled again. Baier stepped in closer. "Don't play games with me. I'll have people come over there and tear that shop apart. I can always think of a pretext." Baier was surprised at how quickly this man had irritated him, and over a subject of such little importance, more a matter of personal curiosity.

"Oh, but I'm not. It's the truth. Legally she remains married to Karl Baier. So perhaps she should be living with you. You did say you find her attractive."

"Don't be ridiculous," Baier shot back. "Is that why you

asked to speak to me here?"

"Have you found a *Fraulein* yet, *Herr Hauptmann*? An American officer could do quite well here. You'd be amazed at how easy it is sometimes."

"Stop it," Baier barked. "You sound like a pimp for your own sister." He paused and studied the other visitors again for a moment before continuing. "When did Baier disappear, and where was it? On the eastern front? That seems to be where so many of you have vanished."

Joachim tossed the cigarette stub at the ground and crushed it with his heel. "Yes, we believe so. Sometime in March. He was last seen during the fighting around Budapest. Do you know of that battle? Very vicious. It was our one last attempt at an offensive to keep the Bolsheviks out of the Fatherland."

"Yes, I know of it. And the losses. As many civilians as soldiers, I might add. Is that when you last had contact with him?"

Joachim shook his head. He fingered another Lucky, then seemed to think better of it and slipped it back into the pack. "Our last letter came from Athens, but we also spoke with him when he returned to Berlin last January, just before his transfer to Hungary."

"What was he doing in Greece?"

"He was assigned to occupation duty and was fighting the partisans much of the time. It was a dirty war down there."

"So I heard. When was the letter sent or received? And what did it say?"

"It crossed paths with him during his stay in Berlin. It arrived shortly after he returned to the fighting."

"And the message?"

Joachim's sly grin returned. "Come now. As you can no doubt imagine, it was a letter to his wife, so it remains a very private thing. She never told me of its contents."

"And there's been nothing since?" Baier pressed. "You're not even sure he's alive?"

Joachim nodded. His left hand slipped back inside his jacket. "That's correct. We heard that his unit had been transferred to Budapest when the Soviets began their encirclement of the city. It seems he got there just in time to be surrounded. We keep trying to find something out. I was wondering if you could help. Is there someplace you could check?"

Baier nodded in turn. So that's what this was about, he told himself. They wanted a favor to find a family member. And he just happened to have the same name. "I might be able to make a few calls." He realized only then that he was staring at Joachim's pocketed hand.

"I, too, fought in some vicious battles, especially in France. I was wounded twice by your army, *Herr Hauptmann,* at Normandy and in the Ardennes. Fortunately, your side did not have very good aim."

"Well, thank Heaven for small miracles," Baier grumbled. "But if you were in the *Wehrmacht,* how come you can't find out more about your brother-in-law's whereabouts?"

Joachim chuckled. "We were not only in different units, but we fought on different fronts at the end. And do you really think it was that easy? That our communications and reporting were that effective or efficient with everything collapsing around us?"

"Probably not," Baier conceded. He studied the murky brown water. "If I find anything I can stop by the shop. Or do you have another address?"

The German shook his head. "No, the laundry shop will do fine. My sister would love to hear any news you might have."

Baier turned to go, then stopped. "One last question, though. I can see why you would turn to me after my visit to the cleaners, but why set up this meeting instead of coming by my office?

Why all the drama?"

"Perhaps it is better if we handle this as a private matter. The fewer people that know of our search, especially people in authority, the better for all of us. I'm sure you'll agree. Eventually."

"That remains to be seen." Baier studied the stranger, partly in an effort to get a measure of the man, but also to decide if this foray into a family's affairs was truly worth the trouble. Then again, there was the matter of the name and the house. And the wife had seemed so intriguing and interested. "Before I do anything else, however, I want a real name."

"Ah, yes. You'll need to run traces on me. Well, I've got nothing to hide. It's Hartmann. Joachim Hartmann." The wide, sly smile returned with another Lucky. "And I have a question for you, *Herr Baier*. Two, actually. Have you wondered at the marvelous coincidence of your name and your arrival at that very house? It's as though fate has thrown you in our family's path."

"Yes, I have wondered at that. I'm intrigued, of course, but I'm not sure how far I'll pursue all this."

"Pursue what, *Herr Baier*?"

"The man's history, his fate. I'm happy to do what I can to help, but nothing more."

Hartmann nodded. "I see."

"And what's the other question," Baier asked. "You had two."

"Ah yes. Have you ever been to Greece?"

"Not yet," Baier answered. "Why?"

"It's a beautiful country, with beautiful women and good wine. The food is not so bad either. But most of all, there is so much to learn there. So much about our history and ourselves."

"That's good to hear. I'll keep it in mind."

Hartmann tipped his hat and ambled towards the gate and

the trees of the *Gruenewald* beyond. Baier watched him go, wondering just what was so damn important about Greece.

There still remained the issue with Perkins. Baier had too many questions about his driver's role in this unfolding affair. It could, of course, be as simple and straightforward as Perkins had stated. Hartmann's claim to have recognized the driver from the visit to the laundry shop had supported Perkins's story that he had acted as a simple messenger.

Maybe so. But there could also be more to it, and Baier had been nagged by doubts about this seemingly worldly-wise and street-smart companion for several days now. The more he thought about it, the more Baier realized how little he knew about the man and his extracurricular life. Given their differences in rank, Baier did not feel comfortable just asking him outright, particularly as Perkins might mistake Baier's curiosity for solicitation. Instead, he decided to try some undercover investigating of his own, prepared to play the innocent should Perkins stumble across him. If things worked out well, Perkins could actually be a valuable ally. That is, if Baier was going to continue his search for the German with his name. His driver probably had some useful contacts in the city.

The very next evening he tailed Perkins to the Harnack House. That building had started life as the headquarters of an academic and scientific lodge established by the *Kaiser Wilhelm Gesellschaft* in the early 1920s in the Dahlem neighborhood to promote social exchanges and an *esprit du corps* among Germany's scientific community. It had been a major objective of the Soviets as they raided Berlin for anything of scientific value they could find, especially on Germany's nuclear program, as soon as they occupied the city. It now served as a bar and hotel for the American occupiers, thanks in part to its proximity to their headquarters, which stood no more than a few minutes walk away. Fortunately, Dahlem, a largely residential area on the city's southwestern side and just shy of Potsdam, had not been heavily bombed. Although the US and British air forces had employed a carpet-bombing approach to German cities, most of the bombs deposited over Berlin had been dropped closer to or right in the city center or in the transportation and industrial hubs further north or to the east. So it was not that difficult to find acceptable accommodations in this neighborhood, as well as clubs and social gathering spots for the officers and enlisted men.

Perkins had met up with a young German woman in the street just outside the Harnack House, and Baier had gotten the distinct impression that they already knew each other. And well, at least judging from the length and intensity of their embrace. Not all that surprising, Baier guessed, given their own conversation on the day of his arrival. Perkins appeared to have himself one of those *Frauleins* he had been recommending, presumably one he could ply with chocolate and stockings and liquor, and probably food and ration coupons as well. That, he figured, would be the real prize. Maybe there was even some love involved, but Baier doubted it. On either side. He just hoped it wasn't one of his new-found heroines, the *Trummerfrauen*. They had had to endure enough already, or so it seemed. Then again, he reminded himself, they had to eat, too. And they'd probably enjoy a drink and some chocolate now and then as well, not to mention some companionship. But from the looks of her, this woman did not spend a lot of time sorting rubble. She had striking blond hair that ran to her shoulders and framed the top of a prominent bust she made sure to put on display. Athough Baier could not see much of her eyes, she had a rounded chin and prominent nose that somehow fit together very well. But mainly, her smooth alabaster skin did not appear to have suffered from much exposure to bricks and dust.

41

While Baier pondered these interesting but not very intriguing thoughts, Perkins slipped into the enlisted men's club with his date. Baier swung by the officers' club and grabbed a beer of his own, then sauntered back outside to keep an eye open for Perkins for when he departed. He had a long wait, since Perkins stayed inside for over an hour, closer to an hour-and-a-half actually, while Baier sipped first one, and then a second beer of his own on the steps of the officers' club, which allowed him a clear line of sight to the enlisted men's entrance just around the corner. Baier parked himself off to one side to avoid all the foot traffic and to provide at least a minimal cover.

Shortly before nine o'clock Perkins and his girl left the Harnack House and wandered down a residential street off to the side, arm-in-arm, half hidden in the deep shadows cast by the trees and houses set against the setting sun along *Brummer Strasse*. Baier followed at a distance of about thirty yards. He was new to this game, and he realized he needed to keep some distance, but he was also afraid of losing the couple.

Eventually, they reached *Thiel Allee,* where the two lovebirds kept strolling for several more blocks until they found a stand of trees just off the street corner, which they probably hoped would provide some cover. There they embraced, and Baier had to look away repeatedly as they exchanged a series of kisses that grew longer and more passionate with each effort.

When Baier looked again, the woman was on her knees in front of Perkins, his head rolling from side to side against the tree trunk. Baier turned away, disgusted with himself for allowing his suspicions to turn him into a voyeur. But he could not afford to lose their trail. He wanted to see where they finished the evening and how Perkins spent it. If it was at the girl's place, then Baier would have an address he could follow, something tangible to trace. Something better than a laundry ticket. Then again, if she had her own place, why stop here? But that, he thought, might be even better, because if she shared a flat, it could point to the involvement of others and give Baier additional leads and information on Perkins's social life.

Then Baier realized he was getting well ahead of himself. He looked back and saw that Perkins had propped the girl against the tree, her arms encircling his neck and her legs pinned to his sides, with her feet flat against the tree trunk. Perkins's trousers lay rumpled at his feet as he thrust himself repeatedly against her.

Baier pivoted in the opposite direction, turning his back to the couple. This, he told himself, he did not need to see. Then he heard the shot.

Baier threw his head around, expecting to see the poor woman lying on the ground in a bloodied heap. It just seemed natural for the German to be the one doing the dying.

But instead it was Perkins who had fallen. He lay on his back, arms spread in an imitation of a crucifixion, and his pants still bundled at his ankles. It was not, Baier thought irreverently, the pose of a conquering hero in death.

He ran to Perkins, his heart pounding and his breath coming in short, staccato bursts. When he reached the trees Baier dropped to his knees to check on his driver, looking at the same time for the woman to see if she was all right, but also to make sure that the danger did not come from her. But she was nowhere to be found.

Not at first. Then he heard the sounds of someone running. Baier jumped up and sprinted over to the streetcar tracks that ran in a broad, open trench just beyond the shaded street corner the lovers had used. He saw a female running in the opposite direction, back towards the city center, alongside the tracks. Baier yelled for her to stop. She hesitated and looked back at him, just long enough for Baier to catch a glimpse of that same pretty face framed in flowing blond hair. This time, though, he

43

saw her blue eyes, and they were wide with terror. Then she turned and disappeared into the shadows and darkness that swallowed the tracks.

Baier momentarily considered pursuing her. Until he realized, that is, that only the dumbest luck would allow him to catch her. He returned to Perkins's shattered corpse, half the poor man's brains spread in a spray that ran four or five feet from his skull. Clearly, there was nothing to be done here. He looked in every direction to see where the shot might have come from. Then he realized the shooter might still be out there, somewhere near, and Baier dropped to one knee and scrambled to the side of the tree. All he found, however, was a night of silence and darkness, the air broken by intermittent sparks of light and the sounds of lives that continued for others, but not his driver.

Baier's shoulders dropped as he turned and walked back up *Thiel Allee* to return to Harnack House and call the M.P.s. Only then did he realize that his face and shirt were soaked in sweat. It was the first death he had witnessed, and the war was over. But it looked as though the fighting was not.

CHAPTER FIVE

"Well, it didn't take you long," Dick Savage exclaimed, leaning once more against the doorframe at the entrance to Baier's office. His suit this time was a navy blue, double-breasted number that was set off by a solid red tie. Savage was not alone this time, however. Just off his right shoulder stood Major Frank Younger, Baier's immediate superior.

Savage straightened himself and ambled into the office, then grabbed the chair in front of Baier's desk. Younger marched slowly and purposefully behind Savage and assumed a spot just to Savage's right in a stance that resembled a relaxed version of parade rest.

"Yeah, you could say I stepped into it last night," Baier conceded. "But man, what a shocker." He sighed, rubbing his eyes. "It was one hell of a night, for sure."

"What time did the investigators let you go?" Younger asked. His crisp pronunciation on each word reflected the military bearing an observer would find in his physical presence. The light brown buzz cut that left maybe a half-inch elevation along the crown of his skull with the sides shaven clean, the starched shirt collar and sleeves, the tight knot of his tie, and the strict pressed line in his trousers all spoke of a man who enjoyed the discipline and regularity that came with military life. Unlike Baier, who had found himself in the Army in the summer of 1944, had hated boot camp, and was relieved when his university education and high intelligence scores had diverted his path from the infantry into the OSS and then military intelligence. And unlike Baier, Younger had seen a fair amount of combat during and especially after the Ardennes offensive, rejoining the front lines after he had been wounded as the Americans breached the Reich's frontiers along the Rhine and raced east, temporarily bypassing the industrial Ruhr region. He had been involved in some of the heavy fighting inside Germany, particularly at Heilbronn, as the Germans responded to their *Fuehrer*'s order to turn every city of the Fatherland into a mighty fortress. Younger once told Baier he could never forgive the Germans for sustaining their hopeless defense as long as they did and thereby escalating the senseless casualties on both sides. Strangely though, in Baier's mind Younger never displayed the hatred or resentment he claimed to feel. In fact, Savage's casual attitude and seeming indifference at times actually appeared more heartless. Baier suspected that despite their crimes and all the devastation and suffering they had caused, Younger still admired the Germans for their military discipline and prowess.

"Oh, I got home around two," Baier answered. He fiddled with his tie and the collar buttons on his khaki shirt to make sure they were buttoned and tight. "There wasn't a whole lot I could tell them. The only other person I saw was the girl, and I never got a good look at her."

"Too bad," Savage interjected. "It sounds like she was a hot one."

Younger frowned and shook his head. He shuffled his feet and turned towards Savage. "Please, Dick. We've got a dead US soldier here."

Savage sat upright and glanced at Younger. "You're right. I apologize." He turned back towards Baier. "Could she have been involved?"

It was Baier's turn to shake his head. "I really doubt it. When I did get a glimpse of her face she looked scared to death. Those

46

eyes were wide enough to reach her ears." It struck him that Savage actually looked contrite, red cheeks and all, and for the first time since he had known him. "Anyway, the investigators wanted to know why I had followed Perkins, how well I knew him. That sort of thing."

"And?" Savage pressed.

"Well, hardly at all. Knew him, I mean." Baier glanced out the window then back at his visitors. "I've only been here a few weeks. We chatted some during our drives, and I learned he was a Badger from La Cross, Wisconsin. And that he liked German girls."

"He wasn't alone, from what I've seen," Younger replied. "But why were you following him? That is kind of unusual."

Baier repeated the line he had given the military police. "We hadn't discussed our schedule for the rest of the week, and I was hoping to get an early start this morning with some interviews and files of the chemistry and physics professors from Berlin University. That is, what and whom I could find. I know there was a lot of work done here in Dahlem, but the University sits over in the Russian sector, or at least most of it." He shook his head again. "We're in a bit of a race with the Soviets there, you know," he added by way of explanation.

"You can say that again," Savage agreed. "But don't." He pointed a finger at Baier and smiled.

"Do they have any ideas why this happened? Any leads, or suspects?" Younger asked.

Baier shook his head once more and blew out his breath. He pulled his chair in closer to his desk and leaned forward on his forearms. "Not that they passed to me. I asked to be kept informed, of course, if only to make sure I did not become a target through our association."

"Makes sense," Savage added. "But do you think that's possible?"

Baier sat back and shrugged, thinking of Joachim Hartmann's strange approach and the puzzle the German had left. "Who's to say, especially since we know next to nothing. I mean, it could've been something as simple as a jealous boyfriend, for all we know."

Younger nodded. "Or perhaps he was shot because of his association with you. Do you think our allies in the east wanted to warn you off? Have you been getting close to any sensitive information or people?"

Baier paused. He wondered if perhaps there was some sort of link to his work, something he had not thought of before. But the link was too tenuous, too speculative. He shook his head. "Hardly. I haven't gotten very far yet." He studied the major. "Besides, that would seem pretty dramatic, not to mention drastic. Do you really think they'd try something like that?"

Younger shrugged. "Hard to say at this point. But there have been cases of Germans disappearing, kidnapped by the Soviets in all likelihood. I wouldn't put it past them."

Baier thought for a moment, his gaze on the desktop before looking back at Younger. "The investigators did say there might be a black market connection. I didn't get the sense they had anything concrete there, though. More like that's often the case in these killings."

Savage looked at Younger. "Have there been that many?"

"Not that I'm aware of," the major replied.

Savage turned back to Baier. "That or, like you said, a husband finds his way home and kills one of our boys *in flagrante* out of rage," he suggested. "Of course, thus far there have been damn few that have made it home."

"One thing they did not bring up was the possibility of it being one of the werewolf guerillas," Baier added.

Savage shook his head. "The Army has pretty much dismissed that as an ineffectual rumor the Nazis spread. Some SS guy was supposed to build that force, but he was essentially worthless."

"Still," Baier responded, "it could have been a lone wolf of sorts, protesting the perceived rape of German womanhood."

Younger nodded. "Yeah, perhaps. But did you get any sense that Perkins might be involved in something like that?" he asked. "The black market, I mean."

"Not really." Baier leaned back, again thinking about how much he should reveal, or how much he actually knew. "He did sound pretty street smart, but I never got the feeling that Perkins had unexplained income or was absent for periods that were not noted or justified." Baier ran his hand over hair considerably longer than his superior's. "It's really a damn puzzle, not to mention a tragedy. I haven't been able to concentrate or get a damn thing done all day."

"Well, that's certainly understandable," Younger consoled. "But don't let it incapacitate you, or even slow you down for long. You've got important work to do, Captain."

"Yeah, let me know if there's anything I can do to help," Savage added, leaning forward. "Let's meet for dinner. We can chat some more. Let you clear the air a bit."

"Thanks, Dick. I appreciate that."

"Harnack House okay? Not too shook up by the memory of that place, I hope."

Baier smiled. "No, that's okay. Perkins was shot somewhere else. I'll see you at seven."

Savage nodded as he rose. Younger saluted when he left, surprising Baier, who hastily returned the salute to his superior officer, wondering why his boss had saluted a junior officer first. Perhaps it was his way of offering support at a difficult moment. If so, it was another heartfelt gesture from a man more understanding of human nature and its vulnerabilities than he appeared to be behind that stiff military bearing. Baier found himself liking and respecting the man the more he worked with him. Baier also realized after they left that he had now lied to the investigators, his boss, and his friend by withholding the story of his pursuit of the man whose name and house he had assumed here in Berlin. True, it hadn't gotten very far, and thus far there did not appear to be any great mystery involved. Yet he was intrigued. And now he was hiding what little there was. He asked himself how much further he'd be willing to go to chase what was still little more than a whim.

Before meeting Savage for dinner, Baier decided to walk over to the Allied *Kommandatura* building, also situated in Dahlem at the junction of *Thiel Allee* and *Kaiserwerther Strasse*. It was not all that far from the Harnack House, ironically. The AK, as it was known, had been established as a sort of joint Allied command post, with each of the four major powers maintaining an office and a small staff there. If he was going to attempt to learn something of his namesake's disappearance and fate, Baier thought it might be worthwhile to approach the Soviet staff there first rather than have his driver—Perkins's replacement had yet to be named—take him to the eastern side of the city, or even to the Soviet intelligence headquarters at Karlshorst, a suburb just outside the city. The convenience, Baier reasoned, at least made it worth a try.

The *Kommandatura* occupied a three-story rectangular building of red brick, which had been constructed during the latter years of the Weimar Republic and had housed an insurance company before the war. Like many buildings of that period, it had a pseudo-classical appeal, most pronounced in the three cement columns in the front that lent it a solid, almost imperial air.

Baier found his way along the second floor corridor to the small office of a Major Ivan Kucholvsky a few steps down the hallway from the main Soviet office. Kucholvsky was a short, squat, broad-shouldered man, whose nose appeared to have been broken more than once. Baier wondered if it had happened in combat with the Germans, as a result of the brutal Soviet discipline he had heard about, or from an entirely private affair, perhaps before he even joined the Red Army. His haircut looked remarkably like Younger's, but Baier doubted this man had the innate sensitivity and understanding he had seen in his own superior. Maybe it was the bristles along the side of his scalp that extended to his cheeks. Maybe he was also selling the Soviet short. Or maybe it was the glare of the afternoon sun that poked through a double set of window panes that looked as though they had been last cleaned at some point in the Weimar Republic.

"Please," the major said, extending his hand in the direction of one of the two chairs to the front of his desk. He leaned forward, both arms extending over the top of the desk, the hands clasped together. "What can I do for you?" His English was heavily accented but understandable. Baier didn't think it would be diplomatic to propose a conversation in German.

"Well," Baier began, "my presence here is not really official."

The major's eyebrows arched, and a slight grin rippled the stubble along his cheeks and chin.

Baier held up a hand. "No, it's nothing like that. I'm looking for some information on a German whose trail was lost on the eastern front. I was hoping you could at least point me in the right direction."

Kucholvsky sat back, assuming a more relaxed pose. "Goodness, there are so many. So many died, and so many have been lost."

So I've heard, Baier thought. "Yes, I imagine it will be a nearly impossible task. But I've been asked by a friend to see what I might do."

The major's grin widened. "A *Fraulein?* You needn't follow

51

up, you know. She probably has no alternative." A silent chuckle escaped. "We could even make sure that he does not return, if you'd like."

Baier suddenly disliked this man. Now he understood better the tales circulating about the Soviet capture of the city and their behavior since. It gave Baier an uncomfortable feeling in the pit of his stomach, almost as though the Soviet officer had threatened him personally instead of some faceless German. Baier sat upright and leaned forward, almost touching the desk. "No, it's nothing like that. Not at all. The man's name is Baier, Karl Baier."

Kucholvsky's eyes strayed to Baier's own name tag. "I'm sorry. Was this German a relative?"

Baier recognized the past tense in the Soviet's phrasing of the question. He also recognized an instant excuse if this activity ever came to light with his superiors, and he cursed himself for not thinking ahead and preparing a line of reasoning to use beforehand. He was beginning to realize that he would need to be a lot more careful and a lot smarter. "Well, that is something I'd like to find out if I can."

"Yes, I understand there are many Americans of German descent. Was it hard on you fighting the Germans here?"

Baier relaxed back in his seat, shaking his head. "Not really. We're all fully American now, and very few of us shared any sympathy for the Nazis. We're all glad to be rid of them."

Kucholvsky nodded, then leaned forward again, his arms back atop his desk. "That is, of course, good to hear. I will try to help. Let me make some inquiries for you. When was this man Baier last heard from? Do you know where he was fighting?"

"Budapest, I believe," Baier answered. "And sometime in March."

Kucholvsky grimaced. "That was some very tough fighting.

The Germans did not give up in Hungary easily, and the losses on both sides were quite heavy." He slapped the desk top. "But I will see what I can find. Where can I contact you?"

Baier hesitated. "Let me reach out to you. I can come by since I live in the area. How much time do you need?"

The Soviet shrugged, then stood. "As you wish. Perhaps a few days. In any case, I will keep whatever information I have here in my office until you return."

Baier stood and held out his hand. "Thank you very much, Major. I really do appreciate this."

"Good. To our cooperation, Captain." Kucholvsky offered his hand.

They shook. Baier found himself wondering as he walked down the corridor and on to the entrance on the first floor just what Kucholvsky had meant by their "cooperation." This was more like a favor in his own mind. Baier reminded himself of the need to get smarter and more cautious. And quickly.

Walking back from dinner at the Harnack House, Baier pondered something that had come up in his evening conversation with Savage. They had been discussing the prospect of Nazi "werewolves" launching acts of resistance, even though remarkably few had materialized as yet. It had been a follow-up to Baier's remark earlier in the day. Savage had downplayed the suggestion, arguing that most likely all the able-bodied true believers had either been killed or were rotting away in P.O.W. camps. The conversation had then turned to the roving courts martial and grenadiers, virtual execution squads that left a trail of corpses throughout the crumbling Reich in a last-ditch effort to shore up collapsing morale and commitment among the military and civilian populations. Savage noted that he had expected a wave of reprisals and revenge killings, but of these there had been remarkably few. Baier suggested that the

Germans who survived were probably just grateful to have done so, and that they appeared to be a broken and demoralized nation for the most part. At least insofar as it involved political activity or dealing with the past.

But his route home led Baier to wonder as well about the past of Joachim Hartmann, something he wished he had pressed the German about during their meeting at the *Jagdschloss*. Or the other Germans at the cleaners. Or even his own namesake, Karl Baier, who may have been spared all that if he had been taken prisoner at the siege of Budapest. Then again, he had a pretty dismal fate awaiting him in a Soviet P.O.W. camp, it that was indeed where he ended up.

When he reached his door, Baier was surprised, and concerned, to find it unlocked. He couldn't be sure, since his movements whenever he left his house had evolved into a routine, but he was pretty sure he had locked the door behind him when he left for work that morning. He entered the foyer cautiously, his eyes probing the dark for any movement or unfamiliar shapes. He also hung close to the wall and gave the entrance to his living room a wide arc to minimize the threat of an ambush.

Then he saw her. The dress and long hair made it plain to Baier that it was a woman. She sat in a chair in the alcove at the back of his living room, buried in shadows cast by the hall light at Baier's back. She must have been looking out into the backyard, because her head rotated slowly in his direction, as though his appearance held absolutely no surprise for her. She had pulled the chair up to the writing table and appeared to have pulled out the drawer that held the folder of pictures and other memorabilia, like the laundry claim check. Much of the folder's contents was spread over the tabletop.

"How did you get in here?" Baier asked. He surprised himself at how calm he sounded, given the pounding inside his chest and his shortness of breath. "And who are you?" He stepped inside from the hall, glanced quickly around the room, and peeked into the others to make sure they were alone. He listened for a sound of movement on the floor above but heard nothing beyond the rustle of trees in the yard at the back.

She swiveled in the chair. Baier noticed how the dress had been pulled up and bundled at the knees. It was then that he recognized her. The woman from the cleaners.

"I have a key," she replied. "I used to live here, you know."

Her German had a faint southern accent, but Baier could not place it anymore closely or precisely. It was definitely not Bavarian, though. Perhaps she came from somewhere in Saxony, he thought. "You're Frau Baier." She nodded. "Why did the man at the cleaners call you his wife?"

The woman shrugged, then waved her hand at Baier as though she could never hope to explain such an arrangement to an innocent, young American. "We're living together in an arrangement. I owe him that much."

"Why?" Baier pressed. "What did he do for you?"

"Well, he saved my life, for starters. Twice, you see." She motioned towards the sofa set against the wall opposite the table. "Come. Let's sit. I'll explain. And I have something for you."

Baier noticed the small bundle wrapped in brown paper and held together by a ribbon of white string. "What's that?" he asked. He did not move any closer.

"It's your laundry packet. My husband's clothes, that is, but I believe they might fit you as well."

"I could have picked them up."

"I wanted to deliver them myself after your visit the other day." She moved to the sofa and patted the cushion next to her. "Come. Sit."

Baier walked to the couch, his gaze locked on the woman. His eyes wandered once or twice to examine her exposed legs, maybe more often. He didn't keep count. "First, tell me why you're here and what you're looking for. Besides the laundry, I mean. I wasn't aware you had a delivery system."

"Certainly," she answered, smiling. "I wanted to see what else you had of my husband's here. This is my house, you know."

"Not really," Baier responded. "Not anymore."

"Ah, yes. The victor's justice."

Baier sat. "We seized homes that had either belonged to officials of the Nazi regime or those that had been confiscated from Jews. We'll return the latter once we identify the owners or their surviving relatives. And we went about it with a good deal more consideration than you Germans in the lands you occupied."

This explanation brought out a laugh from the woman. She waved again at Baier. "Oh, please. Spare me your moral drivel. You took the homes that looked the nicest. My husband was no Nazi." She smiled. "And we are certainly no Jews."

"Whether he was a Nazi remains to be seen. I'm trying to find some trace of him now."

Her eyebrows arched. "Really? Is this official or private?"

"We'll see soon enough. It will depend on what I find." Baier pointed at the folder. "What have you found?"

"Not much. Do you mind if I take the photographs?"

Baier sat back. "I suppose not. But leave me one in case I need it for identification later." He studied her face, outlined clearly by the light brown hair pulled back behind the ears in what his sister had referred to as a ponytail. It struck him that this woman was actually quite attractive and that she seemed to have come out of the war with her beauty intact. Of her morality and innocence, he couldn't speak. Not yet anyway. "Tell me about your arrangement."

She stood, smoothed her dress over her legs, then sat back down in the corner next to Baier. "Ernst has been a great help in this time of trouble. But I'm afraid his usefulness is coming to an end."

"How so?"

"Well, I never really found him attractive, you see. But he was an acquaintance of my husband who had worked for the regime in Berlin, and he was able to produce identification and ration cards when I needed them. Then he took me in after he opened his shop."

"What did he do under the old regime?"

"He was a supply officer in the *Wehrmacht*." She stared long and hard at Baier. "He also had contacts in the Gestapo."

Baier bristled at the mention of this organization. To any American ear it held the ring of oppression under an official guise and sanction, and in the service of a criminal regime. His words came crisp and short. "Just what kind of contacts?"

She reached over and patted his arm. She also let her hand linger there for several seconds. "Oh, stop it. They knew each other from school or something, willing to do a favor now and then."

"You make them sound almost innocent."

The wave came and went again. "Many of us did what we had to do to survive. I'm sure they had their reasons, too." She paused. "Berlin was not exactly Nazi territory, you know."

He did recall that the city known as "Red Berlin" had never given the Nazis anything close to a majority in any of the German elections. "Still, the city seems to have gone along easily enough."

She stared at Baier again for several seconds. Then she inched closer on the sofa and leaned forward to rest her hand on his arm. This time she left it there. By now Baier's eyes had grown accustomed to the darkness, and in the dim evening light he could see her figure as she bent forward. The top few buttons of her dress, a light flowered print, were undone, and Baier looked down at the inside lines of her breasts. She was not wearing a bra. He could not be sure how long he let his gaze rest on the soft curve of her chest.

She smiled and squeezed his forearm. "You remind me of my husband." She tilted her head, as though to get a better view. "You even look a bit like him."

"Perhaps we are related," Baier said, mostly to relieve the tension that had built inside him.

She pulled away, still smiling. "Oh, I think just you being here in this house is coincidence enough." Suddenly she stood. "I should go. I'm sure you have important work to do, to search out the bad Nazis and to help rebuild our country."

Baier couldn't tell if she was being reverential or sarcastic. "Whatever." Then he looked into her eyes, and the image of the terrified woman on the tracks reappeared. He could not understand why, since Karl Baier's wife did not resemble her at all. He shifted his eyes and stared at the floor.

"Is something wrong?" she asked. "Have I offended you? If so, I'm sorry. I didn't mean to."

"No," he shook his head. "I just remembered something that happened recently. I lost somebody at the Command." He tried to hide a shudder that brought the picture of Perkins lying dead and shattered on the ground by the tree.

"Then I truly am sorry. Would you like to talk about it?"

He shook his head again, harder this time. Then he looked up into her eyes once more. The image of the other woman did not return. He smiled. "No, thank you. I don't want to discuss it. In fact, I probably shouldn't. Besides, I'm through for the day."

"In that case, I should be getting back. But may I come to visit again?" She looked around the room and then beyond to the rest of the house. "I have many memories here."

"Yes, of course. You're always welcome." Baier was surprised

58

at how readily he had agreed, and he wasn't sure what else to say. So he changed the subject. "In fact, I may have news about your husband soon. I spoke to a Russian officer, who offered to make some inquiries. Perhaps the day after tomorrow, or better yet, the day after that."

The woman clapped her hands in delight, then stepped over to Baier and kissed his cheek. "Thank you so much. That would be wonderful."

She paused, then kissed Baier again, this time on the lips. When she moved back, she swung around, her dress rippling the air around her legs. She moved towards the front door, glanced over her shoulder and gave Baier a final wave, this one more an invitation than a dismissal. Or so it seemed to him.

When he walked back to the desk, Baier realized what else it was that had made her seem so appealing. She had carried a pleasant smell but not one that he associated with a perfume or cologne of any kind. She was one of the few Germans he had met and gotten this close to who had not carried any body odor. He suddenly realized how difficult it must be for the locals to bathe with any regularity, but she had clearly taken the time and trouble to make herself as presentable and attractive as possible within what he assumed were very limited means. He also noticed that she had left one photograph behind, as he had asked. It was one of those from Athens.

CHAPTER SIX

Baier spent the next few days reviewing two boxes of files his office had located at the *Kaiser Wilhelm Gesellschaft*, ironically, in the basement of the Harnack House. Perhaps the Germans had forgotten to destroy these, or they had been misplaced and even the Soviets had missed them. Both would be understandable, given the chaos that must have reigned in the closing days of the *Reich* and the war's immediate aftermath. In any event, Baier was only getting to review them now because the Army's Counterintelligence Corps had been holding them to cross-check the applications of locals for work permits as one means of ensuring that none had been high- or even middle-ranking Nazi party functionaries, or, more important, involved in any war crimes or atrocities. Baier's work had begun to focus more and more on the German missile program, which had exploited thousands of slave laborers at the underground facilities several hours west of Berlin in the Harz Mountains. Baier noticed that these records contained nothing incriminating in that area, simply details of the research done at various universities and institutes, including at Pennemuende. He did wonder, though, if the men in Counterintelligence were holding additional material they were waiting to share. He would raise the issue with Younger, Baier concluded. After all, his work was important, too. And there were several leads here on scientists that might still be in Berlin, whom he would love to interrogate.

Late in the afternoon of the second day, Baier walked back

over to the Allied *Kommandatura,* looking for Kucholvsky. Baier's luck this day traveled with him. Kucholvsky rose, snapped to attention, and extended his arm towards the chair once more.

"I have found something," the Soviet announced proudly. "Not much, I am afraid, but something all the same." His chest stayed puffed out in obvious pride.

Baier noticed for the first time how sparse the Major's office appeared. He had been so focused on the major and dodging the glare of the sun that flashed across the Soviet's desk on the first visit that he had not paid that much attention to the surroundings. There were just two pictures on the wall behind his desk: the ubiquitous—at least in Soviet buildings—portrait of the Soviet leaders Stalin and Lenin, the man who started it all. Baier wondered why there were no pictures of Soviet military leaders, like the general widely seen as the real strategist behind the Red Army's victorious march on Berlin, Zhukov. Perhaps, Baier guessed, Stalin did not like the idea of popular competition. The other walls were bare, and the chair Baier occupied offered the only seat in the room, aside from Kucholvsky's.

"Well, every little bit will help in some way," Baier consoled. "Or at least I hope so."

Kucholvsky sat down and shuffled some papers in his desk, then searched his pockets. His brow was knit in puzzlement, but then he released a smile of relief and reached into the center drawer of his desk. "Yes, yes. Here it is." He held up a sheet of looseleaf notepaper for Baier to see, presumably as a sign of proof. "And so it begins."

"Excuse me?" Baier thought this sounded odd, even a bit ominous. He did not intend to launch a full-scale expedition. He just wanted something to pass along to the man's wife, no matter how preliminary or inconclusive.

Kucholvsky shrugged. "You cannot expect a final answer so soon, Captain. After all, we have almost three million German

61

soldiers prisoner now . . ."

And how many thousands more simply deported, Baier asked himself.

". . . And I must admit, our records are not as complete as we would like." Kucholvsky smiled. "We are not like the Germans, you know."

"Yes," Baier said, "I can certainly understand that. We've had some problems of our own," he admitted. Baier thought of the thousands he had seen sleeping in the open air in camps across Germany, soldiers and civilians crammed together with little in the way of shelter or sanitary facilities. Still, he doubted they'd be held nearly as long as those seized by the Soviets. The British and American authorities were already preparing some releases. The French, however, were another matter.

"But I can tell you this much," Kucholvsky continued. "A Colonel Karl Baier was taken prisoner shortly after the fall of Budapest in February. However, it seems he disappeared shortly after that."

"You mean he escaped?"

Kucholvsky shook his head. "No, I can't say that." His finger pressed down on a particular spot on the sheet. "That's not the word that was used in the records." He thought for a moment, his eyes fixed on Baier. "I believe the best German word for it would be 'verschwunden.' "

"Disappeared?" Baier pondered that for a moment, returning Kucholvsky's stare. "So it could mean that he escaped. Or possibly that he was killed?"

A slight hiss marked Kucholvsky's intake of breath. "I don't think that's very likely. Probably the first."

"And why is that?"

Kucholvsky sat back in his chair, obviously more relaxed. "Because my colleagues in Karlshorst expressed some interest in locating this man as well." He laughed lightly before continuing. "They were actually quite excited when I mentioned you and ordered me to arrest you. I assured them that you are indeed who you claim to be." His index finger rose. "I checked."

"How reassuring. But what is this particular Baier alleged to have done?"

Kucholvsky shrugged again and reached for a cigarette pack on his desk. He offered one to Baier, who declined. "I'm not sure," Kucholvsky continued. "There were probably denunciations of some sort that we need to check out. It's not unusual, you know, for someone who was in the *Abwehr*, the German military intelligence."

That bit of news put Baier back in his chair. The *Abwehr*. No one had said anything about that. And a colonel. This put an entirely new light on things. Then again, how much stock should he put in information like this from the Soviets? That was the equivalent of an accusation, certainly in their eyes. True or not, Baier saw no reason to doubt that the Soviets would want to find this man, or that any German associated with any kind of security service would receive pretty short shrift from the Soviets. Their chances were not a whole lot better with his own side, from what he could tell. There were already rumors of deals circulating, freedom in exchange for assistance or information. Perhaps that was what the Soviets wanted.

"So, you see," Kucholvsky stated. "We would like to find this man as well. That is why I spoke of a beginning. We would like to work together on this."

Baier tried to think of an appropriate reply. He was certainly not going to jump into any project with the Soviets on his own. And this entire case was intended to be nothing more than a curiosity piece and personal favor.

"This is getting out of my league," Baier replied. "I'll have to speak with my superiors."

He stood to leave. Kucholvsky stood as well. "As you wish.

But I believe we would be able to share more and move more quickly together if we, er, acted unofficially, as it were."

Of course, Baier thought. He may be new to Berlin, but he was not that innocent. "But that would create a new set of challenges as well." He extended his hand, which Kucholvsky shook vigorously. "But in any case," Baier concluded, "I'll be in touch."

Baier let himself out as quickly as possible and remarked to himself how he avoided walking past the American offices.

His next stop was the cleaning establishment. It had taken about twenty minutes to walk there, and by the time the bell rang above the door when he entered, Baier had broken into a sweat, thanks to some unusually warm and humid air in Berlin. The same solid and dour-looking German entered the shop from the room at the back. He wore a similar outfit of a rumpled, brown cotton shirt and dirty gray slacks. Baier assumed that these were his work clothes, although he did not see much evidence of work and only a smattering of actual laundry. His mouth was full, the cheeks bulging, as he chewed slowly and studied Baier with a disdain that was only barely hidden. In his right hand he held a small roll stuffed with some kind of sausage.

"You again?" It was more an accusation than a question. The words escaped in a garble from the mouthful of food blocking their path.

"Yes. Is the woman here?" Baier asked. "I have some news about her husband. Not much, I'm afraid. But it's something all the same."

The German motioned with his head towards the door. "You can tell me. I'll pass it along to Sabine."

Baier realized he had not confirmed her first name when they met the other night. What he had heard on his first visit had been more like a mumble, but without the food. He cursed his awkwardness, his lack of concentration and attention to detail.

64

He would need to wisen up, he told himself. But he had been in a mild state of shock then, learning of her presence. And there was her physical appeal, the warmth he felt from just her presence alone. Baier had never learned how to be comfortable in the presence of attractive women during his initial and fumbling forays into romance. And he really did find her attractive.

"You can tell her that her husband was indeed captured at Budapest, but the records are a bit confused after that."

The German grunted. "No surprise there."

"If she wants to know any more she can get in touch."

With that, Baier turned and walked out the door, the bell ringing once more as he entered the street. The German was still chewing as he stared after Baier, eyes narrowed and focused on the American, as though wishing him somewhere else, far away.

She came to him that same evening. She was wearing a different dress, although one in a similar style and material. But this one had a solid color of light blue. It also fit her more tightly, revealing a figure full in the chest that tapered towards the waist and legs. Baier found himself staring at her body, which appeared to have very little on underneath the dress. Or maybe it was just wishful thinking. He noticed once more the shape of her legs, the muscles in the calves outlined through her stockings. He wondered briefly where she had come across a pair of stockings, but quickly focused on the shape of the legs, remarking at how well she appeared to have kept her shape. She had clearly learned how to survive the war and its aftermath, he told himself.

She slipped through the front door when he opened it, then threw her arms around his neck. "So you found some news. That is wonderful. I can't thank you enough."

Baier appreciated the feel and shape of her body, as her

breasts pushed against his chest. At this point he wasn't sure what she had on underneath. He hugged her in return, his arms sliding around her back and waist. Her scent this time was more pleasant and powerful. She had clearly found some perfume which covered her with a light smell of lilacs. He shook his head to clear his mind. "It isn't much, I'm afraid." He reluctantly pulled away and then led her by the hand to the sofa in the alcove. "But it does give us some hope, and something to go on."

She took his hands in hers and leaned in close. "Tell me all." She surveyed the room. "But first, do you have something to drink? This calls for at least a small celebration."

Baier walked to the kitchen and poured two glasses of wine, a white Bordeaux he had picked up at the commissary. Unlike some of his colleagues, Baier had not discovered a stash of liquor in the basement of his house. He was wondering just what he might find hidden away in the dark recesses of his home until he approached the sofa, realizing that a mere laundry ticket had opened a bigger door than any liquor or firearm. He offered Sabine Baier the wine, then sat beside her. She held the glass in one hand, his fingers in the other.

"Well, as I said, there isn't much to tell," Baier continued. "As I told your companion back at the shop, there is some record of his capture at Budapest. But then the trail disappears."

She squeezed his fingers, and her eyes narrowed. "Disappeared? Really? That can mean a number of things. So there is no clue as to what might have happened?"

"Not that I heard. But it's really just a beginning. We can keep trying."

She smiled. "You're right. We have just started, thanks to you. This is more than we've known before, although it could still turn out badly."

"Yes, but I think he's still alive. The Soviets seem to think so, anyway. They're also looking for him."

Sabine sipped the wine, staring at the rug, then off in the distance. "That is not good. It means we must find him first." She sipped again, nodding in agreement with her own conclusions. "You will help, won't you?"

Baier drank some of his wine. He noticed the clear, dry flavor for the first time. Wine had never been this appealing or appreciated before, at least not that he remembered. "Well, I'd like to. But it's going to get complicated. The Soviets also expect to be involved. They asked me to work with them."

Her hand pressed Baier's fingers hard enough to hurt. Sabine studied the backyard, sipping more wine, as though she might find her husband out there hiding among the pines. She looked back at Baier. "No," she said, "we must avoid that at all costs. They'll kill him for sure."

"How can you be so sure? It sounded like they only wanted to question him."

Sabine shook her head lightly and smiled. She leaned forward and kissed Baier on the cheek. "Karl, you obviously have not dealt with the Soviets very much. If they catch him, he will definitely disappear, but this time forever." Her forehead rested on Baier's. "I need your help. I need you to be with me, Karl, to make me strong for this."

Sabine released his hand and lay back against the sofa, studying Baier's face with an easy smile. Her right hand rested against the side of her head, while her left stroked Baier's forearm. Then her smile widened, and she nodded as though she had just made up her mind about something. "You remind me a great deal of my husband."

Baier was at a loss for words. He listened to his amplified heartbeat and could see little more than the light from the ceiling reflected in the glasses of wine. He was drawn then to her

67

eyes, which seemed to grow darker and more piercing. He was grateful that the image from the other night did not return. In fact, he realized at that moment that he had not thought of Perkins's murder once in the last two days. It was as though this new quest and the increased pace of his work had helped him shove that whole incident further back in his mind.

She took Baier's glass and set both on the window ledge behind the sofa. Then she leaned in closer than before, close enough for her to press her lips to Baier's. Her mouth opened just barely enough for her to rub her tongue over his lips, before she pressed her own lips hard against Baier's again. He was powerless to resist. Together they held the kiss for what seemed to Baier like a full minute. Maybe, hopefully, more. Then her lips broke from his and brushed his eyelids, his cheek, his ear. Her left hand sank to her dress, and she unfastened the top two buttons. She took Baier's hand and slid it over her right breast. Baier was stunned. His breathing grew hard and sporadic. His fingers probed the soft flesh as he stroked the curves along the slopes of her breasts, then moved over her nipples. He could no longer sit comfortably, so he started to lie back. Abruptly, Sabine stood, took both his hands, and pulled him up.

"Come, Karl," she whispered. "I remember the way."

Together they walked towards the stairs.

Afterwards, Baier and Sabine lay together, coiled under sheets that reached to their waists. He had created a nest with his arms, and she lay with her back tight against him, their legs intertwined. He rested his nose in her hair, breathing in deep and often.

"Tell me about yourself, Sabine."

She rolled over to face him. "What would you like to know?"

Baier ran his lips down her cheek, across her nose, then let them rest for a moment on her own. "Everything. Or at least as much as you'll tell me. I want to know as much about you as I can."

Sabine smiled, and her eyes danced with his. "Well, I came to Berlin from Franconia. You know that area, in northern Bavaria?" She frowned. "Yes, of course you do. Anyway, I came to Berlin in 1937 looking for work as a model."

"Were you successful? I'd have hired you."

Sabine glanced away and laughed. "Yes, well, you were not here then, unfortunately. I ended up working first at Siemans as a secretary, but then I found work at the end of 1938 in the Foreign Ministry, again as a secretary." She looked back at Baier. "I was lucky. I only had a degree from the local vocational school, not a proper *Gymnasium*. You know the difference?"

Baier nodded. "How long did you work there?"

"Until the end of 1944. By then everything was coming apart. It was when Ernst first became helpful to us."

"I don't want to hear about him. But tell me how you met your husband."

Sabine rolled over to face him, her smile gone. "Karl, must you ask about him now?"

He leaned back to put a little space between them. "I can't help it if I'm curious about your life." He remembered the reference to the *Abwehr*. "You never told me, for example, what your husband did."

"We met at a reception at the Foreign Ministry, and a year later we were married. Satisfied?"

"I'm sorry. Believe me, but I need to get things straight in my head. There are things I want to know about you, and that involves the others in your life as well."

"How romantic." She sighed. "What do you need to know?" She shifted her weight so that she was facing him with her entire body. "Your timing leaves much to be desired, you know."

He leaned up on one elbow. "I'm sorry. I want to be with

69

you, Sabine, but there are things I need to know before we go on. We must be open and honest with each other. Otherwise, we're not going ahead with this. I can't. Don't you see? Not with my position." He tried to control the speed and volume of his words as they tumbled from his lips.

She gave him a skeptical look, almost grinning. "That doesn't seem to bother your compatriots all that much."

"I'm not like them, Sabine. Not all of them, anyway. And this could involve much more than most of my compatriots can offer, or will do. I've already gone farther than I had expected, talking to the Soviets, I mean."

Her hands rose and stroked his face. "Yes, yes, of course. But I know so little. And I will tell you what I do know."

"The Soviets said your husband had been in the *Abwehr*. Is that true?"

"Yes," she confessed. "He had been an intelligence officer. But he was in the military. That's what the *Abwehr* did. It was not like the Gestapo. He could never be a part of that."

"Why?"

"Because I know the man and what he was . . . is . . . capable of. Besides, he only talked about his work with the *Wehrmacht.*"

"Did he have a specialty?"

"I know he worked against partisans in Greece, but he was transferred from there after we pulled out in October and was then sent to Budapest when the Soviets made their big push through Hungary."

"Your side was not gentle with the partisans in the occupied countries. He must have some blood on his hands."

"As did the other side. It was not a gentle time for anyone, Karl."

"What was he supposed to do in Hungary?"

"I'm not . . . I'm not sure. Our manpower situation was desperate. And there was little he could tell me. For all I know, he was given a rifle and sent to the front line as a regular soldier." She looked into Baier's eyes, and her hand stroked his chest. "The *Fuehrer* and his gang did not trust the *Abwehr* after the putsch attempt, you know."

"Yes," he replied. "I can understand that." Baier knew that Admiral Canaris, the head of the *Abwehr*, had been implicated in the coup and assassination attempt against Hitler and executed for it in the final days of the war. "But do you have any idea where he might have gone if he did escape?"

"No." She laid her face against his neck. "He avoided Berlin to avoid the Soviets. He may have filtered himself in with the thousands of *Wehrmacht* troops fleeing to the West in hopes of being captured by you or the British."

"And what about your brother and that other German? Why aren't they in a P.O.W. camp?"

"My brother was. The British held him in one of their camps in Schlesswig-Holstein. But they let him go during the summer. They are much more relaxed than you Americans. He was one of the lucky ones."

"Has he found work?" Baier asked.

"Yes. The British have put him to work with others they've hired to clean up the rubble."

"I thought the women were doing that."

She sighed. "For the most part. There are still so few men around."

"What about you?" Baier inquired further. "Are you a *Trummerfrau*?"

"Oh God, no." She pulled away from Baier. "I worked at that for a few days. But I'm not going back. That's a big reason I'm staying with Ernst."

Baier pulled her back close to him. "Now that you mention it, what's with that brute? How did he keep out of a camp?"

Her face found his neck again, while her body curled up

71

against his in a tight semicircle. It left Baier with the impression that she was pulling herself into a defensive coil. "Ernst had been one of the defenders of Berlin when the final call went out. Most of them were in the *Volksturm,* the militia. My God"— her eyes rolled—"what a waste. It was truly criminal of the regime to throw old men and mere boys at the Reds. Ernst was able to hide in the cellars for several weeks before the Soviets finally grabbed him. He escaped from a transport that was shipping German prisoners east to work in the Soviet Union and made it to the western part of the city. He refuses to leave the American or British sectors."

"And his role during the war?" Baier pressed.

"Ernst was called up to serve as a grenadier at the end of last year. He's in his forties, you know."

"I thought he had been a supply officer."

"Initially, yes. But by 1945, they were looking for soldiers to enforce discipline and order against desertion."

"So he was one of the ones killing his compatriots."

Sabine nodded. "Yes, that's also how I see it. He claims he was just enforcing order in the ranks to prevent the Soviet onslaught."

How convenient, Baier thought. "I knew there was a reason I disliked him." And perhaps I'll think of a way to lure him east, he thought. Karlshorst is always waiting with open arms. It would serve the bastard right.

"But enough of this, Karl." She straightened herself and rolled over on top of Baier, her legs wrapped around his. "I'm here with you now." She kissed his forehead, then his lips. Her body pressed down on his, her buttocks tightening as she moved against him. "I feel almost as though you are my man now. I want to be with you. It's like I have my husband back."

Baier moved in rhythm with her and felt his body grow loose and tight at the same time. Yes, he thought, it's as though we are back together. He felt himself sink into a deep pool of longing, warmth, and openness. He embraced not just her body, but the very idea and feel of it against his own. I'm with you now, inside, he told himself. And I'm going to stay there as long as I can.

CHAPTER SEVEN

When the Soviets followed up with Baier two days later Kucholvsky was no longer involved. Apparently, it had moved beyond his level. And the follow-up occurred at Baier's door on *Im Dol*. More like a pursuit, or so it seemed. Baier had actually forgotten about his approach to Kucholvsky at the *Kommandatura*, having spent the past two days following the investigation into Perkins's death. The lack of information kept him unsettled and at times preoccupied by the seeming lack of progress.

"You sure you never saw any indication of black market activity?" Younger had asked the day before. Baier had been called into his office, where he met a nameless major and captain from the Criminal Investigations Division, or "El Cid" as Savage had labeled them in his own inimitable and typically irreverent way.

"He drove me back and forth between meetings and visits to industrial sites or former German government offices. That was it," Baier replied. "Sorry."

"What did you talk about?" the major asked. Baier wondered why he wore no name tag.

"The difficulties the Germans were having adjusting, mostly. That and girls."

"Was he unusually sympathetic towards the Germans?" the major continued.

"Hard to say," Baier responded. "Their country, hell, their world has collapsed. But you can't say they didn't bring it on themselves."

"Would you say that summed up your driver's outlook?"

"Pretty much," Baier said. "He may have wondered, like all of us, if the truly guilty Germans were the ones suffering."

"They're all guilty," the captain announced. It was his first statement of the afternoon.

Baier studied the hard, square jaw and beady eyes set under the thin gray eyebrows and guessed he would be a quick man to judge. "Perhaps," was all he said.

The major continued the interview. "Did you get the sense that Perkins might be taking advantage of the Germans' plight, of the chaotic conditions affecting their lives here in Berlin?"

"Yeah," the captain chipped in, "did he have a stable of women he could use for anything other than his own pleasure?"

"Well, he was taking advantage of the surplus of women, but I don't think it went that far." Baier thought for a moment. "I never saw any indication that he was enriching himself materially. He did like to get laid, though."

"We all do," that judgmental captain interjected. "Most of us just go about it differently."

"Differently? Are we talking about positions now?" Baier couldn't help himself, his dislike of this man suddenly intense.

The captain stared for several seconds before answering. "You know what I mean. We don't take advantage of their plight."

"Well, that's open to debate," Baier said, "at least from what I've seen in my brief time here." He paused to take in his visitors. "What have you guys found? Anything incriminating? About Perkins, I mean."

Both men ignored his question. "Did you ever see him with any non-Germans?"

"You mean besides Americans?" Baier was even beginning to enjoy this.

"You know what we mean," the major interjected. His jaw tightened, and his eyes narrowed. "How about the Soviets?"

Baier wondered if he had pushed them too far. He shook his head. "Sorry, guys." He thought for a moment. "What about the possibility of a werewolf killing? Maybe some old Nazi didn't like him infringing on the purity of an Aryan maiden."

The major and captain stood. "There doesn't appear to be any of that going on." The major nodded. "Thank you for your time, Captain. We'll be in touch."

After they left Baier turned to Younger and spread his arms wide, his face stretched with puzzlement. "What the hell, Frank?"

Younger shrugged, then waved in the general direction of the door, through which the two investigators had just disappeared. "Don't worry about those pricks. Unless you're lying, of course."

"Well, I'm not."

"Oh, hell, I know you're not, Karl. Those guys may seem like assholes, but they're really just doing their jobs."

"But have they got anything?" Baier asked. "You know, I'd like to find the creep responsible, too."

Younger shook his head. "They only tell me that Perkins had been seen at at least one locale known for its black market activity."

"And that would be?"

Another head shake and a wave at the door. "Oh, they wouldn't tell me that."

"It's nice to be trusted."

"Well, you're not to worry about it," Younger reassured him. "You got more important things to do."

Which was true enough, Baier told himself. The Soviets, however, were not interested in Perkins, his death, or the black market. Not during this particular visit to *Im Dol*, at least. It came under the cover of night, and this new officer appeared to be alone.

"Good evening, Captain Baier," the Soviet officer said. "May I come in?"

"Yes, certainly." Baier hesitated, then stepped back and held the door open for his visitor. Baier had not wanted the Soviet officer to come inside, much less stay for very long, if only because Sabine was waiting upstairs. Moreover, he doubted it would impress his colleagues and superiors if they knew that he had hosted, in a manner of speaking, a Soviet officer. He guessed that the man was Russian. He could not tell from the man's bearing and the string of medals and ribbons that covered his chest, but it was an association most Americans made instantly and easily. Baier, however, had dealt with a few Soviets, and he realized that the man in his doorway could just as well have come from the Ukraine or one of those Caucasus states. He did not have the Asiatic features Baier associated with Central Asia. In any case, Baier hoped the Russian or whatever had not noticed his reluctance.

The Soviet officer had noticed. "Are you busy, Captain?" He shrugged and smiled. "I promise I won't stay long. I thought I should stop by, though, because it has been several days and you have not responded to our offer." He held out his hand. "But first, let me introduce myself. Colonel Sergei Chernov of the Soviet Military Administration." So I guessed right, Baier concluded. They shook. The Russian's English was impeccable. "And you, I believe, are indeed Captain Karl Baier of US military intelligence."

"Actually, I work as a liaison officer with the civilian administration here," Baier tried to explain.

Chernov immediately dismissed Baier's attempt to apply his cover assignment with a frown and a wave. "Let us dispense with these silly games, Captain." He took Baier's arm and led him through the foyer and into the living room. "I know very well why you are here in Berlin." The smile widened. "I, too, come from that world. I have spent the last fifteen years working for the NKVD. I only tell you that because I know your people will inform you accordingly tomorrow, and to show that I have no intention of deceiving you."

"That's comforting to hear. And if that's the case, then you can tell me what you want."

"I should have thought that was obvious," Chernov stated. "Karl Baier." The smile was still in place, but now his eyes sparkled. "The other one, of course."

"Why exactly?"

"Well," Chernov explained. "We believe he has information that will be valuable in identifying war criminals among the Germans, but also among those who helped in their criminal campaigns in the east." The smile disappeared, finally. "Isn't that why you're searching for him?"

"But I'm not. I simply sought some information for his family," Baier explained. "That's all."

"And not for what he could tell you about German scientific capabilities and endeavors?" Chernov looked around the room. "May I sit?"

"I'd rather you didn't. I have an engagement this evening."

"Ah yes, that's right. I must be imposing," Chernov apologized. "So I will refrain from smoking a cigarette and take my leave. I can see you were not prepared for this. But let me make an offer before I leave. And to give you a warning." He held up a hand quickly, while the smile came back. "Not a threat, mind you, but a warning."

Baier was silent. Something in the Soviet's easy manner, his self-confidence, and his penetrating gaze told Baier that he was in the presence of a true professional. And one who could become a very dangerous foe. The Russian also had an impres-

78

sive physical presence. Although thinner than Baier, the Soviet officer stood equal in height, and the brown military overcoat hung naturally on his shoulders as though attached at the epaulets. It looked as though the man practiced his moves dressed just like that in the morning before a full-length mirror. Baier did not want to encourage this man or open himself to the difficulties an unofficial relationship with an NKVD officer would entail, especially one of this caliber.

"The offer is this," Chernov continued. "We, too, have information on the German scientific community and their works, especially their missile and nuclear programs. After all, as you are aware, we have found German professionals as well and persuaded them to work with us. I could arrange for us to share some or all of it, depending on how forthcoming you are with information on your namesake's whereabouts." He patted Baier's arm. "All I ask is that you think about it."

"And the warning?"

Chernov had turned to leave. When he swung around, a cigarette had suddenly materialized in the fingers of his right hand. The same hand brushed the hair on his forehead back into place. His manicure was meticulous. "Oh, that's right. The warning is this." He glanced towards the ceiling. "There are others interested in Karl Baier and his whereabouts. Not just you and me. So be careful. Choose your allies wisely." The smile returned. "I will be in touch."

"How?"

This time the smile evaporated. "I'll find you. It will be easy enough." He paused and considered the ceiling above him, as though he was aware that someone was waiting upstairs. "And you should be aware that I will be the person to represent our side in this affair."

Baier stepped back. "Just what does that mean?"

The Russian's eyes seemed to drill through Baier. "It means

you should not try to work this case through anyone else from our side. You are only to contact me. If necessary, you can reach out to Kucholvsky, but only to request a meeting." The smile returned briefly. "I can make it worth your while on several fronts, Captain."

Baier could not resist the obvious follow up. "In what way? I'm already paid more than enough for my needs."

This time, the Russian actually laughed. "I think you'll find there are other things more valuable than money, Captain. Information, in particular. There is much available in that line in Berlin and many uses for it."

Chernov glanced once more at the ceiling above, then turned and walked out the front door, leaving Baier alone in his living room, more puzzled than ever about just what Karl Baier had been up to during the war. And what could he be up to now? If he was still alive, that is.

"So, what did that fucking Russian want?"

Baier was struck not just by the obscenity of Sabine's question, which greeted him as soon as he reached the top of the stairs, but also by the vehemence with which she delivered it.

"Come, Sabine. The war's over. You can't hate them forever."

"Not for them it isn't. And yes, I can."

"Well, he wants your husband, Sabine. And his side seems to want him very badly. Why is that?" Baier asked. "What aren't you telling me?"

Sabine Baier ran her hand through her hair and turned towards the bedroom. She had removed her dress and was barefoot, wearing only a bra and a loose white slip. "It's very complicated. And it would take a long time."

"Try me," Baier directed. "We've got all night. But first explain something for me."

"Yes?"

"Why is it that I've never seen any customers at the cleaners and yet you, Ernst, and your brother appear to be doing quite well. At least you're well fed. You haven't once asked me for help in getting food or ration cards or anything of the sort."

Sabine spun and fell on the bed, but then immediately sat upright. She looked at Baier almost with pity. "You really haven't figured that out?"

"I think I have. But I want you to confirm it."

"Yes, we deal in the black market. Ernst got it started."

"How?"

"Through some of his assignments he was able to establish connections to storage sites the *Wehrmacht* had prepared in the region. They were supposed to provide provisions and supplies during the retreat, but the collapse after the Red Army's offensive in January was so sudden they were left largely untouched."

"And Ernst found them?"

"He already knew about them. That's why he was able to get into them before the population looted them. It's what kept us fed this summer."

"But for how long? Winter isn't very far off, and there hasn't been much food produced in Germany."

"Of course not." Her vehemence had returned. "What can you expect with the loss of so much of our land in the east, the war, the destruction, the loss of men." Her eyes searched the floor, and the words softened. She slid back across the bed, and the slip rose up across her thighs. "But we have enough supplies for ourselves and for trading to get us through the winter." She looked up at Baier, her eyes pleading. "You won't tell anyone, will you? Please." Her hands came together in prayer.

"Was my driver Perkins involved?"

Sabine considered this for a moment. She propped herself on her elbows and frowned. The lamp from the nightstand cut the bed in half with its shaft of light crawling across the middle of the blanket. She had already turned the top sheet down, and Baier wondered if she had watched the Russian leave the house from her perch upstairs. "No, not that I'm aware of. I only saw him that once with you."

Baier nodded, then sat beside her on the bed. "Now, about your husband . . ." He paused when her eyes narrowed and Sabine blew out her breath in frustration. "You promised to tell me all you know."

"Yes, yes. All right, I will." Sabine took his hand in hers, then kissed his cheek. "I don't know everything. But what I do know is that it started in Greece."

"Is that why you and your brother keep steering me there?"

She pulled his hands to her lips. "Yes, it's because you can go there and we can't. And it's because you are Karl Baier."

"So let's start at the beginning."

She nodded. And then she began her tale.

CHAPTER EIGHT

"You see, it started when he was stationed there. He was not with the original invasion force. Too bad, though, because that was more like a picnic outing."

Sabine sat on the edge of the bed, her knees tight together and drawn up to her chest. The slip fell past her knees and almost to her ankles. She wrapped both arms around her legs and stared straight ahead at the bedroom wall. The room itself wore a dark shroud, deeper than any night Baier had experienced in Berlin. A ray of moonlight split the open window of the bathroom off to the right, and the glow of the table lamp had shrunk to a small arc. Sabine continued in a low voice, a few tones above a whisper.

"It only took our troops about two weeks to reach Athens, and then the Greeks surrendered. The Greeks had done much better against the Italians, but that surprised no one. Karl also missed most of the first year of our occupation. That was fortunate. It was a horrible time. Thousands starved. No real preparations had been made to feed the civilian population."

"Worse than occupation by the SS?" Baier interrupted. "There were terrible reprisals there, as elsewhere in Europe."

Sabine nodded, then her chin fell back to her knees. "Oh, yes. Much worse. I'm sure many more died this way. At least, that's what Karl said. And those reprisals probably came later, when the fighting with the partisans broke out. There were so many requisitions, and so little food was left. And there was no system or government established yet. Except our military, of course. And Karl said they just took everything they could find."

"So when did your husband arrive in Greece, and how did he find all this out?"

"Near the end of the first winter. It was March, 1942, and I was quite happy, you see, because it meant he would not have to go to the eastern front. Even when our army was so far advanced in the east, the fighting was growing bitter and cruel after our first offensive failed to take Moscow. So Greece seemed like a good posting. Our soldiers all thought it was a good one. Perhaps as easy as France. But Karl saw all the starving people, especially the children, and he learned how brutal that winter had been."

"What was his job there?"

"As an *Abwehr* officer he was to set up an intelligence network aimed primarily at the British, to block their infiltration and sabotage efforts. That gave him great autonomy and freedom of movement. And that's how it began."

"How what began?"

"His treasure hunt. Or that's what he called it. I think he got the idea when he saw how much suffering there had been."

"So he looked for a way to exploit that?"

"Or to provide some help at the same time. He claimed he quickly found he could make money on the side by facilitating the movement of Greeks who sought to flee to the Italian occupation zone. Occasionally, he was able to seize a shipment of Red Cross supplies that started coming in 1942 and sell them to the Greeks."

"So he had a traffic in humans going?"

She nodded.

"Like Jews?"

"Yes, some Jews. And others, too. Whoever could pay."

"That's horrible. Your husband stole food from starving

people and bartered with people's lives." Baier turned away from her, his lips twisted in disgust. "He should be tried as a war criminal."

"Don't be a fool," she spat. Her eyes grew wider and hard as she leaned towards him. "And don't be so quick to pass judgment before you have all the information. He never took food away from people once they had it. Enough was distributed eventually. He claims he sold only extra supplies to the well-off, who were always demanding more." Her visage softened, and she settled back into her huddled pose. "And those he helped escape at least got away from the SS and the Greek fascists."

"So he claims. Or claimed."

"Yes, so he claimed."

"Where was he stationed and how was he paid?" Baier asked.

"At first in the north, in Macedonia, and occasionally he traveled to some of the islands. He mentioned Chios and Delos. But then after we occupied the entire country, he was moved to the Peloponnese. And he only took gold as payment. The Greek currency was worthless, he said. And after the Italians surrendered in 1943, he said it was obvious we would lose our position in the Balkans, and possibly the war, in view of what was happening elsewhere. That's why he started hoarding it."

"Did he continue to sell food then?"

"Yes, of course. There was always a market. Sometimes he simply had it shipped from one area to the next where there might be a shortage."

"And he continued to profit from that?"

"Stop it, Karl. I see American soldiers profiting here every day in Berlin."

"It's not the same. For the most part we're helping you. Besides, he would have needed collaborators."

"Yes, of course. But he never told me the particulars of how it all worked."

"You said he started hoarding it later. In the second half of 1943. What did he do with it before that?"

"He brought some home. Fortunately, we were able to save some of it in the later years, and later it helped start our own black market activities here in Berlin. Ernst still had to pay off some people to get those supplies from the *Wehrmacht* depots."

"How was he able to avoid detection? By the German authorities, I mean. The SS and *Wehrmacht* were all over that place, or so I thought."

"Don't forget, the *Abwehr* was part of the *Wehrmacht,* so Karl would have known how to operate there. And there was always competition with the SS and Gestapo. So the *Wehrmacht* would instinctively protect one of their own against them. And Karl once said he had a special protector. Very high up."

"Such as?"

Sabine raised her head to give it a slight shake. "He never said. Not exactly, anyway."

"Not exactly? Did he give a hint?"

"Only that General Lehr and Minister Neubacher admired his work against the British and the *andartes,* or bandits, and that they were both very supportive."

"And who were they?"

"Lehr was the military commander, and Neubacher was the Foreign Office minister in charge of Greece, and most of the Balkans as well, I think."

"What did he do to win their trust? Did he pay them off?"

Sabine shrugged, and her chin fell back to her knees. "I'm not sure about any payments. Perhaps. But they liked his networks and the information he provided. Karl did not believe in the random hostage taking or reprisals. He said they were counterproductive. He even tried to prevent them in his areas. He claimed they would disrupt his networks. It's one reason he was able to build up trust and continue to earn gold. That kept up until we left Greece last October. But while he was there he was able to gain a lot of autonomy for his operations."

"Sabine, please be honest. Did he help round up Jews, like all those who were deported from Salonika?"

She turned her face towards Baier and studied him with eyes that had gone dark and distant, like small stones in a stream. "They all did, Karl. No one had any choice. They may not have enjoyed it or believed that it was right, although I'm sure many did. But they all participated in some way." Her face turned away. "My husband never talked about it."

"So how much did your husband collect after all this?"

"He never gave an exact figure. He probably doesn't know. I doubt he kept a record. He once said something about a half a million Reichsmarks. I'm not sure how much that is in real money now." She smiled for the first time that evening. "Or in Lucky Strikes."

"Jesus." It was all Baier could think to say at first. "So where is it?"

Sabine broke the clinch around her legs and leaned back across the mattress. Her eyes had regained some of their natural light and color. She gazed at Baier for nearly a minute, as though she was taking his measure for a new suit of clothes. Or his courage and sense of adventure.

"That's another story. It's one you may get to write. That is, if you wish."

"What do my wishes have to do with it?" Baier was puzzled, even stunned. He stared at Sabine, his forehead wrinkled with uncertainty.

She sat up, her eyes glistening. A half-smile lit her face with a look of mild surprise. "Doesn't the prospect of all that money interest you?"

"I certainly don't wish to have money I don't deserve. That money doesn't belong to me. It doesn't belong to you either. Or to Ernst, or Robert. Or even your husband." Baier found it difficult to speak the man's name. This surprised him, and he thought about that for a moment, studying the way Sabine's face passed in and out of the shadows in the room. "What he did was wrong, Sabine. Simply wrong."

The smile evaporated, and her spine stiffened. She leaned away from Baier, her arms folded across her chest. "And just what do you propose we do with it? That is, if we ever find it."

Baier shook his head in disbelief. "We have to give it back, of course."

Sabine slammed both hands on the mattress. "Back to whom? Are we supposed to hunt down every Jew and Greek and ask for their receipts so we know how much to return?"

Baier waved his own arms in frustration. "No, of course not. But there must be some organization, some charity you can give the money to."

"And how can you be so sure the right people will ever see this money? Shall we try the Catholic Church? Then the Vatican will most likely be able to afford some new jewelry and art works for Saint Peter's."

"Don't be ridiculous . . ."

Her fists pounded the mattress again, then they slammed into Baier's chest. "Don't you be ridiculous." A grin, more like a leer, spread across her face, and she brushed her hair back past her forehead with her hands before they fell to her waist. "Or perhaps we can give it to the Communists. After all, they represent the working class, the truly oppressed. Just ask them. Surely they deserve it after all these years of toil and suffering. Maybe that's why those fucking Russians are so interested."

He wanted to calm her now, block the anger that was erupting as the words flew from her lips in a wave of saliva and aggravation. Baier took her hands in his and drew her closer. "Sabine, please. Calm down." Small pools of tears started to form above her lower eyelids, then several thin streams creased her cheeks. Baier kissed the wet skin and stroked her hair. "Please, Sabine. It's all right."

"It's those fucking Russians, Karl. They're the ones who really want the money for themselves. It's why they're after my husband. That's all they want. Don't speak to me of justice."

"How can you be so sure?"

"Because I know them and what they're capable of. I saw it, Karl. We all did. Here in Berlin. And the rest of Germany to the east. Just ask anyone. Especially the women."

Baier folded her in his arms, kissed her forehead, and placed his face against her hair. Then all her pent-up emotions seemed to burst at once. He felt her shoulders shake with sobs, her face buried in his shoulder and neck. He let her rest there for several minutes, hoping she would calm down enough to go on. There was still so much more he needed to know, so much more he wanted to know.

"Tell me about when they came, Sabine, why you distrust them so." He pulled back a bit to look her in the eyes. The weeping had stopped, but her eyes were still wet and rimmed in red. An occasional tear trickled down her cheeks. "Do you want to talk about it? Can you?"

Sabine nodded and sighed, wiping tears away with the back of her hand. Balled fists came to rest in her lap, and she stared at some distant spot on the bedspread.

"After the big Red offensive in January, we all knew we were lost, that it was only a matter of time. There was an air of fatalism here. It even came through in a gallows humor. You know, for example, that LSR stood for *Luftschutzraum,* but those were changed in popular talk to mean *Learn Schnell Russisch.* Berlin is famous for its wit, you know?"

"Yes, so I've heard," he replied, nodding. From "air raid shelter" to "learn Russian quickly."

89

"We heard such terrible stories from all the refugees that flooded in here from the east. The Soviets were so horrid when they first got to East Prussia. And it continued all through the eastern advance. Karl, they even raped Soviet women who had been brought here as forced labor. Many tried to flee. Except me. I was too frightened of all the uncertainty and the danger of running away in the open. Your planes, Karl, and those of the other Allies often strafed people. And if the Russians caught you in the open, there was no hope at all. I mean, they would just run over people with their tanks.

"By April, the Red Army was close to Berlin. I shall never forget the morning of April 16 when the artillery started to bomb for the assault on Berlin. Karl, the earth here in the city shook, even though they were still dozens of kilometers away and none of the bombs actually fell inside the city itself. A few fools still believed in the *Wunderwaffen* that would turn things around, or that the Allies would split, or that some relief column would break through. There was even talk that you Americans would drop your paratroops here to seize the city first. Or that you might even join us to fight against the Bolsheviks. It was a surreal and hopeless time. You didn't think it could get any worse. We lived like cellar rats, scrounging for food and water. After about a week the Red Army broke through into the city."

"How long did you live like that?"

Her eyes were red and pleading. Her hands twisted the slip between her legs. "Karl, you no longer had any sense of time. We lived in the dark, only venturing out when absolutely necessary. We could hardly sleep with all the shelling and fighting. Some fled whenever rumors of another Soviet advance or the capture of another neighborhood spread, and others tried to hide in their buildings. But it never did any good. They always found you. And there were bodies and filth everywhere. That and the constant fear, which gnawed at your insides like a cancer."

"Fear of what, Sabine?"

She looked up at Baier. "Fear of death, of course. Or worse. Capture and deportation, or, for the women, rape."

"Were you raped?" Baier's head slumped. "No, I'm sorry," he said. "I shouldn't have asked." He leaned forward to take her in his arms again.

Sabine held up her hands. "That's all right, Karl." She covered her face for a moment or so, then lowered her hands slowly. "No, not at first. I hid for two days under a pile of clothes in a wardrobe. I was hungry and cold and thirsty. I even wet myself. But I was too afraid to move. Still, I was very lucky. Others were not, though. I could hear the screams and pleading of the other women. Often at first, but then only occasionally when I ventured out for food and water." She looked up and then through Baier. "The mornings were safer because their soldiers were usually sleeping off their drunks. At first it was the common soldiers, brutes really. They would often stand in line. You had to be strong to survive." She looked back into Baier's eyes. "Many didn't, Karl. There was a rumor that the Soviet command gave their troops three days to do as they pleased. Then they restored order. That's when the officers took over."

"The officers? Did they participate in gang rapes as well?"

Sabine sighed and looked down again. "No. They chose some to be their kept women. We had little choice, Karl. It was that or starve. Or worse. You would lose their protection and be back at the mercy of the brutes. I was eventually found and shared by two officers from the Ukraine and White Russia. I don't remember their rank. I've tried to block all that out."

"When did it all end?"

She smiled, and her face rose to Baier's. "When the Western Allies came. In July. That's when we had a safe part of the city

91

to go to." She lay back on the mattress, her head resting on her arm and her legs curled up against her stomach.

"I'm so sorry, Sabine." Baier, of course, had heard the stories before, but they had always been something abstract and remote. Seeing Sabine shrunken and curled on his bed brought a human dimension to it all, one that was now personal enough to pierce his heart and shake his sense of confidence and understanding. He lay down beside her, pulling her close and wrapping his arms around her shoulders.

"I can never forget, Karl. And I can never forgive those bastards. They are not going to get that money. Nobody else is, Karl, nobody. I swear it."

"Rest now, Sabine. Try to sleep. Everything will be all right."

He didn't know if anything at all would be all right, and he wasn't sure if he was able to convey the confidence in his words that he lacked in his own mind. Nor did he know yet what he could do, or what he might try to do. But he knew that he wanted to make sure no further harm came to Sabine Baier.

CHAPTER NINE

"Where to again?"

Baier and Younger trotted to the circular driveway of rough, pale gray paving stones that ran in front of the American headquarters on *Kronprinzen Allee*. Baier's new driver, another corporal from the Midwest, but this time from Rockford, Illinois, waited by the jeep in a loose approximation of parade rest, the car's engine running. His name was Kopp. A fellow German-American, Baier had thought when he first met the new man. He would have to probe to learn more about his family and background. Two other jeeps also waited with their engines running, and two trucks as well.

"*Osnabruecker Strasse,*" Younger replied. "It's just across the Spree from the garden behind the Sophie Charlotten Palace. It's tucked back in that warren of streets with the apartment complexes. Or what's left of them. It's in the British Zone," he reminded Baier.

Not that he needed to. They had gotten the address from the British after sharing some information, although just what it was remained unclear to Baier. If there was one security obsession that held Younger it was the "need to know," a euphemism he had come to know well in this new world of intelligence. Baier, of course, thought he had every right to know, given that he had discovered the identity of the man they were now pursuing. He had come across the name in the files the boys in Criminal Intelligence had finally turned over after weeks of prodding and pleading. There had been a certain SS General Baumgartner—his membership purely ceremonial, Baier suspected—who had escaped from the missile works at Peenemuende just ahead of the Soviets and apparently ran for all his life to Berlin. The escape was fortunate, but he made it to the *Reichshauptstadt* just in time to be caught in the Soviet encirclement and on the eve of its final death struggle, the *Endkampf* in the Nazis vainglorious vocabulary. His odd luck had continued, as he dodged first the Soviets, then the Western Allies for months. Apparently, he feared that his membership in the SS would be remembered more than his scientific work, even if it had been in the service of the Nazi war machine. But that work was a major reason Baier was so sure that his SS membership had been more perfunctory than ideological, more professional than political. The man had been a first-class chemist until his recent unemployment, and Baier vaguely remembered his name from some article or textbook he had read as an undergraduate. Baier also doubted this Baumgartner would ever face any kind of trial. His scientific prowess was simply too valuable to all the victors.

"That was good work you did in finding this guy, Karl." Younger climbed in beside Baier in the back of the jeep. "How did you figure the British would help?"

"Well, the files mentioned his studies at Cambridge in the 1930s, so I thought he might prefer hiding in the British Zone, thinking he would feel more comfortable in surroundings slightly familiar. So I dropped the name and a description to the British at their office at the *Kommandatura.*"

Kopp pulled the jeep out of the parking lot at the head of the column as it sped down the Kronprinzen Allee.

"Well, it worked," Younger noted. "Even if we did have to trade for the right to keep the guy if we find him. Some guy named Thompkins proved to be pretty helpful. Jumped right in on the case."

The column swung right after about half a mile and rolled down *Hohenzollerndamm* until it reached *Fehrbelliner Platz,* familiar territory to Baier from when he first arrived in the city. There were still crowds lingering by the makeshift bulletin boards, searching for news of their lost or wandering family members, and Baier wondered if any had found their missing loved ones since he last passed this way a little over a month ago. The *Trummerfrauen* continued their work in front of the buildings that resembled little more than shells. It was October now, and already the nights had grown chilly. With winter approaching Baier felt his first inkling of concern for the inhabitants of this city despite the horrors their regime had inflicted on themselves and the rest of Europe. The column veered left at the *Platz* and continued in the direction of Charlottenburg on a street that, as far as Baier could tell, had no name. The street sign must have been blasted away at some point, Baier guessed. They crossed *Kant Strasse* and *Bismarck Allee,* and soon the ruins of the Sophie Charlottenburg Palace rose on their left. Allegedly, Frederick the Great had built the residence for his queen because he didn't really care to have her present at his favorite haunt, *Sans-Souci,* over in Potsdam. Then he probably wouldn't mind all that much, Baier figured, to see the shambles the bombing and fighting had left it in. Baier asked himself how much art and architectural history had been shattered and possibly lost there, and whether any of it would be restored at some point in the future. It would have to be a pretty distant future, from what he could see.

"Pretty sad, isn't it?" Younger must have been thinking the same thing. He surveyed the ruins as their jeep breezed past the crumbled palace and crossed a small pontoon bridge the British had erected over the Spree. Baier was struck by how narrow the river was at this point.

"Here we go, sir," Kopp barked as they pulled up in front of an apartment complex just a few blocks from the river. Baier was amazed that anyone could live there. It appeared to be about sixty or seventy percent destroyed. Only one of the buildings, the one at the center, looked habitable. Baier guessed that it must have been supported by the structures on either side to allow it to remain standing. Most of the windows and doors were still in place, unlike the other buildings, and it still had its roof, which looked complete and solid. Only two other buildings in the neighborhood could say as much. Groups of people milled outside each of the structures, and all turned to look as the column sped into the courtyard. Two jeeps had sprinted around behind the building to guard against any possible escape from the rear.

Baier and Younger leaped out of the jeep and raced behind the squad of soldiers climbing the stairs to a third-floor apartment. The team burst through the door of an apartment on the left side of the stairwell with no warning. Baier heard shouting and screams from inside. Several neighbors threw open their doors to see what was happening, but they shut themselves in again as soon as they saw the uniforms.

Baier jumped through the doorway and threaded his way between the soldiers and German civilians, desperately searching for the face he had seen in the file. Two middle-aged women stood in the center of the living room, trying to block the squad from proceeding any further into the apartment.

"What the hell are they saying, sir?" one of the soldiers asked Baier.

"They're saying that we have no right to be here, that this is the sort of uncivilized behavior one expects from the Soviets."

"Screw that," the soldier, a private first class, stated. "We do have the right, don't we, sir?" His hands gripped the M-1 tightly while his eyes roamed the room with a hint of fear that he might

96

actually have to use his weapon.

"Yes," Baier noted. He tried to sound reassuring to calm the young G.I. "We most certainly do, and I doubt these people will put up much resistance." He turned to the women, both of them wearing tattered shawls over dirty house dresses that had faded to an indistinguishable color close to gray, and ratty slippers over woolen socks. It did not feel as though there was any heat in the room. *"Hor auf,"* he ordered, or "Shut up," in American parlance. An old man sat on a sofa that looked as though it had exchanged most of its stuffing for a thin layer of dust, a grin on his face and his arms folded as though he was enjoying the entire spectacle. *"Unser Fuehrer, wir danken dir,"* he kept mumbling. Baier had found a few of the old posters around town that bore an image of Hitler and the saying, "Our Fuehrer, we thank you." Pretty ironic, considering the state of Berlin these days. But Baier did not recognize the old man's face.

He slipped into the kitchen, and that's where he found the man he was looking for. Baumgartner sat placidly at a long oak table, slicing some cheese, which he set on a piece of brown bread. He was wearing woolen slacks with suspenders extending over a grimy white shirt on its way to becoming a brown one. His feet sat inside worn and peeling black leather shoes. He studied Baier's face while chewing some of the bread and cheese. He set the knife down on the table.

"Americans?" he asked in English.

Baier nodded. "Yes, from Military Intelligence. General Baumgartner?"

The man nodded in turn. "Please, I prefer Doctor Baumgartner now." He shrugged. "I always did, as a matter of fact."

He stood, then strode over to Baier. "I'm glad it was you who came." He held out his arms. "Shall we go?"

Baier took him by his elbow and lowered the man's arm. "That won't be necessary. I never planned to use any restraints."

97

Two soldiers stepped inside the kitchen; each grasped one of Baumgartner's arms. Together, all four walked out of the kitchen, through the apartment, and down the stairs.

"Don't forget your friends and family when you're in America, Ulrich," Baier heard one of the women shout. Baumgartner just smiled.

As the jeep column sped back to headquarters, Baier asked Kopp to cut across two streets and hook up with *Gruenewald Strasse*, which became *Koenigen Louise Strasse* as they entered Dahlem. He gave the lame excuse that this might actually be shorter. His real reason was to seize another opportunity to catch a glimpse of Sabine. It was more a matter of curiosity for Baier than concern. But he found himself thinking of her more frequently these days. She had been strangely absent for the last week, and he had wandered past the shop several times in hopes of seeing her. Baier had no plan, no idea exactly what he would do if he did encounter Sabine on such an occasion. Invite her for a drink? For dinner? Hardly. Then again, why not? In the end he realized he'd just be happy for a chance to see her once more.

He had not found her on those days, and he did not find her this time either. Instead, he was shocked to see a group of American and British soldiers gathered at the sidewalk in front of the cleaners. And just as they drove by, several British troopers led Joachim and Ernst out the front door and into a waiting lorry. Baier strained to see if Sabine was also being apprehended, but he saw no trace of her.

His shock must have been apparent to Younger. "That was our tradeoff."

"What?!" Baier shouted. It seemed as though the word erupted from his lips. "A laundry establishment?"

"Actually, a big time black-market headquarters. The British seemed pretty eager to shut it down. I could have sworn that

guy Thompkins was just about rubbing his hands with glee."

"Did they say why? I mean, what's it to them if there's black-market activity going on in our zone? We can handle it." He looked into Younger's eyes. "Did we know about it?"

Younger shrugged. "They didn't give any particulars. Thompkins said something about a grudge match. We didn't think it was all that much to give up to get our hands on Baumgartner." Younger leaned back and studied Baier. "I don't believe we knew it was that big an operation." He jabbed Baier's arm lightly. "Why the concern? Anyone you know?"

A thread of fear ripped through Baier's midsection, and he turned his face to stare into the Gruenewald as the jeep pivoted onto *Kronprinzen Allee.* "I've been there once or twice, that's all. I had to pick some things up."

Sabine was waiting at the house when he returned from work, just as Baier had hoped she would be. The rest of the afternoon had been lost in a haze of worry, confusion, and anxiety. Savage had stopped by, but Baier blew him off with a mumbled excuse about a headache, the same one he had used with Younger when the secretary told him the Major wanted to review the Baumgartner operation. Baier was not a particularly religious man, but he found himself praying, half consciously, as he neared *Im Dol* that he would find her and soon. She was pacing back and forth in the living room, treading a path through the middle of the light brown carpet. Only then did he notice how close the color of the rug came to that of her hair and wondered if that was why she, or they—Sabine and her husband—had chosen that particular color. Sabine maneuvered around the furniture as though she were navigating an obstacle course, her eyes focused down towards the floor and her hands wrestling with one another.

She glanced up when she realized that Baier had entered the

room. "Oh, Karl, they've taken Joachim and Ernst."

"I know," he replied. "I drove by there a little earlier as they were being taken away."

She stopped in mid-stride and stared at him in horror, her eyes wide with confusion. "Did you know about this?"

"Don't be ridiculous." He discovered that for the first time since he had known Sabine Baier, he was actually angry with her. After their time together how could she suspect such a thing?

"Then how did you come to drive by at just that moment?"

"I was returning from a trip to the British sector and asked the driver to detour past your place. I was hoping I might see you. I certainly did not expect to find the street swarming with military police." He paused to study her face, the eyes still wide with fear and uncertainty. "How did you manage to escape?"

"I . . . I was so lucky. I had gone out for a moment and saw those military police when I was returning. I stopped a block away and watched with some others." She glanced out the window, then back at Baier. "I . . . I don't think anyone recognized me."

"What happened?" Baier asked. "You didn't have any warning that they were coming?"

Sabine's hands fell to her side. "What do you mean? Of course, I didn't know." She stared at him for a second, then her hands started flapping at her sides as though they were causing her pain. "I just told you I was so lucky. I . . . I don't know what to do."

He stepped toward her. "But what happened, Sabine? How deep into the black market are you people? That is why they raided your place, isn't it?"

She started to pace again while her hands continued to flail. "Yes . . . yes, of course. At least I think that's why they came. That's what you said, isn't it?" She stopped in the middle of the room and stared at Baier, her face a force of concentration and sudden inspiration, as though a great insight had just now come to her. She almost smiled. "Perhaps Ernst and Joachim had been involved in something else after all."

"Such as?"

"I . . . I don't know. I can't be sure. Perhaps they were smuggling things." She raised a finger. "Yes, they could have been smuggling people." She shook her hand and looked down at the carpet again as though she were noticing her footprints for the first time. "But I should have noticed something. I'll have to think what it was."

"Why would the British want to go there?" he asked. "I'm sure there are many places where that is happening. My boss claims they were especially eager to raid your shop." He paused to examine her face. "Have you heard of a Brit named Thompkins? He apparently ran the operation."

Sabine Baier shuffled over to a chair by the fireplace and lowered herself into the seat. She sank back against the cushions, the fabric of her forest green woolen dress pressing against her body and outlining her legs. She turned her face to Baier, the eyes ablaze with a conviction and indignation that easily matched anything Baier had seen from her before, even on the night when she had spoken of the Soviets and the personal consequences of their victory in Berlin.

"Of course, it's the money. Our money."

"You mean this horde of gold your husband has supposedly hidden away somewhere? What does any of that have to do with the British?"

"They're after it, too. Karl must have had to contend with them down there. It was their territory, after all. And they're back down there now that we're gone. I'm sure they want it."

"But I thought it was the Soviets we . . . I mean, you have to worry about."

She shook her head and her hands as her gaze swung to the open hearth before her. "No, not just them." She rammed her fist into the arm of the chair, once, twice, then a third time. "That must be it."

Baier shook his own head. "But how would they even know? Are you saying that some of the people your husband exploited ran to the British and tattled on him? Did your husband ever mention any names?"

She stood and marched over to Baier, who had yet to move from the spot in the doorway between the foyer and the living room where he had first encountered her. Sabine walked up close and grabbed Baier's arm. Her face was inches from his.

"I can't remember, but those creepy British bastards must know," she said. "Either they found out in Greece and are looking for it there, or someone betrayed us back here."

"But who and why?" Baier pressed. "They don't have any more right to that money than you do."

Her grip on his arm tightened. "That's what we have to find out, Karl. We have as much right to it as any of them. More even. That's what I've been trying to tell you."

He strode over to the chair Sabine had just vacated. He sunk into it, his gaze roaming from Sabine to the floor and back. What had he gotten himself into? The raid, the romance, the stories of hidden treasure. It had all seemed like a bright adventure, an exercise in curiosity, but he had not foreseen anything this troubling when he walked through the door of that laundry shop. How, he asked himself, could he walk away? He knew it might well be too difficult, too late even. And did he even want to? His gaze wandered over to Sabine, and immediately he knew the answer to that question. He would do almost anything to help her.

Things were now moving fast, certainly too fast for him. It was then that Baier remembered the words of caution, of warning actually, passed by the Soviet colonel in this very house. There were others trying to find his namesake, not just the Soviets. Just who and how many, Baier asked himself, and why? And what would it take to find out? He couldn't be sure the raid and the treasure hoard were linked, but it was something he would have to explore. He needed information to give him some context, the additional background and history to figure out a way forward. He would reach out to the one man who had approached him from another side. He would contact the Russian.

CHAPTER TEN

Colonel Chernov had agreed to meet for drinks in the French sector of Reinickendorf, just across from the Tegel forest, a place Baier considered neutral territory. Sabine had initially resisted when he first raised the subject over breakfast the following morning.

"Why do you need to talk to that fucking Russian?" she protested. "It would be best to keep him at a distance."

"He has a name, Sabine."

She nodded while she chewed a piece of toast. "Yes, that's right," she agreed. "He's that 'fucking Russian.' He's also a snake, and snakes bite."

"Then how can you distinguish between them?" Baier asked.

"There's no need to. Those bastards are all the same."

Given what she had been through, Baier was certainly not going to argue with her.

"What about the English?" she asked.

Baier examined the woman who sat opposite him. She wore one of his white T-shirts as a substitute nightgown, her hair pulled back in a bun after a morning bath. She leaned over the table, a knife in her right hand as she sliced an apple, the second half of her breakfast after a slice of cheese and some toast. Baier could see the outline of her breasts as her body pressed against the edge of the table. "I'd have thought you'd consider them to be snakes as well," he said.

"They are. They're just not as venomous."

When he had suggested the possibility of a meeting to Kucholvsky at the Allied *Kommandatura,* the Soviet representative had beamed with pleasure and satisfaction. The light emanating from his smile had been almost bright enough to warm the old building in the damp October cold, and the vodka he offered Baier would have completed the job. Baier had declined.

"I think that's a bit premature," he had reassured the Soviet officer. Baier wanted to avoid any hint of collaboration, or even cooperation. He politely declined several more offerings, which did not, however, dissuade Kucholvsky from celebrating with several shots of Russia's national drink on his own.

Baier had begun to reconsider the wisdom of choosing a rendezvous in this part of town as he drove in what seemed like circles through deserted streets strewn with rubble and lined with the shells of shattered buildings. The problem, he decided, was that they all looked like any other street in Berlin. And it did not help that he had chosen to drive himself in order to avoid any prying questions or spreading knowledge about his extracurricular activities. After about half an hour of searching, Baier had found the location, a three-story structure that actually appeared to have served as a restaurant before the battle and occupation.

"They have food here as well, I understand," Chernov offered.

"So you've been here before?" Baier found it interesting that Chernov had come dressed not as a Soviet military officer but as a civilian, in a light gray woolen suit and a white shirt and deep blue tie, all of which looked as though they had not been out of his suitcase or duffel bag or whatever he used since he had left the Soviet Union, or even before. Baier surveyed the room with its exposed brick walls and wooden beams providing the ambience of a romantic wine cellar. All it had to offer for drinks was beer, however, which Baier was happy to see tempered the mood a bit. As did the fact that it was now the only fully habitable part of the building. The upper floors were little more than skeletal ruins, with only the roof and three walls intact. This did not deter the many Berliners desperate for living space, however. The ground floor still had all four walls, and it looked as though three families were sharing that. Baier assumed all the help lived just above. If anything, it eased the commute.

"Oh, yes," Chernov replied. "I was pleasantly surprised when you suggested it. How did you know of it?"

"My colleague, Richard Savage, recommended it. I believe he meets his French counterparts here."

"This Mr. Savage, does he work in your office?" Chernov inquired.

Baier was happy to discover that he must be learning more about how to play this game, because his warning antennae rose immediately. Chernov was clearly fishing for a more complete list of the people working in Baier's office. He shook his head. "No, he's a civilian. He works with the political parties here, trying to re-establish a semblance of democracy as Germany rebuilds."

"That would do us all some good," Chernov agreed, which brought some elevation to Baier's eyebrows and wrinkles to his forehead. He had laid a particular emphasis on the word "democracy" to make a point to the Soviet, but the man appeared to have missed the point entirely, considering how the Soviets were managing their part of Berlin and Germany. "Yes, of course," was all he said as Chernov's gaze roamed the cellar, presumably in search of a waiter. Baier found himself wondering about this man's personal history in the Soviet system, how he had advanced his career or even survived the momentous purges, whether he had a family, and just how committed a communist Chernov was. Eventually the Soviet spied a waiter, and Chernov signaled him over, ordered two more beers and two bowls of gulasch. "I'm buying," he insisted. Baier was damned if he'd let him pay, though.

"So, are you ready to cooperate in finding your namesake?" Chernov pressed.

"I'm afraid I don't have much to offer. Not yet, anyway. In fact, I still find this episode, this whole story, very confusing." The Russian's eyebrows arched as he sipped his beer. "Perhaps if you could tell me more about how he came to escape from your side, that would help," Baier countered.

"Help how?" Chernov replied.

"Help me in knowing where to look and what to look for. For example, I understand he was captured at the fall of Budapest last February. But what happened then?"

Chernov paused to think. He watched the waiter deposit the bowls of gulasch and the basket of sliced brown farmer's bread, the Russian's face impassive and focused on the steam rising from the rim of the pottery. Chernov lifted his spoon, spun it several times in his hand, then sifted it through the thick, meaty stew. Finally, he let the spoon rest in the dish and grabbed a piece of bread, which he ate by breaking off small bits, dipping them in the stew, then tossing them in his mouth.

"Are you familiar with the battle for the city?" Baier shook his head as he started to shovel gulasch into his own mouth. He was surprised by how rich it tasted and at how hungry he suddenly felt. He guessed that the owner must have some sort of connection with the local French authorities to be able to serve food this hearty. Baier studied the Russian over the rim of the bowl as he ate.

"You are correct. It was in February. We had a siege laid on for about one hundred days and advanced steadily into the center of the city. Unfortunately for the Germans, they tried to break out only after the relief efforts had failed, and by then it

107

was too late. We were well prepared, and few of them made it out. Still, our losses were very heavy."

"As usual," Baier had wanted to say. Instead, he stuck another spoonful of gulasch between his lips.

"The German Baier had been with a group that survived the initial assault out of the city center in Buda and broke through into the woods to the north of the city. Several hundred made it to a series of hills with some of those horrible sounding Magyar names like Csobanka and Norgykovacsi. It was there that we captured him."

Chernov paused to stir his stew, then ate a couple mouthfuls before continuing. "I'm talking too much. This is losing its heat and its head." He ate several more bites. "But that may have saved his life."

"How so?" Baier inquired.

"He and some of the others were held in the woods to get them ready for transport. When the Ukrainian regiment holding them realized Baier was an *Abwehr* officer, they got ready to execute him."

"So how did that save his life?"

"First of all," Chernov raised one finger, "it prevented him from being transported with the mass of prisoners taken from there to the east. He would have been lost in the crowd and ended up in Siberia or the Urals in very short order."

"Second," Chernov held up another finger, "it gave him a chance to use his wits. He told the Ukrainian fools that he had important information to pass along and demanded to see a Soviet intelligence officer. So they called for me."

"You mean you were already there?" Baier dropped his spoon into an empty bowl. There was a loud ringing sound that made him wince. "How was it you were called?"

Chernov shrugged. "I was the closest one there." He finished his gulasch and proceeded to wipe his bowl clean with another slice of bread. Baier did likewise. "And your namesake was very persuasive. He told me he had been in charge of *Wehrmacht* funding for intelligence operations in Greece and knew where a large sum of money had been left behind. When I pressed for details, he claimed that only he could find it and that only he could approach his local friends and collaborators."

"Why did you believe him?"

"Because he provided a small bag of gold coins right there. He tried to give me Reichsmarks at first, and I told him I had no use for those. So he gave me a handful of gold coins instead."

"So what happened next? Obviously you never shot him."

"No, obviously not," Chernov conceded. "He was able to slip past his Ukrainian guards during the night." Chernov held up a third finger. "They, however, were shot."

"You mentioned the other night that others were looking for Baier as well. Whom did you mean?"

Chernov smiled as he sat back in his chair. "Not quite, Mr. Baier. I've talked enough, and you've had little to say. That you will have to find out on your own."

"I'm afraid that at this point I have nothing to add."

"Oh, come now." Chernov leaned forward. "Certainly you know more about the money in Greece. If not the exact location, then surely a general idea. His family, whom you've gotten to know quite well, must have some idea. We could even search for it together. You and me, I mean. We can eliminate any middlemen. That will keep our circle tighter and make it safer for both of us."

Baier caught his breath when he heard the word "eliminate," especially from a member of the Soviet forces. And "safer" for both of them? How so? Just what dangers were out there? "Together?" Baier repeated. "I hardly think that will be possible."

"And why is that? Are you afraid of me? Suspicious? Or

perhaps you think yourself better than a Soviet officer."

"Why does this have to be personal? I can assure you this has nothing to do with you," Baier tried to reassure him. "Do you think we can simply walk into Greece together?" He realized then that he was also trying to convince himself.

"Of course, it's personal. Don't be so foolish. At this point it has everything to do with me. And we needn't travel together. I can keep track of you well emough." The Soviet officer studied Baier. "Is it possible you want to keep it all for yourself and your German whore?"

Baier paused, his eyes focused on the empty bowl as he worked to subdue his anger. "I hardly think that's worthy of you, Colonel, or called for. Just what do you mean it has everything to do with you? That money, if it does exist, does not belong to you. And I have no authorization . . ."

Chernov's voice rose, and his words rang out clearly with an emphasis on each separate syllable. "Captain Baier, there are some things in this city you will need to do on your own. That is, if you intend to benefit from your time here. Or even survive, considering what you are now involved in." Chernov paused as much to get his breath as to consider the American. "Do you have any idea what's going on here, and how desperate some people are? Just what did you hope to accomplish this evening?"

Baier was surprised at how quickly he replied. "I had hoped to learn more about Karl Baier so I could help his family."

Chernov moved in closer so that his entire upper body stretched over the table. "Well, that will not do. Do not try to make me believe that you are only an angel of mercy for a German family you've only just met. And I know that you have learned much more than 'nothing,' if only from Baier's wife, who now shares your bed. So do not act so superior and shocked by what I propose. You are hardly the innocent angel you would like to have me believe you are. If you think it can simply end

110

there, then you are truly a young fool."

Baier sat upright and shoved his bowl away from him and in the direction of Chernov. Sabine had been right, he thought: you couldn't trust these men. One moment Chernov had been friendly and collegial, and then he had turned threatening and insulting. "I came here in good faith . . ." Baier began.

"No." Chernov slapped his palm on the table. "I came here in good faith, and it has not been repaid. In fact, you have abused it." He pointed a finger at Baier. "Do you think you can operate in such splendid isolation? Do you really think I am unaware of what you are doing?" Chernov brushed Baier's bowl away from the space between them. "You should remember that we occupied this city for several months before you arrived, and that we had many opportunities to prepare our own network of informants in every corner. I have friends in your sector as well, and I can monitor your every move. So I will find out one way or another." A smirk broke across his face. "There could even be benefits in that for you, if you're wise. You'd be surprised at what I am willing to trade for information on Karl Baier."

"Your friends?"

Chernov's hands spread out beyond his body, as though he would embrace the entire room. "Perhaps I misspoke. I have no friends over here, only assets. And assets are often for trading."

Baier stood his ground, arms folded across his chest. He smiled as though he had just uncovered some secret. "All this makes me wonder what else is at stake here. Are you really so interested in some alleged money chest, or is there something else involved. In fact, it makes me even more hesitant to leap into anything with you."

Chernov rose to go, tossing a handful of rubles on the table. "Believe what you like, my young American. We can do this as allies or as enemies, Captain Baier. But you won't find out what you need to know unless we do this as the former. It is your

choice. The former would certainly be easier for the both of us."
He stared long and hard at Baier. "And you would do well to
remember what happened to your first driver."

Baier nearly exploded as he leaped from his seat. "What did
you say?" he demanded. "What do you know of Perkins's
murder? Were you behind that?" Baier moved around to the
front of the table to confront the Soviet, who placed a hand on
his chest. Baier slapped it aside.

"No, Captain Baier, I was not behind that killing. But I know
of it, and it should remind you that there are many actors in
this and other dramas in this town. Some of them are connected, some are not. But it is clear that you know nothing of
them, that you are walking on unprotected ground and you are
very vulnerable." Chernov held up another finger. "And be very
careful if you touch me again like that."

With that Chernov stomped up the stairs and out into the
street. Baier worked to settle himself for several minutes, then
asked for the bill and paid the waiter in American dollars, leaving the rubles for a tip. At first, the waiter looked as though he
would leave the rubles on the table. But after a second thought,
he returned, scooped them up and stuffed them in his pocket,
then walked back behind the bar.

With the British there was less drama. But even more surprises.

It had not been hard to find a pretense to meet with his colleagues in British intelligence. Baier had approached his boss
with a proposal that they probe their special allies for other opportunities to cooperate, like the one that had brought the
chemist Baumgartner to the American side, possibly to see if
their interrogation of the German scientists back home had
turned up any leads in Berlin. Younger had leaped at the idea
and suggested inviting them to lunch, preferably at the Harnack
House. "Get 'em on our turf," he had plotted.

At the *Kommandatura* the British officer, a Captain Mac-Donald, had suggested contacting a Colonel Thompkins, even offering to make the initial call himself. Baier remembered the name from the raid the other day. It did sound like a good idea. According to MacDonald, Thompkins had a long history of working with the Americans, and he had acquired extensive experience on a broad front during the war, especially on tracking down Germans. Baier, relieved to be dealing finally with someone of equal rank in MacDonald, gave the captain his number, then strode proudly past the American office, even nodding to the secretary seated just past the open doorway.

Thompkins had called later that afternoon and sounded almost gleeful when he accepted Baier's invitation to lunch. Given what he had seen on his one visit to the British command earlier in his tenure, Baier was not surprised by the ready acceptance. The food there looked pretty grim and unappetizing. He was beginning to wonder just how much America's special friend in Europe, indeed, the world, was going to be able to offer to do beyond its own shores. A nice thick steak, Baier surmised, should do nicely to soften this Thompkins fellow up and allow Baier to probe for anything the British knew or were looking for at the laundry shop and the people associated with it.

He would have to be careful, though, since Younger also planned to attend. But it wasn't too long into the lunch before Baier and Thompkins appeared to develop a genuine liking for each other. True, Thompkins had attended Oxford before the war, "reading" History, as he put it. But the man displayed none of the pretension Baier had expected. They had just finished their salads and drunk perhaps a third of the bottle of Bordeaux—or "claret" as the British officer insisted on calling it—that Baier had ordered and which Thompkins showered with compliments when he began to quiz Baier on the Avignon

Papacy and then Charlemagne, but in a manner one would expect from a colleague, not a superior. Thompkins had visited both Aachen and Avignon before the war and offered to accompany Baier there should he ever get the chance to visit either city.

"I suspect Aachen barely resembles the city you once saw," Baier suggested. "But I can always check with Dick Savage, one of the civilian political advisors who worked there early in the occupation."

"Yes, that would be marvelous," Thompkins replied. "Please do. And I'm sure Avignon has not changed much from when I was last there. The SS never pursued any of their grisly business there that I'm aware of."

To no one's surprise, Younger took his leave shortly after the steaks arrived. Besides, he had said almost nothing throughout the lunch, barely touched his wine, and raced through his sirloin. With a sharp salute to the British colonel and a pat on Baier's shoulder, Younger rose, excused himself, and departed.

"Stop by the office when you get back," Younger said. "I'll be interested in any possible followup. And Colonel, I sincerely hope we'll be working together often in the future."

Thompkins rose, offered his own open-handed salute, then shook Younger's hand. "Absolutely, Major. And I apologize if our banter about European History drove you away. It's just that I rarely get the chance to discuss my favorite topic nowadays. I'm sure you understand."

As he sat, Thompkins refilled the wine glasses. "I hope you aren't in trouble, Captain."

Baier waved the thought away. "Not at all. He understands. Besides, the major is too nice a guy to let something like that upset him. Especially if he thinks it can lead to new opportunities for cooperation."

"Ah, about that." Thompkins sat back. "I haven't heard

anything from Farm Hall yet, so I don't want to raise false hopes. But I will certainly encourage them to be forthcoming." He leaned forward, wine glass poised in front of his lips. "Can you give me a better idea of just what it is you're looking for?"

It was Baier's turn to sit back, wine glass in hand. "Oh, anything along the lines of what we were able to accomplish in the Baumgartner case. I'd say I'm interested in anything that throws light on German industrial and scientific capabilities. Much of that is already available in academic and business circles, however. So what we'd really like to learn is more about how they were able to achieve so much in those fields that had a military application, especially given the constant air assaults they faced."

"Like their missile programs and jet engines?"

Baier nodded vigorously. "Yes, yes. That's why the Baumgartner case was so helpful."

"Anything on the nuclear front?" Thompkins asked.

Baier grinned, then sipped some wine. "I think we're pretty well ahead on that front. At least I haven't gotten much in the way of requirements there."

"Which is just as well," Thompkins conceded. "Mind you, there's no official policy on this, but I note a certain reluctance to share much there, perhaps because, as you've said, your side is pretty well ahead."

"In that case," Baier continued, "can we agree to meet again for lunch next week? You can let me know if there's anything from your people."

"Absolutely." Thompkins drained his glass. "And this time we'll dine at our officers' club over by the Olympic Stadium. We've found a nice intact building over by the stables that is doing quite nicely for that sort of thing."

"And is there anything I can bring in return?"

"Well, yes, now that you mention it," Thompkins answered.

"Of course, I'd appreciate any information on nuclear activities you encounter, if only to test it against what their scientists like Heisenberg are telling us."

"No problem. Anything else? Like black market activity, perhaps? Your fellows seemed pretty eager to break up that ring operating out of the cleaning establishment on *Koenigin Louise*."

Thompkins fingered his glass and studied Baier's face. He glanced down at the tabletop, reached over, and poured the last of the wine into their glasses. He waited a minute more before speaking, and only after surveying the room.

"That operation involved more than just black market, smuggling, and the like." Another pause. "We had reason to suspect that there was also espionage activity underway there."

Baier leaned in close, almost knocking his wine glass over. "Say again. Espionage activity? Who, exactly? How?"

Thomkins reached out a hand to calm Baier. "I use the word 'suspect' purposely, Captain. As it turns out, there was nothing we could confirm. But we still suspect something is up."

"Can you be more specific? I mean, this is practically on our doorstep, as it were." His thoughts swam back immediately to the dinner with Chernov the night before and the Soviet's boast about knowing all that occurred in Baier's surroundings.

Thompkins surveyed the room once again. "You're aware, of course, that this sort of thing is best left to our relationship with your CID and CIC people."

"Yes, of course. But still, I mean, it's practically right around the corner."

Thompkins nodded. "Yes, I understand. And I'm prepared to discuss aspects of this with you, if you promise that it will go no further." Baier nodded. "Good. It involves people working with the Soviets, and the man we principally suspect is this Ernst Hoffmann. He's a brutal sort, who had some involvement with the German Communist Party before the Nazis came to power.

Afterwards, he more than made up for it. He strikes me as the sort who will make amends with whomever is in power."

"But to what purpose? Was he trying to collect intelligence on us?"

Thompkins smiled. "Oh, probably. This is Berlin, Captain. Everyone is trying to collect intelligence on everyone else." He drank some wine. "And usually succeeding, I might add."

"Suspect?"

"Yes, I'm afraid it's not documented yet, and at this stage it appears to be largely circumstantial. But there are foreign links here, issues that extend beyond the borders of the former *Reich*."

"Such as?"

"Captain, may I ask you a question about your past, your family?"

"Yes, I suppose so, although I'm not sure what that has to do with anything."

Thompkins leaned in closer. "Your family originally came from Germany. Is that correct?"

Baier nodded. "Yes, but so . . . ?"

"So, was your purpose in coming to Europe to defend your country and project its power and interests, or to salvage what you could of your ancestors' homeland?"

"I and my family are fully American, Colonel. We have no sympathies for what the Nazis wanted to do here in Europe." Baier felt a rush of heat rise in his cheeks. He had also gripped the spoon firmly in his right hand as though it were a weapon.

The British officer pursed his lips. "That's not quite what I meant, Captain. I did not mean to suggest anything as untoward as Nazi sympathies. But I am curious to know how sympathetic you feel towards the Germans, given your background, and whether your interest compels you to look backwards or forward. We need to keep our focus, Captain, and to choose our allies wisely."

Baier leaned in close to make his point. "My interests and focus, Colonel, go where my country tells me to place them."

Thompkins smiled. "Ah, that's all well and good then. But you see we've only just finished one battle, and now a new one is emerging. So I would not concentrate too much on what just passed and what you can accomplish with those left behind."

"Such as?"

"Such as your woman, Captain. All of Europe is in flux. You are no doubt aware we're entering a new competition for the future of the continent. For example, we're deeply engaged in restoring stability and a constitutional monarchy in Greece, an involvement in which we could use your assistance. That could be the next battleground."

Baier hoped that the sudden intake of his breath had not been noticeable. "Greece, you say. I've heard they're on the verge of a civil war there."

"Yes," Thompkins replied, a slight grin suggesting he had noticed Baier's discomfort. "One stage of that war is over, but the sides are being redrawn as we speak. And I'm afraid we are likely, as I said, to be in need of assistance. Of nearly any kind, Captain, not just military. Diplomatic as well, and especially financial."

Baier felt the sweat beading on his forehead. He dabbed at it with his napkin, then drank the rest of his wine, hoping it would settle his nerves. "Financial? Is London really as broke as I've heard?"

Thompkins nodded. "Yes, I'm afraid it is, or nearly so. It's expensive to keep fighting these Germans, even if we do win. That's why we're so interested in running down leads on all and every treasure chest, as it were, to which we believe we have a legitimate claim. Or the legitimate Greek government does."

"Yes, I see." Baier sat back, hoping to catch some air. The room had lost its focus for him, and he needed to catch his breath. "Well, I'll see what I can find, but I'm guessing I'll have more luck on the nuclear issue."

They rose to leave. Baier was relieved to discover that he was actually steady on his feet. The brief spell of nausea also passed quickly. Outside on the steps of Harnack House Thompkins turned to Baier halfway down as he proceeded toward his car, the driver waiting.

"Oh, by the way, Captain. Your woman is in the clear, at least for now." He smiled and offered his hand. "On the espionage topic, that is. And thanks again for an excellent lunch. I hope you enjoy our kippers and kidney pie as much as I enjoyed your steak."

CHAPTER ELEVEN

"So how'd it go?" Younger inquired.

Baier grabbed the chair by the door to his boss's office, pulled it next to the desk, and sat. He relaxed in the seat, leaning back and resting his arm on the edge of the desk. "Fine. I'm sorry, though, if we drove you off with all that history talk."

Younger waved at nothing in particular. "Forget it. I could see you guys were getting along well, and I didn't want to screw things up. I knew you'd be fine."

"Well, not quite fine enough."

"What," Younger asked, "he change his mind about the wine?"

Baier laughed. "No, no. Nothing as serious as that. But it doesn't look like we'll be getting any new leads from their side. At least not yet."

"Meaning?"

Baier studied the window at Younger's back for a moment before redirecting his gaze at the major. "Well, he hasn't heard much from London, and in particular from the folks working at Farm Hall there in East Anglia where they're holding their own batch of Kraut physicists." Baier leaned in close. "Interestingly, though, Thompkins eventually shifted the conversation to Greece."

Younger's face took on a look of concern. His hands, which had been playing with a pencil, froze. "Greece? What the hell for?" He sat back in his chair, as though to place some distance between himself and the subject raised by his young protégé.

Baier's hand rolled on the desktop while he shrugged. "It wasn't entirely clear. But he suspects fighting to break out eventually between the royalists and the communists there."

"But the Nazis are gone and their king is back in place."

"But apparently not everyone is happy with that. The disarmament of the Communists is incomplete, and he fears they'll return to partisan activity."

Baier paused, rose and walked to the door, then shut it. When he returned to his seat Baier stared hard at his boss. "What I really found intriguing, though, was the hidden plea for assistance."

"Oh, bullshit." Younger shifted his weight forward and set both arms on his desk. "We are not sending troops there. That'll be the day, son. Hell, we can't ship 'em home from here fast enough."

Baier held up a palm. "He wasn't talking about military assistance. It was more financial."

"They want money from us?" Younger snorted. "Hell! We've spent enough to help those limeys out," Younger almost shouted. He rolled his eyes, then shook his head. "Did he ever hear of Lend Lease?"

Baier kept his palm up, almost pleading for a chance to finish. "It was more like helping them find money he claims belongs to the Greeks, which he says is back there in Greece." Baier's hand finally fell. "It would require some intelligence help as well."

"Like what?" Younger's skepticism was clear in the lines of his face, the set of his brow, and the curl of his lips. "I mean, if it's in Greece, what the hell are we supposed to do? And why should we care?"

"I think he believes there are links to people back here," Baier explained. "I'm sure that's why he brought it up. And I think it's tied to that raid at the cleaners we saw the other day."

"But I still don't see why he would talk to us about it?" Younger pressed. "That's not in our lane."

"But it is on our turf. And I think I may be able to help."

"You?"

Baier shifted his weight in his chair as though he was trying to get comfortable again under the weight of Younger's new-found suspicion. Younger's eyes moved to a stage one step short of a glare. "What have you been up to?"

Baier waited, counting the seconds while he tried to determine if this was the right step to take. When he reached ten, he spoke. "sir, don't take this the wrong way, but I've gotten friendly with some locals, and I think they may know something."

"Who?"

"Well, they're connected to the cleaners. And there's a woman . . ."

"Oh, goddammit, Karl. I knew it." Younger shot himself back deeper into his seat, slapping the desk as he pushed all his weight against the back of the chair.

"Please, sir. Hear me out. This woman has some ties to the German occupation in Greece through her husband. They're pretty vague and tenuous, but I might be able to learn more." Baier paused to let the idea sink in and grab some time to catch his breath. He wanted to relay the next point very carefully. "And I might even be able to help down there in Greece."

Younger said nothing. He stared at Baier as though a stranger sat in his office.

"Just consider it, sir. Obviously, I can't promise anything, but it would put the Brits in our favor. They'd have to share more with us, even if there's nothing to this. We'd get points for just trying."

"Hell, son, we won the goddamn war for 'em. That puts them pretty deep in our favor as it is."

Baier stood to go. "I'm afraid they still don't see it that way.

In their eyes, they were holding the Nazis off just fine until we finally decided to jump in. And I think there's a lot here they're not telling us. Our relationship may have gotten a lot closer in these two wars, but they still have their own agenda. It may be tied to their past and not the future, but they still have imperial ambitions." He paused. "And obligations."

Younger looked out the window, his side turned to Baier. He did not look up at first when he spoke. "We'll see. I'm going to think on it, and then I'll probably run this up the chain." He swiveled in Baier's direction. "In the meantime, son, I want you to think long and hard about this yourself. Have you thought about what you might want to do when your enlistment's up?"

"Not really, sir. But I can promise you that I won't do anything illegal or anything that would taint the command here."

"Oh, hell, son, I'm not so worried about that. You're not important enough to taint the command, as you put it. And as for myself, I hope to be out of here and back home before the end of the year or shortly thereafter. My cousin is starting up his construction company again in Montclair, New Jersey, and he's offered me a spot in the front office there. With all the G.I.s returning and getting married and starting families and whatnot, there's going to be plenty of new building going on."

"How does that apply to me, sir?"

Younger sighed. "My point is you have to think ahead. What I don't want you to do is mess up your own future. Can you understand that?"

Baier nodded. "Absolutely, sir." He glanced at the photograph on Younger's desk of the major, his wife, and two teenage sons. It struck Baier then that he had not brought any pictures of his own family to decorate his office. He hadn't thought it possible, going to a war zone. But Younger clearly had an indication, Baier assumed, of the importance the man attached to his wife and children. He may not have a family of his own, but Baier realized how much importance his boss put on things beyond his immediate assignment.

"In that case," Younger continued, "I don't want you to do anything stupid and foolish. There is a lot going on here that you do not understand. Hell, I don't understand a lot of it either. And it would be very easy for you to fall in over your head. Think ahead, dammit. Are you sure going to Greece is a good idea and worth the trouble it could bring?"

Baier surprised himself at how quickly he replied. "Yes, sir, I think it is."

"Well, okay then. But whether you go or not, I especially do not want you to fall in love. That's a goddamn order."

Baier laughed. "I'll do my best, sir."

"Listen, son. I'm just a grunt who made it through OCS, new to this kind of business. It looked like an interesting assignment over here, but it's turned out to be a lot more of a challenge than I expected. Like a puzzle with minefields. You've done pretty well so far, and I don't want to see you get hurt or screw up your future. Got it?"

"Yes, sir, I do." Baier saluted, then left.

"Jesus Christ, Sabine, everyone in this damn town knows about us." Baier was too agitated to stand still. He had been stewing over his push for a trip to Greece, uncertain if he had made the right decision, and just where it all might lead. What had seemed clear and logical at first had become less so over the course of the afternoon. He paced back and forth from the kitchen to the dining room, running his hand through his hair. Sabine Baier grabbed his arm, held it tight, and tried to stroke his hand.

"Karl, calm down. What do you mean by the entire town? All of Berlin?"

He stopped to look at her. "It sure as hell seems so. That fucking Russian, as you call him, spoke about you sharing my bed, and the British refer to you as my woman."

"When did I come up in the conversation? What were you talking about?"

"Both are interested in the money your husband stole, and they seem to think it's somewhere in Greece. And they also believe I know just where it sits."

Baier slipped from her grasp and strode over to the sofa. He fell back against the cushions and studied her. "Just what do you know, Sabine? What have you been holding back?"

She moved toward him. "What do you mean? I haven't been holding anything back. Karl, you know as much as I do."

"I can understand how the Soviet officer knows. He apparently encountered your husband after the failed breakout at Budapest. Although your saintly German *Abwehr* officer told him the gold had been stolen from *Wehrmacht* funds used to finance intelligence operations."

"Surely you do not think he would tell the Soviets where it really came from."

"Why not?"

"Because they'd use that information to run it all down themselves. Besides, that would never happen. Those *Abwehr* monies must have been very tightly guarded."

Baier shook his head and ran his hands through his hair again. "That's not the point right now. The British also know about you. Just how the hell is that possible?"

"What did they say? And who said it?"

"This Colonel Thompkins," Baier replied. "He didn't say so explicitly, in so many words. But he knows about us, he was behind the raid at your place, and he pointedly brought up the subject of money belonging to the Greeks."

Sabine sat on the sofa next to him and ran her arm around his shoulder. "The British must have captured some of Karl's agents or met up with some of the people he helped."

"Helped?" Baier laughed lightly, shaking his head some more. "That's a pretty generous interpretation."

She squeezed his shoulder and kissed his cheek. "He did help them, Karl. And he got paid for it. You can't hold that against him."

"Well, others will. I can assure you of that."

"So what should we do?"

Baier turned to study her face. The moment he did, he knew he'd go through with the proposal he had discussed earlier that day with Younger. "I'll have to go to Greece to see if I can get this thing resolved. Or at least find out more."

"What do mean by 'resolved'? And the money? What will you do with that?"

"I'll have to see. That is, if I find anything. I'm going down there blind, Sabine. I may have to ask the Brits for help."

She shot back away from him, her arm falling to his side. She was silent for a minute, as though trying to determine if Baier was serious. "Karl, if you do that, it will be lost. They'll steal it."

"Or give it back to the Greeks."

"Don't be a fool. They'll either keep it for themselves or use it to prop up their new royal government." She grabbed his arm again. "Which no one there wants, anyway. Those British are crazy for kings. I don't understand it."

"But, Sabine, what do you honestly think I can do with it? Put it in a suitcase and carry it home for you to deposit in a bank somewhere?"

Her arm snaked back around Baier's shoulder, while she nuzzled his neck, then stroked his hair. "I think Joachim may be able to help us."

"Joachim? Isn't he still being held by the British, the very people you want me to avoid?"

She kissed his cheek once more and squeezed his biceps. "No, he's out. I think Karl may have given him more information than he passed along to me, information he expected Joachim to be able to follow up on in case he himself couldn't return."

Baier turned his face to catch the next kiss on his lips. "What sort of information?" He remembered how Joachim had tried to steer him to Greece during their first meeting at the Hohenzollern hunting lodge in the *Gruenewald*.

"Perhaps something about his contacts or some locations in Greece. We can ask. I'm sure he can help."

"I won't promise anything, Sabine. And I'll have to make sure I don't burn any bridges with my own people. I'm willing to help some more, but there has to be something in it for me as well. I have to be able to walk away from this with my life intact."

She kissed Baier hard and long on the lips this time and threw both arms around his neck to hold him close while it lasted. When she finished she rested her forehead on his. "Your life is only beginning, Karl. I'm going to make you the happiest man in Berlin."

CHAPTER TWELVE

The sun was wonderful. Baier enjoyed the the warmth and the glare, something he saw too little of back in Berlin, a city that seemed to sit under a constant curtain of clouds rolling across the north European plain. He could not remember the last time he had been able to sit outside and soak up sunshine and heat like that which penetrated the air in Greece as though it were yet another part of the country's rich historical tradition. He was staying at the Grande Bretagne, a large, square, marble and granite hotel perched on the corner of Constitution Square, the heart of modern Athens. The balcony attached to his room—more of a patio, actually—provided the perfect setting as he scanned the parliament building and the brown hills beyond and absorbed the history and warmth of the city. Several miles away and off to the right was the oval stadium of white marble that had housed the relaunching of the Olympic Games just fifty years ago. And even further to the right stood one of the true historical wonders of the world, the Acropolis. Its marble columns beckoned from the rocky outcrop that in itself struck Baier as a geographical oddity and natural fortress. It was too bad the Turks had also used it as an ammunition dump, whose explosion had erased much of the temple's original formation and outline. For a self-styled student of history, it was as close to paradise as Baier had ever come. The hotel alone had seen its share of history, hosting royalty and statesmen for the last hundred years. Even Hitler had reputedly stayed here on one of his rare trips outside the Fatherland, although Baier doubted he'd find a plaque commemorating the visit. That is, if the *Fuehrer* ever actually visited Athens. Baier had his doubts. The Germans had also used the street out front as a major parade route, but he suspected the Greeks would want to forget that as well.

He had little time to ponder all that now. Joachim Hartmann had given him a name, someone to contact in Pireus, the ancient port attached to Athens and the principal point of departure for anyone traveling to the islands. That was where Joachim had claimed Baier needed to look. He refused to say exactly which island, although he did pass a set of coordinates to help. Joachim had not said any more.

Baier had not been sure just how much he could trust Hartmann, not since the raid at the cleaners.

"He's been in British custody for two weeks, Sabine," he had argued. "How convenient that they let him go now."

"They had to release him," she had responded. "He said they didn't care about the black market activity, and he had not been involved in any spying." She shook her head and held her hands up. "What good would he be as a spy? He doesn't know anything or anyone."

"He seems to know about your husband's hoard down there in Greece."

She had paused and looked at the floor of the bedroom before raising her eyes to Baier. "That's different. He wouldn't betray that."

"Why not?"

She had taken a step back, defiant. "Because it's family. That's all we have now that Germany is gone."

"Are you sure he didn't share any of this with the British, possibly in return for his release and maybe the promise of relocation somewhere? I think that's what he's really after, not the friendly confines of his sister's family, such as it is."

Sabine had moved in close, wrapping her arms around Baier, and resting her head on his chest. "Perhaps you're right. It's all so confusing now."

"And perhaps it's what you want to believe."

She had looked up at him. "Yes, perhaps you're right. But what choice do we have? We can't afford to let this chance slip away." Her head had returned to his chest. "I know that makes it more dangerous. And that means you will have to be extra careful."

"And just what do I do with all this stash if I find anything?"

"Transport what you can. I know that won't be much. But find a way to keep the rest safe." She had looked deep into his eyes and held her gaze there for what seemed like a full minute. "I trust you, Karl. I know I haven't much choice, but we have become close. We're together now."

"Sabine, please." He had gripped her arms and held her at a distance. He had needed a chance to think with his head. "I know no one down there. I know nothing about the country."

"Trust the contact Joachim gave you. He should be able to help. He said Karl saved his life and kept his family out of the hands of the SS."

And there were the British, of course. Baier had no doubts that Thompkins had seen through his story about pursuing another lead on a Greek scientist who had collaborated with the Germans on their missile program because he had been a fanatical anti-Communist. Nor had the backup story of a Greek industrialist who arranged the shipping of valuable potash and limestone been very convincing. But Thompkins had played along and arranged transportation south through the RAF and got Baier his room at the Grande Bretagne. Baier had figured that cooperation stemmed more from a desire to keep track of his movements in country than professional courtesy or allied collaboration. Then again, Baier realized that he had little choice; this was Britain's patch, and he did not have the sort of training or network in place to operate on his own. He just hoped that his tail or tails would be obvious enough to allow him to grab some time alone if necessary.

The taxi ride that evening to the back street address he had been given was uneventful enough. It was the second trip. The first had been the day before, Baier's first attempt at contact. That had taken him to a worn-down, three-story brick structure two blocks from the water. Baier had been given the address by Joachim Hartmann, but it was not actually the contact's address, not the man Joachim had mentioned. The individual who came to the door at first pretended not to know anyone or anything about the affair. His English was nonexistent, so it was difficult to determine what he did know. He had also refused to remove the chain and murmured through a lawn of gray stubble on his cheeks and chin and a small crack between the door and doorframe. Baier was confident he could have shattered the rotten wood with one good kick if he had been desperate enough. But the man did have a smattering of German, which led Baier to assume that he had done some work with the occupiers at least. Only when Baier had shown him the name on the passport and insisted on meeting with Mr. Evangilopokous did his resistance weaken. "Tomorrow night. Nine o'clock," he had said.

"Here? This address?" Baier had asked.

The man's eyes grew wide, and he shook his head vehemently from side to side, waving his palm in Baier's face. "Here no more," he had hissed. "Not good." Instead, he had gotten Baier to understand that they would meet at a tavern straight down the street at the waterfront.

He had held out his hand. Baier passed him a few notes of currency, which the man had crumpled in his fist before the hand disappeared inside. Then it had reappeared while he mumbled something about a location. Baier had passed him a copy of the coordinates he had received from Joachim Hartmann. The door had slammed shut, and Baier had hoped the frame would survive.

The interior to the tavern was spartan. Baier laughed inwardly when the word came to him, considering the country. The walls were bare, and a large ceiling fan sat motionless above him. A tin sheet stretched out over a half-dozen waist-high metal poles separating the dining or drinking area from a door that appeared to lead to a kitchen. Baier chose one of the rickety chairs at a wooden table that had lost its varnish to the years. He hoped the chair would bear the burden of his one-hundred-eighty pounds long enough to last through the evening. The owner—Baier assumed that's what he was; there was no other help that he could see—came over and took Baier's order for a glass of white wine. He returned a minute later with a mostly clean glass—it was difficult to tell in the dim light—and a small carafe of light, golden liquid. To Baier's surprise it tasted cool and smooth.

There was one other patron several tables away. He appeared to be in his fifties, mid-to-late, largely because of the balding gray hair and thin gray mustache that ran around the corners of his mouth and halfway to his chin. A large glass of water served as a companion to a smaller one of ouzo, and the man periodically dribbled water into the creamy liquid.

This lasted for about twenty minutes. Then the creature from the night before wandered in, and Baier was taken aback momentarily by the shabby and broken figure before him. Baier hadn't known what to expect, seeing as how the man had remained mostly hidden behind his door. But he walked—no, he shuffled—on crooked legs that looked barely capable of carrying the hump of an upper body that flowed past an invisible neck and into a face that looked as if it might once have been handsome. The man was clean-shaven tonight and sported long brown hair that cascaded over his ears and neck. He was wearing the same wrinkled clothes from the night before, or at least the same shirt, since that was all Baier had seen, and a black raggedy sweater and brown corduroy slacks, the knees of which were almost transparent.

Baier started to rise, but the look of fear that gripped the man's face set Baier back in his chair. It seemed to groan in protest at the entire business. As soon as Baier sat, a look of relief spread across the man's countenance. He almost smiled. A glass of white wine sat waiting on the countertop, which he gratefully accepted from the owner with a nod, a few words in Greek, and then a single swallow that drained its contents. He turned, glanced at Baier, then stumbled out.

Baier rose to follow.

"That won't be necessary."

It wasn't just that the stranger at the other table had spoken to him that startled Baier. The individual had actually done so in flawless German.

"Andreas is simply your go-between. Unfortunately, it's one of the few ways he can earn enough to get by. I think his disabilities from the war tend to disarm suspicions about him. He's actually quite effective . . . if overly fearful."

Baier wasn't sure how to respond. "What caused his disabilities?"

The man glanced over and studied Baier. "The Germans, of course. Their suspicions were not so easily disarmed."

"Did he work for the partisans?"

The stranger smiled, finished the last of his ouzo, then rose from his seat and approached Baier's table. "He worked, and works, for whomever pays. That's why he was willing to help us.

133

I thought it necessary to have a filter since I had never met you before." He held out a hand and gestured toward the door. "Come. We have a long journey ahead of us tonight."

Baier stood and pulled some bills from his' pocket. The stranger leaned over, took two from the pile in Baier's palm, and dropped them on the table. "My cousin thanks you for your generosity." His hand extended toward the door once again. "Come, if you please."

"But . . . where are we going?"

"To the islands, of course, for your money. And we need to get there before morning." He started toward the entrance, stopped, then turned. "Oh, by the way, my name is Georgios Evangilopokous. I wasn't sure if you were going to ask."

He led Baier out through a small patio that was missing the awning that should have stretched over the metal railings set in a square in front of the taverna. They marched down to the waterfront, where a fishing boat, probably no more than fifty feet long and fifteen wide, sat silent at the sea wall.

"Please." Georgios motioned at the boat. A burly young Greek stepped from the cabin and offered his hand to help Baier on board. He had a fisherman's cap pulled over a bearded face, and Baier struggled to guess his age. He turned to Georgios. "Another cousin?"

"More like an entrepreneur. And thankfully apolitical."

"The captain, I assume?"

Georgios shrugged. "The captain's son. He comes from a family of apolitical entrepreneurs. It's the easiest way to survive amidst all the leadership changes in this part of the world."

There did not appear to be any other crew. When Baier inquired, Georgios simply noted the fewer the better. The journey itself lasted a little over four hours. The boat moved with incredible slowness, but at a comfortable pace, a quality Baier ascribed more to the clear night and calm seas than the seamanship of the young entrepreneur. He almost wished they could have traveled during the day so that he could have witnessed some of the fabled Greek isles. When he tried to inquire of the "captain" where they were or how much longer it would take, Baier was met by a look of incomprehension and a shrug of the shoulders. The only incident of any alarm came when they had to maneuver past a British patrol boat in the harbor as they left. But Baier and Georgios slipped into quarters below the cabin, where Georgios explained that their pilot—Georgios clearly preferred that title to captain—would explain that he was leaving early to pick up a crew in the Cyclades island chain in order to get an early start on the day's fishing. "Besides, that's where we're heading anyway."

"Where exactly?"

"Delos. That's where the coordinates that were passed to me lie."

"How appropriate," Baier laughed. "The location of the Athenian Empire's treasury."

Georgios smiled and nodded. Then he curled up to catch a few hours' sleep. Baier tried to do likewise, but the sound of the engine and the water lapping against the boat let him do little more than doze.

It was still dark when the boat drifted into a secluded inlet on what Baier could only assume was Delos. Beyond a few isolated trees and some scrub, he could see little more than barren, rocky soil and some hills in the distance.

"I hope you got some sleep," Georgios said as they waded ashore. Baier shook his head, shuffling his feet through the ankle-high surf. "Well, we have a bit of a hike. Fortunately," Georgios nodded at a solitary figure next to a lonely pine tree, who was holding two ropes, each one attached to a mule with cloth packs and a large wooden box on its back, "Dimitri is from Delos and knows the shortest and easiest route to any spot on the island."

Baier heard the boat's engine kick into a higher chugging sound and turned to see it pulling away. "Isn't he going to wait?"

Georgios had walked over to speak to the guide, then returned and patted Baier's shoulder. "He'll be back this evening. He has some real fishing to do. Besides, he can't just sit here in the open all day. Someone will see him and ask his business."

Georgios had been right, at least about their guide. They hiked for nearly two hours, and Dimitri seemed to know exactly where they were going. He also seemed to know where every hole and rock was to be found along their path, and Baier stumbled and fell twice, as much from lack of sleep as from the terrain. Dimitri smiled but never stopped or even slowed. He led the way with the two mules who were balancing the cloth packs and boxes on either side of their backs. Baier had not really been able to get a good look at their guide, whose diminished stature seemed to hide a tough, experienced, and solid peasant. Baier inquired once how the man made his living, indeed how anyone made a living on the island, since they had not passed any agricultural land or even a village yet. "Oh, that's all on the other side of the island," Georgios explained. "The soil is really too barren to grow anything, though, so most of the food is shipped in, often by fishermen like our pilot or his father. It's another way of increasing your income."

"So how do the locals pay for it?"

"Well, Delos has always served some larger purpose, either in trade, for pirates, or as a fortress to hold things like the Athenians' treasury. It appears the island may have done the same for your German friends. I'm impressed, though, that you know of the Delian league." He stopped to catch his breath and turned to look at Baier. "And we'll find out soon enough if Delos continues to serve in that capacity."

"And how do we know we can trust this Dimitri fellow?"

Georgios smiled and patted Baier on the shoulder. "It's like Andreas. He works for whomever has the authority and the money. But Dimitri still likes the Germans, unlike many of us. They must have treated him well."

"Why?"

Georgios shrugged. "Who knows? And does it really matter?" When Baier didn't answer Georgios smiled again and even laughed lightly. "You have a lot to learn, my friend."

"And what, may I ask, is in it for you?"

"Oh," Georgios assured him, "you are going to pay me as well." He started to walk again. "Or at least someone will."

They swung past the ruins of an ancient amphitheater as the sun broke over the horizon, spraying the ground in front with a soft glow of yellow and orange. The guide kept moving toward a string of low mountains, more like hills, Baier thought, which they reached after another thirty minutes. They circled around the first set, then climbed the next range in their path, maneuvering around the back to a pile of logs, brush, and boulders. The guide waved them over, and all three set to shoving and pulling away enough debris to clear a path into a cave, the opening of which was just tall enough for the men to enter erect. Once inside, the opening meandered back into the mountain and grew wider and higher. The guide then led them deeper into a cavern for about another hundred yards until they encountered a series of wooden crates set up off the cavern floor by two rows of logs. Baier counted seventeen boxes in all.

"Good Lord," Baier exclaimed. "I can't believe it." He caught his breath and glanced at his companions. "It's actually true."

"Let's open a few to take a look," Georgios suggested. "Perhaps I'll take my fee now."

Baier motioned toward the guide. "Will he want to take anything?" Baier and Georgios stumbled forward, while the guide stepped aside. "Or doesn't he care?"

"Probably not. He has been well paid, so his wishes have been met."

"But he knew where this was all along and never bothered to take anything or turn it in to the authorities?"

Georgios laughed. "What authorities? And how was he to know the Germans would not return." Georgios shook his head. "No, his wishes are not that great, and they have been met."

"Who paid him?"

"Me. When we arrived. That will also be a part of my fee."

The guide brought Baier a hammer and crowbar from a pack on one of the mules, and Baier worked several boards loose on the top crate nearest him. But it was not gold that looked up at him from inside the box. It was an automatic rifle. In fact, the crate was full of them. He held it aloft, a look of incredulity covering his face.

"Do you recognize it?" Georgios inquired.

Baier ran frantically to the next row and ripped the boards off the top of another crate. There were more weapons in this box as well, slightly different models. He pushed that crate from its perch onto the ground and worked the boards loose on another one. This one contained packets of ammunition, 9 × 19 millimeter parabellum rounds, thousands of them.

He glanced over at Georgios and then Dimitri. "Yes, I think so. They're what the Germans referred to as *Maschinenpistolen.*" The detailed specifics from his crash course in German weaponry came rushing back. "The first one was a mass produced thing called the *Maschinenpistole* 40. They could be produced from stamped metal parts for easier manufacture. The second box contains a Beretta model, probably seized from the Italians here in Greece."

He shook his head, as though to clear it of all the useless information. Baier ran in a frenzy from box to box, opening some and pushing the others onto the cavern floor. They had discovered a munitions dump, not a treasure horde. He stumbled forward and leaned against the side of the cave. The adrenaline that had carried him across the island evaporated, replaced by a blend of anger and frustration. "But where's the fucking gold?" Baier shouted at Dimitri. "I don't understand. What happened to the money? Why did we even come here?"

"I'm sorry you're disappointed. But this is where the co-ordinates I received take us."

The guide looked at Georgios, confusion all over his face. Georgios translated.

The guide shook his head. "No gold here. Not anymore. Just weapons." He pointed a crooked finger of leathery, brown skin at Georgios and continued in broken English. "It's what the English are looking for."

"What? Is he saying you're English?" Baier marched toward Georgios, his hands balled into fists.

Georgios shrugged. "We all work for whomever pays, Herr Baier. Right now it's the British. And they're mostly interested in finding arms caches. Although they would have been more than happy if you had come across buried German treasure."

"You bastard. You knew all along."

"No, I only discovered the location when you passed the co-ordinates and the island through Andreas. And I only found what was here when we arrived on the island and opened the boxes. Dimitri mentioned something about weapons after we landed, but I, too, needed to see for myself. Perhaps your informant in Berlin betrayed you."

Baier paced up and down the floor of the cave, circling the cache. "I can't believe this. It was all a set up."

"Oh, come now. Be realistic. You didn't really think you'd

find a horde of gold, did you? And if you had, you certainly didn't believe you could just walk off with it?"

Baier shook his head as he stared at the row of crates. "And I was so careful. I was so certain I had not seen a tail or surveillance of any kind."

Georgios laughed. "Of course not. You were looking for the British. They didn't need to get so directly involved. They had us."

The guide spoke, this time in a mixture of broken English and German. "Gold and money gone. German soldiers took it away. Some came when they were leaving last year. Replace with these." He patted the crates.

"Ask him where they took the money, the gold," Baier demanded.

After Georgios translated, Dimitri simply shrugged and waved towards the wider world.

"But if you suspected as much, why even bring me here? Why play this charade when you could have simply come and grabbed the arms cache on your own?"

"We did what the British wanted us to do. I had my suspicions, of course, but my paymasters wanted to make sure. I guess they wanted to make sure that this was where you actually planned to come, and that there was not some other location." Georgios paused to study Baier's face. "This is where you intended to come, isn't it? You wouldn't be leading us astray, would you? If so, I doubt you'll get away with it."

Baier erupted in laughter, all of his frustration pouring out and echoing off the cavern walls. Dimitri and Georgios pondered this American figure as they would a madman. "Of course not. This is it. Where else would I go in this godforsaken country?" He shook his head, wiping tears from his eyes. He glanced for a moment at the floor of the cave and then up at the ceiling. "I only know to go where I'm told. I'm either one man's pawn or another's."

"Well," Georgios reassured Baier, "you can console yourself with one thought. If there is a treasure, at least the British didn't get it."

It was small consolation on the walk back to meet the boat at the inlet. Baier did get to see the island in daylight this time. It didn't look any better.

CHAPTER THIRTEEN

The trip back to Berlin had been uncomfortable, to say the least. The physical part of the journey had been fine enough. The RAF transport flight into Tempelhof had passed uneventfully. But Baier had suspected or read into the expressions on the faces of the British officers and flight crew he encountered a condescending smirk, a sign of amusement at his expense, as though the old Empire had at long last put one over on the innocent and easily duped Colonials.

The only sense of consolation had come from Georgios, of all people, and that was during the boat ride back to Pireus. The two-hour return hike to the secluded inlet had been mostly silent. The only break in the monotonous journey had been Georgios's offhand comments about the island's other historical significance.

"I suppose it's actually fitting, that we should find a weapons cache instead of treasure. Delos served not only as the Athenians' treasury, you know. It was also Apollo's birthplace."

Baier had to stop to gain control of his temper. His temples seemed to throb with a rush of blood and anger, and he stared for minutes at the ground, afraid that if he looked at Georgios, Baier would strangle him. And the worst of it was that, however pleasing the revenge, it would leave him stranded on the godforsaken island, and probably forever.

So it was a real surprise when Georgios spoke up during the boat ride in a gesture of reconciliation. He had been studying

Baier ever since they had left the island, and Baier, in turn, had been contemplating how he might throw Georgios overboard and still make it back to Pireus. So Baier was surprised when the man moved in close, sat beside him in the cabin, and set his hand on Baier's shoulder.

"You know, this trip was not a complete disaster for you. You have no need to feel entirely disappointed." Baier looked into his eyes for the first time since they had left the cave. "I don't believe your British colleagues are actually convinced there ever was a stash of gold or money here," Georgios continued.

"What on earth are you talking about?" Baier moved aside to get a better look at Georgios. "I thought you were along expressly to determine if there was and to guarantee that they would recover it, however improbable."

Georgios nodded, placed a finger on his lips, then lowered both hands to his knees. "Not exactly. They, at least the ones here in Athens I dealt with, were skeptical. They suspected that any money or treasure would have been long gone by now. And that appears to be the case, according to Dimitri. Their real interest right now is any weapons that could fall into the hands of the Communists."

"But these were German weapons, not Soviet ones."

"True. But Communist partisans would still have found them, in all likelihood. Why the Germans left them there is beyond my knowledge. Perhaps they were pre-positioning them for an eventual return, or to help their fascist allies here. Maybe it was even how they got the local Greeks to allow them to leave with the gold that Dimitri claimed had been there. I cannot say. If you ever find your friend or relative or whatever he is, perhaps he will tell you."

"But why," Baier pressed, "did your British handlers think they would find weapons instead of gold?"

"Oh, I'm not sure they knew what they would find. They

143

simply wanted me to be there to report on whatever it was."
Georgios laughed. "I wish it had been gold, or currency, or
jewelry, or something truly valuable. I don't think there's any
shortage of arms in this part of the world right now." His
eyebrows arched with a smile. "Besides, your treasure would
have paid much better."

"Why do you care?" Baier's puzzlement was evident in the
force of his question, which he nearly shouted. "What difference
would it make to you?"

Georgios shrugged, lifted his hands, then let them drop again
to his knees. "Because then you and I could have helped
ourselves to some of it. And all this marching, this lack of sleep,
this awful boat ride would not have been in vain." He leaned
over and poked a finger in Baier's arm. "But now you can
resume your search when you return. You should remember
what Dimitri said. He claimed that there had been something
there that was removed."

"So what? I'm supposed to put my trust in some shepherd?"

Georgios smiled and patted Baier's arm. "Believe what you
want, my friend. But I shall keep those last comments from my
British paymasters. You, however, are free to do as you wish. You
and your superiors should not be discouraged. But I will tell
you one more thing because you deserve to know it."

Baier eyed the Greek skeptically. "And what would that be?"

"You need to be aware that there are others besides the British who are interested in this alleged treasure." Baier nodded
and rolled his eyes. "Yes," Georgios continued, "you probably
suspect the Soviets, since they have their allies here as well."

"What do you know of them?" Baier asked. "Do you take
their money as well?"

Georgios waved the insult away. "My warning is not about
them. You'll have to deal with them on your own. But there was
another German on the island, just a few days before we came.

Dimitri mentioned it on the walk back."

Baier leaned forward. "Who was this German? Does he have a name?"

Georgios shook his head. "Dimitri would only say that he had been here in Greece with the SS. That is why Dimitri refused to take him to the cave. Or, I should say, he played the dumb peasant. Dimitri can be very good at that."

"Do you know any more? What did this German look like?"

Georgios shrugged. "All Dimitri could say was that he was tall and blond."

"That doesn't exactly narrow it down."

"Yes, but it was probably how Dimitri remembers all of those soldiers." Georgios paused, considering Baier. After a moment, he spoke again. "You would be wise to watch your back where a man like this is concerned. We can all do without SS men as enemies, especially dispossessed and desperate ones." He poked Baier's arm. "Again, I tell you this as a sign of friendship. You may do with it what you wish."

What I wish, Baier had thought to himself during the flight home, is that this trip had never happened. And just what was he going to tell his superiors and colleagues? He sure as hell did not want to talk about SS bogeymen and crafty peasants. He'd be laughed out of Berlin. He just wished at this point that he would be able to put the entire affair behind him.

To Baier's surprise, Kopp was at the runway at Tempelhof to greet him upon his arrival. And to his relief, Kopp's presence was not because of events in Greece. Or so he said.

"This is a pleasant surprise, Corporal. Are you here to take me home? I certainly hope so, because I am exhausted." Baier had slept fitfully on the plane, stretched out on the hard metal floor with only his duffel bag as a pillow, despite having been up most of the night for his excursion to Delos.

"Unfortunately not, sir. Major Younger ordered me to bring

145

you straight to headquarters. I think there's been a new development in the Perkins case."

"Thank God. It's about time." Baier looked over at his driver, who sat stone-faced staring at the road ahead. He seemed to be oblivious to any emotions over his predecessor's death. "Did you know Perkins at all?"

"What do you mean, sir?"

"Just what I said. Did you know the man, either as a person, or by reputation?"

Kopp shifted gears as the car swung along *Hohenzollerndamm* and then onto *Kronprinzen Allee.* "Only by reputation, sir."

"And?"

"And his reputation was that of someone who could get you just about anything you needed."

"Could you explain what you mean by 'anything,' Corporal?" Baier asked.

"Yes, sir. Anything to do with women, booze, war souvenirs, Soviet or Allied contacts, and even some narcotics."

"Narcotics? Here in Berlin?" Baier was dumbfounded. This was the first he had heard of traffic in drugs. "And what do you mean by Allied or Soviet contacts?"

"Well, sir . . ." Kopp paused, glancing over at his boss. "In case there was something you wanted or needed from those folks, like souvenirs or help in getting someone over. Perkins was your man." Kopp hesitated, swallowed, then shrugged. "As for the narcotics, sir, some of the guys who had been wounded got kind of dependent on them. You know, morphine and stuff like that. Perkins was good at finding that, too."

They pulled into the long driveway that led to the main entrance of the American command on *Kronrpinzen Allee,* where Kopp swung the jeep around the bumpy, circular cobblestone driveway and deposited Baier at the front door. Several German laborers were kneeling off to the side, resetting the cobblestones in an effort to create a smoother pavement. Baier wished them luck.

"Thank you, Corporal. This has been a very enlightening drive." Baier paused and leaned on the jeep. "And rest assured that you needn't worry about having been so forthcoming with me. I appreciate your candor."

"Thank you, sir." Kopp saluted stiffly before ramming the jeep into first gear.

The muffled roar of the jeep echoed in Baier's ears as he trotted up the steps leading into the building, then climbed the circular stairway to the second floor, where Younger's office sat at the end of a long, marble-lined corridor to the left. He felt a rush of excitement over a possible breakthrough in the murder of Perkins, tinged with an anxiety over what he should tell his superior about the misadventure in Athens and Delos.

"Good. You're back." Younger waved Baier into his office as he rose from the desk. Younger then gestured toward a chair and maneuvered himself around the side of the desk and took a seat on the corner after Baier sat down.

"So, what do we know?" Baier asked.

A thin smile creased Younger's face. "Well, more than before. On the advice of our British cousins, we've closed down the laundry shop."

Baier sucked in his breath. "Is this in reaction to the Perkins shooting?"

"Yes, the CID people think there's some connection. Apparently, the British are not being real forthcoming with them either. The Germans who worked and lived there have disappeared, in any case. I guess the one fellow we're really interested in is some guy named Ernst Hoffmann, whom CID suspects of being a Soviet agent."

"But they're our allies, at least officially. Is he a communist or something?"

"Apparently he had some ties there before the Nazis took over, but the real link appears to have developed afterwards. The Soviets grabbed him when they took Berlin and either broke him or persuaded him to work for them." Younger sighed. "He's probably skipped back over there. I guess the Brits were getting close to him, and he seems to have been warned off."

"By whom?"

"Hard to say. It could have been almost anyone, but the CID people suspect it might have been Perkins, although how he would have known escapes me. Or why he would do such a thing." Younger glanced at the floor, then up at Baier. "I don't know. Maybe they were buddies in the black market."

Baier leaned forward and looked first out the window, then at Younger. He hoped his anxiety was not too open and easy to read, but his lack of sleep prevented Baier from being absolutely sure of his demeanor. His heart felt ready to leap from his breast. "Were there others involved in that sort of thing?"

"Didn't you say you had done some business there?"

Baier nodded. "That's right. It's pretty convenient to where I live. I remember two men and a woman."

"Well, they're gone as well. I think the other guy, a Joachim Hartmann, works for the British. That's how the Brits found out what this Ernst fellow was up to."

This explains a lot, Baier thought. What a hornets' nest I walked into with that damn claim ticket, he told himself. "And the woman?" Baier realized he had clenched both fists, so he loosened them slowly and tried to wipe off the moisture on his palms along the legs of his trousers.

Younger waited a moment before continuing as he studied the young officer. Baier could not be sure if Younger had noticed the state of his hands or whether his face betrayed him.

"Were you aware this woman had the same last name as you? Her married name, I mean."

Baier nodded, his gaze directed at the floor. "Yes. I thought it was interesting, one of those small-world, historical oddities."

"Was she your lady friend?"

Baier tried to bluff his way through this with a look of disbelief as he sat back in his chair, his eyes avoiding those of Younger. "Chief, what does all this have to do with Perkins? I thought the CID was looking into black market activities."

Younger paused while he studied his captain's face some more. "Should I take that as a 'yes'?"

Baier could do no more than grimace. Younger slid off the corner of the desk and returned to his seat. "Well, the CID was and still is looking into that. That place was a regular black market hive as well. But the theory now in play is that Perkins was mistaken by someone, a Soviet would be my guess, as being caught up in something more serious. And he got a bullet in the head as a result."

"That would fit with what Kopp told me, in a way."

"How's that?"

Baier leaned forward, hesitating when he realized he had just done what he had promised Kopp he would not. Baier chalked it up to lack of sleep. It was convenient enough as an excuse. Then he decided it was too late, so he plunged in. "On the way in from the airport, he told me that Perkins was someone with a range of contacts among the other allies, including the Soviets. And that if you needed something or help in smuggling someone, Perkins was your man."

Younger nodded in comprehension. "Yes, that would fit in with the CID's theory." He looked over at Baier and leaned forward in turn. "But that's not why I asked you in here. How'd it go in Greece?"

Baier smiled and stood, almost relieved. He knew he would have to face up to this sooner or later. "A total bust. We ran across an arms cache, something the Krauts had left behind, which pleased the British no end. So we may get some goodwill and cooperation from that."

"Any sign of the money you thought might be there?"

Baier shook his head. "Nope. None. I doubt there is any such thing. Someone sold the Brits and me a lousy bill of goods."

"It sounds like that movie Humphrey Bogart was in, *The Maltese Falcon*. What was it that fat guy said, something like the stuff dreams are made of?"

Baier looked up at his boss, eager to take the offered hand, such as it was. "That's right. And given what these people have been through, you can see why they'd spin these kinds of dreams." He sighed. "But like I said, the British probably don't see it as a complete loss. They can even arm some more royalists."

"Do you think you're done with this thing now? Can you stay free of it all?"

Baier sighed, then shook his head. "Hard to tell, Chief, but I sure hope so." He thought about the various actors. "The British shouldn't be a problem, given what happened down there in Greece. And if the Germans have really disappeared, I should be able to put this behind me." Baier did not mention Chernov, or the mysterious SS visitor to Delos.

"Well, good then. You can get back to some real work. Check with our British friends, though, to see what we can get out of it."

"Sure. I'd be happy to. Thompkins owes me dinner anyway."

"I hope you enjoy the food, considering what they might feed you." Younger sat back. "And I won't press you on your love life, son. But you may have dodged a bullet there, figuratively and literally. It looks like she skipped town with the others. You need to be a lot smarter, Karl. You can't be thinking with that thing there." Younger pointed at Baier's crotch. "There's a lot going on in this town, above and below the surface."

"You're right, Major," Baier reassured him. "I realize that now. You are definitely right."

Baier strolled back to his office, groggy from lack of sleep and confused by the turn of events. Leaning against his desk and watching an empty sky just beyond his window, he kept telling himself he had dodged that particular bullet and could now put the affair behind him. And he repeated it over and over again to make himself believe it. After a couple of hours and a half-hearted stab at work, Baier stood up, turned off the light to his office, and wandered home.

CHAPTER FOURTEEN

The next few days were a blur. Despite all his resolve since his return, Baier could not keep his mind off the debacle in Greece and Sabine's and Joachim's possible role in all of it. And he could not shake the nagging doubt that, despite his hopes, despite his earnest attempts to convince himself otherwise, the adventure with Karl and Sabine Baier and their alleged hoard of gold had not come to an end. He finally admitted after a day or two of strenuous denial that he would have liked to see Sabine again, if only for the closure a final encounter would bring. He had definitely fallen for her, something he could admit to himself now that their affair appeared to be a thing of the past. And he wondered how vulnerable and gullible that had made him, if it allowed her to manipulate him, if he really had been thinking with his crotch, as Younger had suggested. But he had enjoyed those nights with her and the companionship they brought. Then again, Baier also had to admit that this pursuit of some golden treasure had threatened to turn his world inside out, jeopardize his future, and that he could not claim to have even a remote right to hold on to any of what they might have found.

He spent the next three days in dogged pursuit of members from Germany's earlier scientific elite, but with little success. The leads appeared to have dried up, and the CID had not been forthcoming with any additional files. Even America's good friends the British had little to offer, despite their alleged gratitude for the discovery of the arms cache in Greece. "Be patient, Captain," Thompkins had counciled, "we are working on it. I hope to have something for you soon."

Several incidents also increased his doubts that others had reached the same conclusion about the illusive treasure. In fact, Baier's suspicions grew each time he crossed paths with them in these encounters, and each time for little reason that he could see. And it seemed to be more than coincidence with the messages getting stronger and more direct each time. He could have sworn that at least twice he had seen Captain MacDonald shadowing him, and on one occasion as he left a German *Gasthaus* after a late dinner, none other than Colonel Chernov approached him as he walked to the jeep where Kopp was waiting.

"So nice to see you, Captain." The Russian's voice was slurred, and his eyes were cloudy. Baier was certain he smelled alcohol on the man's breath, vodka no doubt. "It has been quite a while, and we should get together to talk about our mutual friends."

Baier nodded, slipped a smile in the Soviet officer's direction, and started to move past him. Suddenly, Chernov grabbed his wrist, hard enough to pinch the skin to the bone, as though he wanted to impress Baier with his strength, or make certain the American did not escape. "We really should talk. I'm surprised you do not have more of a tan from your journey to Greece. Perhaps you could tell me of your adventures there and any additional information you acquired regarding our friend."

Baier had shaken the Soviet's grip loose and hurried to the jeep where Kopp was waiting.

"Anything wrong, sir?"

Baier stared straight ahead. "No. Just another fucking Russian. Something I'd like to forget."

The following morning, Colonel Thompkins was waiting for

153

him on the sidewalk in front of his house when Baier left for work. He had dismissed Kopp the evening before, telling him that the weather was nice enough for him to walk the short distance down *Kronprinzenallee.* "To what do I owe such an unexpected and early pleasure?" Baier asked. "Something from Farm Hall?"

Thompkins waved as though brushing away the air between them. "Oh, no, not that. No reason in particular." He looked at the ground, as though in thought, then raised his right index finger with his gaze in Baier's direction. "There is one thing, though. You need to be careful when you go out for an evening's entertainment nowadays. You never know whom you will meet. And you must always be careful what you say." He smiled and averted his eyes, trying to make the encounter look as innocent as possible. He failed. "People could get the wrong impression. But perhaps when we next meet I can explain the purpose of your mission to Greece, or at least one part of it. Let's not wait too long."

With that he disappeared into a Land Rover waiting down the block. At least, Baier told himself, there had been no sign of the mysterious SS man. But Baier decided he would have to confront Thompkins to clear the air, and at the earliest possible opportunity. He would figure out how to deal with Chernov later. First things first.

He never got the chance. Two nights later, as soon as he walked through the door of his house the illusion that this could all go away so conveniently, after the first setback and after Sabine had vanished, evaporated. He could tell the instant he passed his threshold that someone had been here inside his home. The set of doors to his patio and backyard stood half open, as though someone had absentmindedly forgotten to shut them. But no one had forgotten. Baier flipped the light switch to push back the darkness and see what else they had done. His dining room chairs had all been moved to one side of the table opposite the doors, and his sofa in the alcove had been pulled away from the wall by several feet. The chairs in the living room had been regrouped in the center in a crooked square. But at least there did not appear to be any damage to the furniture.

Upstairs, his bed cover and sheets had been pulled back to expose the mattress, and the pillows had been piled together in the middle. His towels had been gathered from his linen closet and deposited in the bath tub. Oddly, that was the most destructive act he found to any of his property. The problem was that the towels were no longer clean. They were covered in blood, which he initially assumed belonged to Ernst Hoffmann. Baier's assumption was based on the fact that Hoffmann was lying in the bathtub on top of the towels. And he was clearly already dead, a dark red splash on his chest and a hole in the front of his forehead. Vacant eyes stared up at the ceiling of Baier's bathroom.

He was too stunned to move, or even look away. Baier could not be sure how long he stood there staring at the dead man before he stumbled out the door, searching for balance as the walls of his house swam around him. He nearly fell down the stairs, then waited at the bottom step to calm himself and gather his wits. He walked slowly outside in a daze. Guided less by a rational plan than some instinct to keep his hands busy, he found himself before the wood pile that had been stocked the day of his arrival. He selected half a dozen logs, some kindling, and small branches from the yard and brought them inside. He laid a fire in the small stone fireplace in the living room. He left the back doors open just a crack, as though the movement of more fresh air would clear the stench of death and invasion from his home. After about ten minutes of lighting matches, shuffling paper and twigs, and rearranging logs to get a proper air flow, he had a small flame started. Baier pulled a chair from the broken square close to the hearth to try to enjoy the heat that spread from the fire against the late October night.

Baier sat motionless for half an hour, considering the implications of what he had found. He realized then that he could not simply sweep the events and people of the last few weeks away, that his resolve on the walk home several evenings ago had brought him no more than a momentary reprieve. He was no longer certain if it had been the Soviets or the English, or some German players. Perhaps the SS ghost had finally made an appearance. That would explain the change in tactics and the introduction of this new brutality and violence. But whoever it was that had entered his home may well have been searching for something, whatever that was and for all the good it would do them. But they had also left something behind, more than a body. It was clear to Baier that their real intent had been to leave a message. Two of them, in fact. The first was that there was indeed some kind of treasure out there, and they had searched the house on the off chance that they might find some clue as to its size and location. And second, they were not going away. No matter what Baier might wish to happen, they would continue to press him for cooperation and information. They were convinced this tale of treasure was true, and they meant to have it. They could harass him at will, even exert some control over him by violating his sanctuary and manipulating his emotions. And by leaving Ernst behind, they wanted to demonstrate just how serious this business was, and how much power they had over their opposition.

Before he could begin to find any more about this treasure and all the players involved, though, he would have to tell Younger and those stiff necks from CID about the body upstairs. The real challenge would be to determine how much he could withhold and when to share what information he had now or obtained later. Baier stared at the fire for a moment

156

longer, gathering his wits and courage, willing his heartbeat to slow, and strengthening his resolve. Then he stood and walked to the telephone.

CHAPTER FIFTEEN

"Any chance this is connected to your little escapade in Greece?" Younger asked.

He and Baier stood at the entrance to the carport just to the side of Baier's house. Younger glanced at the kitchen door, through which he could see the four-man team of CID investigators as they crossed the hallway on the ground floor. Baier peeked at his watch, then at the night sky as streaks of gray clouds sailed past a half moon. He wondered if he'd ever get to bed, and if he did, if he'd ever sleep. It was already a little past two o'clock. "I'm not sure, Major, but it's a pretty good guess. In any case, it's something I believe I'm going to have to find out."

Younger studied his subordinate while peeking intermittently at the kitchen door. "What else could it be?" He paused. "And what aren't you telling me?"

Baier turned to face his superior. "Major . . ."

"I think at this hour and considering the circumstances, 'Frank' will do."

Baier nodded. "All right, Frank. I'm not really sure just how much more there is. The only thing I'm relatively sure of is that there is a heck of a lot more I don't know and that I need to find out."

"Like what?"

"Well, in the first place, that we were wrong about this thing being over. For someone it clearly isn't."

158

"That's a no-shit observation. What else ain't you got?"

"The main answers, like where this is heading. And where it's really coming from. I feel like I'm standing on the tracks and I can hear the train, but I can't see it. I mean, what did I miss in Greece and before? And who all is really behind this?"

"You care to say anymore about who they might be? Besides your woman, that is."

"Hell, Frank. I don't even know where she is or what might have happened to her."

"It sounds like you don't know a whole hell of a lot, son."

Baier nodded and blew out his breath in frustration. He looked into his boss's eyes and simply shrugged.

"Don't you think those guys in there are better equipped to do that?" Younger nodded at the door. "I doubt those years at Notre Dame prepared you for this, no matter how good their football team is. You're also awful new and fresh here. Just look at the pile of shit you've landed yourself in already."

Baier sighed. "I know what you're saying is true, Frank, and that it makes a lot of sense. But those guys don't know where to begin or who all might be a part of this."

"And you do?"

"I have some of the characters, and I know what's driving them. Or at least I think I do."

"And your *Fraulein* is one of 'em. You think you can still trust her?"

Baier grimaced. "Fair enough, Frank. But that also proves my point."

Younger stared. "You're losin' me, son."

Baier swept his head toward the kitchen and glanced at the upstairs window that led to the bathroom. Inside, he could hear the CID team pass instructions as they lifted Ernst Hoffmann's body from the tub and placed him in a plastic bag for transportation to the morgue. "Those guys will never find her, and if they do, they won't get anywhere."

"And you will?"

Baier looked back at his boss and shrugged again. He glanced away at the dark, empty street in front of his home. "Maybe, maybe not. But I'll have a much better chance than they ever will."

"Even so, you'll never get them to call off their investigation."

"I know that, and I wouldn't dream of it. But I need to do some searching on my own, Frank."

"I realize I can't put a leash on you, Karl, because I know you're going to go after this thing no matter what. You've already displayed a willingness, no matter how crazy, to pursue this thing, and it isn't every day you get a gift like that in your bathtub. But I can watch you very closely. And if you cross their path, or screw up their efforts, you'll be on the next boat home. You know that, don't you?"

"Absolutely. And this will not absorb all my time. I promise, Frank."

Younger nodded, then grabbed Baier's arm. "You're damn right it won't." He shook his head. "I must be getting a soft spot now that this damn war is over. But I want you to keep me informed of every fucking step you take, son."

Baier impulsively gripped Younger's hand as it slid from his arm. "You've got my word, Frank."

Younger turned toward the sidewalk. "I'll need more than that. I'll need results and continued good performance at your real job." He marched away from the carport and toward the jeep he had left parked at the curb. His voice drifted back over his shoulder. "And we're back to 'Major.' " He waved over his shoulder. "Captain."

He decided to start with the English. Colonel Thompkins, to be precise. At least they spoke the same language, or something similar, and the British had emerged from the war as America's closest ally, which Baier hoped would count for something. And it did not cost him the sufferance of an English dinner, at least not right away. Instead, he joined Dick Savage for dinner the following day in hopes of getting a better feel for British perspectives and objectives. Baier felt confident enough in dealing with what was emerging as America's closest foreign relationship, but he wanted to make sure that there were no aspects of the British world view or imperial policy that he was neglecting. Granted, this came in at a pretty elevated and strategic level, but Baier had convinced himself that a better understanding might help him grasp Thompkins's motives if they were going to be in regular, or even infrequent, contact. He also wanted to discuss this without giving too much away at home about just what lay at the heart of his quest. And his friend Dick Savage was as good a place to look as any.

"Dreams and delusions, that's how I see it." Savage was always happy to hold forth on the subject of America's European allies and their history. "And a failure to recognize how much the world has changed. That's what they're laboring under."

"How much the world has changed?" Baier responded. "Can you elaborate? I mean, aside from the war being over."

"Sure. I mean, just look at Bretton Woods. It redrew the lines of global economic power by securing open trade and the pre-eminence of the US dollar. It will take the United Kingdom years to rebuild its economy and pay off its debts. And we're the ones holding those chits. If you ask me—and you have, Karl," Savage continued, "our British friends think they can salvage their Empire and continue as before. That's what this war was all about for them. In fact, it's what the last one was about as well. And the settlement of that one only delayed the inevitable, which is going to come true after this one."

161

The Harnack House was serving a chicken Kiev special this evening, and Baier made sure he kept the Riesling flowing to keep Savage's tongue loose. "Don't tell me there was no concern about the Nazis' philosophy and the crimes of this regime," Baier countered.

"Of course there was, although I'm not sure how much they were actually aware of what was going on over here in the camps and all." Savage drained his glass and held it toward Baier for a refill. "But don't forget, even Churchill expressed his admiration for Mussolini back in the 1920s. I don't think those guys really cared what form of government you had in Berlin."

"So how did this war help them preserve their Empire?"

"It's true, I believe, that Churchill provided great leadership during the war, but it's also true that he is an unreconstructed imperialist. And this war achieved a principal objective for him. It rid the British of their two most formidable competitors: Japan and Germany." Savage shrugged. "Of course, now they have to contend with the Soviets, who have a lot more in the way of resources than the Krauts or Japs ever did."

"And don't forget us," Baier reminded him. "Roosevelt made it pretty clear that we were not in this thing to preserve their imperial dreams and delusions, as you put it."

Savage nodded. "I certainly hope not. Sometimes, I'm not so sure, though."

"How so?" Baier queried.

"Well, it looks like new lines are being drawn, both here in Europe and elsewhere in the world." Savage raised his eyes from a plate clean of any chicken; just a small pool of butter remained at its center and spots of mashed potatoes and broccoli at the edges. "Look at how the Soviets have pushed their borders further westward, and they've expelled every living German they could find. That is, the ones that they or the Poles or Czechs haven't killed."

"So, you're saying we'll be in dire need of friends in this part of the world?" Baier paused to mop up the rest of his chicken. He soaked up what butter sauce was left with a piece of thick German *Bauernbrot*. "Does this mean we won't be withdrawing back into our 'splendid isolation' like after the last war?"

Savage took another sip of Riesling, then shrugged again. "Not for me to say. There will probably be a bit of a learning period and adjustment, during which we'll need the help of our special friends, even as they adjust to the loss of that damn Empire. Take Greece, for example."

Baier's gaze shot across the table as he leaned in closer. "What about Greece?"

"Hell, Karl, there's a civil war about ready to break out. That could be Stalin's next big push. And don't think London is just going to give up and walk away. They're still worried as hell about protecting the Suez Canal and the pathway to their real jewel, India. And things are getting increasingly shaky there as well."

"So that's where their 'dreams and delusions,' as you put it, could prove useful. It will keep them occupied and unwittingly helpful down there in the Aegean until we're ready to assume the mantle of global leadership. Assuming we decide to take it, that is."

Savage laughed. "That's one way of looking at it, although I'm not sure our compatriots back home really care all that much." He laughed again, slightly louder this time. "And as long as it doesn't end up costing us in the end."

"And just what do you expect to happen in Greece?"

"I think, Karl, that it will come down to some hard fighting. One round is over, you know, the one right after the Krauts pulled out. But I don't think it was truly settled there. And in the end, the Brits will have to ask for our assistance. But they won't do it gladly." Savage set his newly empty glass back on the table. "Why do you care so much about that place? Did you have an epiphany recently? Too much ouzo?"

It was Baier's turn to laugh. "Hardly. But this does help me understand where our British allies are coming from."

"Have they been giving you a hard time?"

"Oh, it depends. Let's just say their cooperation has been kind of grudging lately. And they have seemed preoccupied with places like Greece." He paused. "Plus, there is the inescapable bit of arrogance."

"It depends on whom you deal with," Savage responded. "But, yeah, I can see that happening."

The following afternoon, Baier sat in Captain Ashley Mac-Donald's office at the Allied *Kommandatura* across from an ebullient Colonel Thompkins. Baier felt more comfortable meeting with Thompkins at the AK, as he wanted to be as close as possible to the American headquarters, preferably within walking distance. After his escapade in Greece, Baier decided that he had given his British allies the advantage of place for the last time, at least as much as he could ever help it. He was willing to forego that dinner for now, and even lunch.

The King's portrait beamed down on Thompkins, who sat parked at the desk and at ease in MacDonald's chair. A bright, autumn sun shone through the window, and Baier relaxed in the unexpected warmth. "At least you were able to eliminate a weapons cache, even if there was no treasure, buried or otherwise," Baier said.

Thompkins leaned back in his seat, mirroring Baier's pose. "Quite right, Captain. We do appreciate that, rest assured. Although I must say I'm puzzled as to why the Germans allegedly left those weapons and the ammunition there for storage. Any ideas why?"

"Allegedly?"

Thompkins shrugged, grinning. "Figure of speech, is all."

Baier shook his head. "Well, in any case, I can't think of any reasons why. Who knows what those guys were thinking at that point." He glanced out the window, then back at Thompkins. "They probably left the stuff there from their earlier stay and never had the chance to pull it out. Then again, maybe they were hoping to assist the Greek fascists, or even the royalists in case they ever come back." Baier nodded at Thompkins. "That should make you guys happy."

Thompkins laughed. "Well, yes, as long as the supplies ended up with the royal forces and not the fascists. Although I doubt the latter are much of a force in that country now that their sponsors are gone." He leaned forward and pulled himself close to the desk. "I have another theory, though."

"And that would be?"

"What if there actually had been a gold stash on Delos, and the Germans purchased the assistance of the locals with the finest currency at their disposal, i.e., those weapons? I doubt bundles of Reichsmarks would have gone very far."

"But why would the locals have settled for weapons when they could have gotten gold or other valuables?"

"Perhaps the Greeks were unaware of what was actually sitting there under their very noses. Or perhaps they were desperate enough for the currency that counts most if you expect to be fighting again in the future."

"Interesting theory," Baier responded. "So you believe there was a treasure of some sort hidden there. I had the impression that your colleagues were less enthusiastic about that. In fact, I'd say they were downright skeptical. Why are you so consumed with this, Colonel?"

Thompkins smiled and seemed to weigh the wisdom and value of confiding in Baier. "I'll admit, Captain, that not

165

everyone in my service shares my opinions. On this and other matters."

"Was it Joachim Hartmann who sucked you in?"

If the name or its revelation shocked Thompkins, he failed to show it. "Joachim Hartmann? The fellow we pulled in the other day?"

"That's right," Baier continued. "What ever happened to him anyway? I understand he's disappeared."

"Yes, I gather he's left Berlin, along with his sister." Thompkins smiled again to see if his revelation in turn left a mark on Baier's bearing. Baier hoped the heat he felt in his cheeks did not show too openly. "I heard something about Hamburg," Thompkins continued. "Is that how you learned of the gold and other valuables? From Joachim or the other one?"

Now it was Baier's turn to lean in close. One forearm rested on his leg, the other on the desk. "I know next to nothing about this damn treasure, as I tried to explain the last time we met. I traveled to Greece practically at your bidding." The vague, impersonal reference to Sabine had angered him. "Just what makes you so goddamn sure there's anything to recover? And if it wasn't Joachim Hartmann, then how did you learn of it? If we're going to establish a more cooperative relationship here in Berlin, Colonel, you're going to have to be a lot more forthcoming. And trustworthy."

Thompkins sat back again, almost as though Baier had begun to crowd him. The smile returned. "Well stated, Captain. You remind me of the American pilots I helped rescue and sneak back to safety during the war. Always very direct, coming right to the point. It's what I admire about your nation. But I'm afraid I'm not at liberty to divulge my sources. One thing I will give you, though, as I suspect you already have it, is that the Soviets are eager to find this as well. Or at least Colonel Chernov is."

Baier stared straight ahead for what seemed like minutes, working to bring his beathing under control and recapture his voice. When he spoke, he just hoped he didn't stutter. "Yes, I'm aware of that. And how do you know of Colonel Chernov and his interests?"

"Oh, come now. He's one of our principal competitors. It's my business to know of the man. And I have heard of you meeting with him on occasion, like the other night outside the *Bier Akadamie*. Wonderful name, that." He paused to consider Baier. "So how are you aware of his role in all this, and how did this Soviet officer hear of it?" Thompkins pressed.

Baier decided he would share this much with Thompkins to see what he got in exchange. "Karl Baier told them about it, or he told Chernov at least. It's how he purchased his life after the fall of Budapest. It also gave him an opportunity to escape, as it turns out. What I can't figure out is whether Chernov is so eager to capture this hoard, and Baier in the bargain, out of love for the international proletariat, or just for personal revenge and profit."

"That's an interesting point, Captain. How about this?" Thompkins proposed. "I'll send over our file on Chernov so you can educate yourself on the man and his background. It might help enlighten you as to his motive."

"I can always check our own," Baier replied.

Thompkins shook his head. "I doubt your people have much at this point. You're still new to the game. Are you aware, for example, that this Chernov began his career in counterintelligence?"

"Is that why he was stationed with the troops at the front?"

Thompkins nodded. "Yes. That's right. But since he's been in Berlin, the Soviet has been working on foreign intelligence matters out of Karlshorst. It's been my impression that he feels a bit like a fish out of water. CI, that is, Counterintelligence, has been the man's bread and butter as it were."

Baier could have sworn he saw a smirk on Thompkins's face. "So, you've been observing him?"

"Yes, of course. Like I said, it's a part of my business." Thompkins stood and held out his hand. "But by all means, see what you can find out to supplement our material." They shook hands, and Baier noticed that Thompkins was practically beaming. "Now this is more like it," the British officer nearly shouted.

On his way out the door Baier stopped and turned back toward Colonel Thompkins. "By the way, you never told me how you came to know of the gold that is supposedly floating around out there. And why this has become a personal crusade for you."

"Why do you characterize this as personal, Captain?"

"Because no one else on your side appears to give a damn about some mythical treasure."

Thompkins smiled once more, his hands resting on his hips. He paused, as though weighing a decision, then stepped forward. "I assure you, this is no myth. And you were right about this Hartmann chap. He did help some. But you see, I also met Herr Karl Baier. It was in Greece. I had been captured on Crete fighting the German air drop but won my freedom in a prisoner exchange. I decided to return to Greece as an SOE operative. That's where I helped your pilots. Unfortunately, I was captured again and should have been executed as a consequence of Hitler's Commando Order. You're aware of that?"

Baier nodded. "Of course. He had ordered all captured British commandos shot."

"Yes, quite right. I guess you could say I had the good fortune to be captured by our friend and your namesake. He transferred me to Athens for interrogation, during which I suggested he start preparing for the unthinkable, that Germany might actually lose the war." Thompkins snorted. "Oh, I confess that it was sheer bragging at that point, more a defensive mechanism than a prediction or matter of conviction. But he surprised me when he said he was in the process of doing precisely that. He claimed he was making sure that he did not end up broken and impoverished, as he feared his country would become. He probably assumed his secret was safe with me, but it was his misfortune that I escaped. It was Joachim Hartmann who brought me up to date."

"And were you able to convince others in your organization of the truth of this story?"

"Oh, I haven't really tried, Captain. In fact, I've done my best to ensure that they don't become interested and involved. That was one of the benefits of your trip to Greece. It increased their doubts. How about you?"

"I'm not sure I believe it myself," Baier replied. "But tell me why you're trying to keep your colleagues at a distance."

"Because I'm still disgusted by how shortsighted our policy in Greece was, and I'm not sure we've progressed much beyond that. We coddled the damn communists in the interests of preserving their cooperation against the Germans. Do you have any idea how they operated, how treacherous they were?"

Baier shook his head. "Not really."

"I once saw them return to a village after the local headsman and priest had regained control from the communist thugs left behind and had to watch as they were both hung, along with a dozen other villagers as an example." Thompkins studied the floor for several seconds, then shook his head in disgust, his face in a grimace. Baier thought he might spit on the floor for a moment. When he spoke, he spat the words at the tabletop. "I will never, never trust those bastards."

"Which ones?"

Thompkins looked up. "Both, actually. The communists are

169

sods, of course. But I'm going to make damn sure I have all the facts to this story before I let anyone else in."

"I'm sorry you had to witness such a thing. And I'm sorry you've had to carry that memory."

"Well, we all have our crosses to bear, Captain. I suspect you have yours as well. In fact, I've noticed some of that same innocence and ignorance in your country's leadership. I hope you're not prone to those same miscalculations, Captain."

Baier shook his head and glanced towards the window. "I believe I've gradually lost my innocence in this town."

"Well, that's good then, in a way. You see, so have some of your countrymen, I believe."

"How so, Major?"

"Well, you may not realize this, but there was a hell of a lot of gold and other valuables making their way across the various highways and byways of the collapsing Reich in the last days of the war. And not all of it has been accounted for, Captain. I'd suggest that this is something worth looking into. Who's to say that Karl Baier's loot wasn't a part of that?"

Thompkins paused, his finger to his lips as though he was trying to remember something. All of a sudden his face lit up, and the finger extended in Baier's direction. "That's right, the woman. We haven't seen any sign of her lately, Captain. Have you had any word?"

Baier turned to leave. "No, I haven't. Do you know something? Is there anything you're not telling me?"

The smile widened. "No, Captain, I don't have anything for you. It's just that I'd expect her to return at some point."

"Why is that?"

"Because you're her meal ticket, as you Yanks say. She hasn't anything else, you know. Not now. Not after we closed that laundry shop."

Thompkins gave another one of those awkward British

salutes. Baier did not return it but turned quickly and marched out of the office. Just when you think they're your friends, he mused.

Thompkins was as good as his word, though, as far as the Chernov file was concerned. Baier did wonder if Thompkins would follow up, since he appeared to be assuming some of the condescending superiority Baier had initially expected. The man remained an enigma of his own for Baier. He could never tell if Thompkins was a friend and ally, or an opponent playing a hidden hand of his own with the Germans. Thompkins was definitely not the great pal Baier had thought he might find, but instead was displaying characteristics he would expect to find in someone with his own independent and possibly competitive agenda. At other times, he actually did provide some helpful advice and assistance. And, after all, the United States and Britain had not agreed to share everything, certainly not when it came to personal wealth or stolen loot. Moreover, Baier did have to admit that he hardly came across as the equal of an experienced intelligence professional like Thompkins.

So Baier found himself considering just what Thompkins's motives were in providing Chernov's file and if it really was complete. And not only was Thompkins sharing it, he had agreed to let Baier take notes while he read the file in Captain MacDonald's office at the *Kommandatura*. MacDonald flitted about, offering coffee or tea and biscuits, while Baier responded with provisions of Lucky Strikes, Coca-cola, and Fig Newtons from the American office down the hall. Anything to keep the man occupied.

And the file was informative, even enlightening. Chernov had come from a well-to-do family, what the British categorized in the file as upper middle class. He was born in 1902 to a prosperous St. Petersburg family, his father a very successful merchant exporting sable furs, among other things, but young Sergei Chernov had run off to join the Red Army in 1919 as his country found itself torn apart by civil war. Despite his service, it was speculated in several personnel assessments that Chernov felt the need to demonstrate his commitment to the revolution and Marxist-Leninism by joining a communist youth organization at Moscow University, from which he had been recruited by the NKVD. His rise through the ranks was steady, although not what anyone considered rapid. He performed admirably in the war, escaping the German encirclement at Kiev, and first distinguishing himself in the defense of Stalingrad. What Baier really found interesting, however, was the existence of family in Europe, principally Berlin and Paris: an elder brother and a sister who had escaped the Communists and fled to the West in 1918. Chernov had served in Prague and Paris during the 1930s, working out of one of the Soviet trade missions, well known as operational bases for the NKVD. His job had been to infilitrate and report on counter-revolutionary émigré groups and their Western patrons. During this time, he had reportedly been in periodic contact with his siblings, something for which he had been briefly imprisoned during the purges in the 1930s. But as far as the British could determine, the links had been broken in 1940 and 1941 when the Germans swept through France and then invaded the Soviet Union. There was no indication in the files of what had become of Chernov's siblings.

Interesting, Baier concluded, and perhaps helpful for future encounters with the Russian. He wasn't sure just how, though. Not yet anyway. Now if he could just get a look at Thompkins's file, he wished, assuming one existed.

When Baier returned to his office on *Kronprinzen Allee* he immediately approached Younger with a proposal for another trip. But this time Baier suggested he return to Frankfurt to visit his old office in the I. G. Farben compound for another look at the document files.

"And just what do you expect to find there that you can't here?" Younger asked.

"Hard to tell until I search them. On the one hand, I never really had the chance to exhaust whatever possibilities there might be in those files that Farben left behind," Baier explained. "I mean, it's pretty much impossible to get through them in one lifetime, but at least now I have a much better idea as to what I'm looking for."

"And that would be?"

"You're aware of that German sub, the U234, that surrendered at the end of the war and docked at Portsmouth? It was on its way to Japan when the Krauts finally gave up."

"Vaguely. And?"

"Well, those two guys in our section from ONI, Kuhn and Shoger, passed some interesting reports from the interrogations and inspection of the cargo."

"Like what? I heard it was carrying jet engine parts, but why would that interest you?"

"But that wasn't all. There was material and plans for the jets, their fuel, for ballistic missiles, electronic targeting and firing programs, and guided bombs, as well as a whole host of other stuff. They also had plans and diagrams to help the Japs set up their own production programs."

"So what does Frankfurt have to do with any of this?"

"That's why I want another look at these files. I could easily have missed something since I wasn't fully informed. I didn't know what I was looking for. For one thing, these reports give a brief mention of several chemists who were critical to their advances not only in poison gas, but also in synthetic fuels. And they seem to have disappeared."

"So," Younger continued, "you think you'll come across clues as to their whereabouts?"

Baier nodded, then shrugged. "Hopefully. But I'll never know unless I take the time to look. And there's no way they'd transfer the files here."

Younger thought for a few seconds. "No, I suppose not. Is there anyone there who could do a search for you?"

Baier leaned forward and shook his head. "I doubt it. Hell, I'm not even sure what to look for myself."

Younger studied his young protégé while Baier shifted his weight uncomfortably in the chair in front of his desk. "Are you hiding something? Is this connected to the body in your bathtub?"

"Maybe, but that would be a stretch, Major. I really do believe I can spend some useful time on my real job in Frankfurt. Especially since I'm not getting much help from our British friends at this point."

"Why is that?"

Baier shook his head and met Younger's stare. "I can't figure out their agenda, Boss."

"So why did you say 'maybe'?"

"Well, while I'm there, I might try to find out what I can about the movement of valuables right after the collapse of the regime here. But that's only if I do get the opportunity. That will be secondary, I assure you. There is real work to be done there."

Younger seemed not to have heard the last part of Baier's speech. "Valuables? What kind?"

"I'm not sure about that either. It's really no more than a hunch."

"A hunch? Not a whole lot to go on."

"That's why I don't plan to spend much time on it."

"But how does this help you explain—maybe—the dead guy in your bathtub?"

"I'm not sure it does, Chief. It might surprise you, but I haven't been able to spend much time on that. And I haven't heard squat from our own cops."

Younger shook his head. "Captain, you're speaking in riddles again."

Baier paused to collect his own thoughts. "Major, remember that phrase from the Maltese Falcon, about dreams and what they're made of?"

"Yeah, but there wasn't anything there."

"But in this case there might be. That's where the corpse in my tub comes in. And remember what happened at the end. They all got up to continue their quest for the bird."

"Except for the woman, of course. Bogart turned her in."

"Like I said, it's just a hunch."

In the end, Younger relented and agreed to give Baier "two-to-three days" to hunt in the archival material stored in the basement of the new American military government headquarters, now conveniently located in one of the few complexes large enough to house the American command: the I. G. Farben compound in Frankfurt. Ironically, it had also emerged from the Allied bombing campaign virtually unscathed. Another fine example of precision bombing, Baier thought.

Fortunately for Baier's ulterior purpose, the old I. G. Farben building was also next door to the former Reichsbank office, which had also been largely untouched by the Allied bombers. Baier spent the better part of a day and a half searching the records from I. G. Farben's chemical research division and was pleased to uncover leads to two of the scientists he had encountered in the documents from the U234 episode: one whose trail faded after his flight to Hamburg, while the other appeared to evaporate after a stop in Luebeck. Both cities had been hit hard in massive bombing raids, and Baier wondered if the two men had literally gone up in smoke along with any clues of what had happened to them. They had apparently gone there because of family connections and responsibilities, and Baier guessed they may well have joined countless other Germans searching the rubble and the makeshift bulletin boards for information on loved ones. That is, if they themselves survived. But Baier could at least pursue these leads, slim as they were, although he would once again be in British territory in both cities, since they lay in the British zone of occupation, and dependent on their cooperation. A third name Baier had come across, a Doktor Wehrli, had headed further east to Breslau. Baier guessed that he had probably ended up in the Soviet Union, conscripted for work in their scientific establishment, if he was lucky. The alternative would have had him swept up in either the vicious fighting in that city, one of those Hitler had designated as a fortress to be defended to the death, or in the turmoil of those Germans expelled from the eastern provinces given over to Poland, such as Pomerania and Silesia, or seized by the Soviets, principally East Prussia. That meant either death at the hands of vengeful Poles or Russians, or expulsion to the West. For all Baier knew, the man could be scrounging for food and shelter somewhere in the Rhineland these days.

The remainder of Baier's time in Frankfurt—roughly a day—was spent next door in the office of the former Reichsbank. During his brief tenure in the city, and before his assignment to Berlin, Baier had gotten to know several of the officers assigned to the Allied—mainly American—efforts to locate the gold and currency transferred primarily from the Reichsbank's main headquarters in Berlin out of the city as the Russians closed in on the German capital. Two of the individuals were Lieutenants Esser and Lisson, and Baier hoped that his superior rank would dissuade them from asking for his authorization to study the files he wanted. A third friend had been working as a secretary, a Corporal Hunnicut whom Baier had even dated for part of his stay in Frankfurt. And they had parted on amicable terms. She might be of help if Esser and Lisson proved to be too reluctant. Baier couldn't be sure what he might learn beyond a sense of what monies had been shipped where and how, but even that would at least give him some context.

In the end, all three were happy to see Baier again, and he offered to spring for a round of beers and schnitzel when they closed for the day. No one bothered to check for his authorization, presumably assuming that anyone working for military intelligence in Berlin was free to read any files he deemed necessary. They had only a vague idea of what Baier was doing in Germany, and he explained that it was useful "to follow the money trail." Which, in a way, was what he was doing, even if the trail was more of a detour. In the end, he assured them, "It's all about the money." They nodded knowingly.

"Just let me know what else you need to see, and I'll help you find it," Corporal Hunnicut offered. "The records are kind of scattered," she explained. "I'm afraid the officers leading those teams were not real good at writing up their reports, either." She leaned in close to whisper in Baier's ear. "In fact, there are some gaps in their activities, which leads me to wonder what they haven't been telling us, given that a good deal of the bullion and currency is still out there somewhere." She winked. "Or so I've heard."

"Just what have you been hearing?" he pressed.

Hunnicut's eyes rolled between long brown eyelashes and even darker eye liner, apparently the only cosmetics of any sort she allowed herself to wear on the job. "Just rumors, you know. Corridor gossip. But from what I gather, people have been playing fast and loose out there."

"Any particulars you can divulge?"

She shook her head. "Sorry. I don't know anything more."

She looked at Baier apologetically. "It's just general talk and stuff."

"I'm not surprised," Baier confided. "There was a lot of that stuff moving around, and it was a pretty turbulent period. Is anyone still out there searching for it?"

"Well, a lot of that fell to the Third Army, since they were in charge of the area in the south where the money was first found. But I hear they're turning the whole business over to the CID." Her eyes glanced over at the door but then resettled on Baier's face. "I hear they might even bring the CIC in."

Baier smiled. "I'm sure that'll help."

"Oh, tell me about it. With types like that involved it won't be long before we're giving gold to the Germans. Someone had better alert Fort Knox."

"What do Esser and Lisson have to say?"

Hunnicut laughed and waved her hand at Baier. "All those two care about is transferring out and going home. As far as they're concerned, we should just leave it all to the Germans. It's theirs anyway."

"But who would claim it and what would they use it for? I think that's the main concern at the top. We have to make sure it doesn't fall back into the wrong hands. There's still a lot of that turbulence around."

"Yeah, and from what I hear it isn't about to settle down anytime soon." Baier must have looked confused, because Corporal Hunnicut rolled her eyes and patted his forearm. "You know, the Nazi werewolves or guerillas or whatever, and now the Russkies are getting all demanding and frisky. You must be seeing a whole lot of that up there in Berlin."

Baier assured her that his job and life were loaded with excitement and mystery in Berlin, and he promised to fill her in at dinner. "I can't wait," she bubbled before walking back to the registrar's desk near the entrance.

As best Baier could pull it together from the piecemeal and scattered evidence, several shipments of gold bars and bullion, coins, and currency had traveled south to the Bavarian and Austrian Alps in the hope of hiding and preserving the German treasure from Allied hands. As the Germans involved were either captured or surrendered, they eventually led the American teams to the various hiding places, which ranged from caches buried in caves and forests to flowerpots and vegetable gardens in small Bavarian villages. A great deal had indeed been turned over to Patton's Third Army and then transported back to Frankfurt. Some, as Susan Hunnicut had revealed, remained at large, as did a few of the Americans assigned to the teams. Hence, the talk about possible CID and CIC involvement in an effort to track down the rest of the money and those looking for it.

That, however, was of little concern to Baier. Others in the US military would have to run that down. What he did not find was any evidence of gold, currency, jewels, or other valuables transported back home from outside the Reich, except for gold shipments that had been looted from the Hungarian and Belgian national banks. Baier wondered for a moment if his namesake had been involved in that, perhaps instead of his mythical horde back in Greece. But all that gold had been found and accounted for, which would not explain why the Baier family was so obsessed with finding that other treasure.

What struck Baier, though, was the realization that none of these individuals, none of the Germans involved, had acted alone. And when he read the reports of the efforts involved in shipping the materials, in hiding and securing them, Baier realized how it would have been nearly impossible to handle anything of the magnitude Sabine and Joachim and the others talked about all alone. How could I have been so blind, Baier asked himself. Of course, it would have posed a difficult and challenging logistical problem to move anything of the value his

Germans had mentioned. That would also explain the effort to bring me in. Something must have fallen through, either the loss of an important ally or the means of secure transport. But what if it was still in transit? It seemed as though everyone involved, except perhaps the infamous Karl Baier himself, had lost track of the cache, and now he had disappeared as well. But there had to be others out there who had been involved at some point, if not all along the way. Baier suspected that Sabine and Robert and Ernst knew who. But Ernst was dead, and the other two had disappeared. When he returned to Berlin, Baier knew he would have to discover just what had become of them. He had always suspected that they knew more than they revealed. And he was determined to find out just how much they had been holding back.

CHAPTER SIXTEEN

The biggest or most important piece of the puzzle missing, of course, was Sabine. She had been the principal architect for Baier's involvement in this adventure, luring him in with her beauty and passion, driving him deeper and deeper and then pushing him to Greece. And now she had disappeared. He couldn't even be sure she was still alive.

There was also the personal element for Baier. He had been shaken by Sabine's disappearance, the sudden void she had left behind with her departure. He had already come to question her loyalty, her feelings toward him, and now Thompkins's words and his own research in Frankfurt brought these concerns into a much sharper focus. Was he really nothing more than a "meal ticket"? Did he really serve only that one purpose, a glorified logistics officer and security cover? Even then, Baier still knew one thing for certain. He knew that he wanted to see her again. He was simply unable and unwilling to deny the emotional tie he had built to her during those days and nights after he had fallen into her arms and into her life. That had also brought him into her past, which he could learn to deal with, to manage as a part of his present. The more he thought about Sabine Baier, the more he realized that she was what had brought him to this point, not his namesake, Karl Baier. Ultimately, it had been the woman. And now she was gone.

For lack of any better alternative, Baier had spent a little more than a week, nine days to be exact, surveilling the laundry shop, its windows dark and boarded. He could only do it intermittently, of course, principally during the evening, but occasionally in the early morning as well. There were always the drive-bys during the day and the casual stroll and stop on his way home from work with a slight detour. But the month of November had delivered colder weather, which discouraged long stays. Once, he thought he saw a light in a back room, and another time he could have sworn a candle drifted briefly from one window to the next in the floor above the shop. But Baier had not gone in to investigate further for fear of exposing his interest and inciting renewed visits by Thompkins or Chernov or any of their minions. They might even have been the ones in the shop. But they had kept their distance, as best he could tell, and Baier was determined to stay as far away as possible from them as well until he had assembled more pieces of the puzzle on his own.

On the tenth day, there had been another flash of light in the upstairs room, and Baier could have sworn he saw some kind of movement, a shadow darting about, both upstairs and on the ground floor. This time, he crept in closer, but by the time he reached the storefront whoever or whatever had been inside appeared to have gone. He strolled up and then back down the block and peeked between the boards and broken glass but saw no more sign of life. A glance at his wristwatch told Baier that it was approaching eleven o'clock, so he hurried home.

She was waiting for him there. Sabine Baier sat on the sofa, now safely back in place in the alcove, bundled against the cold, late autumn night in a dark green woolen overcoat. She had tied a navy blue scarf over her head, either for warmth or disguise. Baier couldn't tell which, but he never really gave it much thought, torn as he was between relief and suspicion, concern and anger. He noted that she occupied the exact spot on the sofa from which she had first seduced him, and that she held almost the same pose. Those same thoughts and feelings from that night came rushing back. He raced across the room, fell onto the cushions next to her, and grabbed her hands.

"Goddammit, Sabine. Do you realize what I've been through? All that has happened?"

She squeezed his fingers and drew his hands to her chest. "Yes, Karl, I do. Joachim told me about Greece." She hesitated. "At least he told me as much as the British told him. It's why I stayed away."

"So you know Joachim works for them? And that Ernst is dead, and that he was working for the Russians?"

She nodded. "Yes, I always suspected that they were working for someone else. Both of them. But after the raid I knew for sure about Joachim."

"And Ernst?"

She looked away and then back at Baier. "I was afraid that he was dead. I think they must have kidnapped him, tried to force him to go back to the east. But he always talked of his hatred for the Soviets and the Russians. He said it was all the same."

"He's an old Communist, Sabine. Both were reporting on you and this damn treasure hunt to their masters. And God knows what else." Baier paused and studied Sabine's deep hazel eyes that looked almost like clouds against her skin. Her lips still looked full, and the round cut of her chin and the smooth curve of her cheeks pulled at him once more. But try as he might, Baier could not get past those eyes on this night. So much of her was drawing him in deeper, but her eyes pushed him back with their secrets. She had kept so much hidden for so long, and he wondered how much more was buried there. "I need to know where you've been, Sabine, and what you've been doing. Why you stayed away. What was it about the trip to Greece?" he pleaded. "You're the one who pushed me to go there."

183

"Oh, Karl." She tightened her grip on his hands and brought them to her lips. "Look at how that turned out. The British were a step ahead of us the whole time. I feared all was lost. And I've been so frightened ever since that raid. I . . . I didn't know what to do." A tear from a small pool in her left eye drifted down her cheek. "I didn't know if you were a part of that, if I could trust you anymore. I mean, there were American soldiers there, too."

"Oh, Sabine, please. You came here that night. I explained everything. And if you had been honest with me about those two we could have avoided these lost days. So much has happened, and there's so much to do."

"But I didn't want to say anything, because I couldn't be sure. And I didn't want to scare you off. Karl, I got so frightened and confused when you were away. I was so alone."

"But I went to Greece for you. You knew that."

She lowered his hands, then raised them to her chest. "No, Karl, don't you see? My whole world fell apart again. I couldn't come here while you were away. I didn't know what to do once you had left. I didn't know who might be watching, what informers might be out there."

"Sabine, please, we don't have the Gestapo anymore."

"How can I be so sure? You have no ideas what it was like to live here under the Nazis. There were informers everywhere. And the Communists have rebuilt that system in the east already. I've been hiding in empty cellars or staying single nights with different friends. I even risked going back to our shop to hunt for food and money."

"So it was you."

"Were you there? Did you see me? Why didn't you say something?" she pleaded.

"I wasn't sure. I never got a good look at whomever was there."

"Do you think there were others?"

He shook his head. "I can't be sure."

"I know it was dangerous, but I took that risk because I was so desperate. And I didn't know if I was being watched, so I was afraid to approach you, even if you hadn't been involved in that raid." More tears ran down her face. "And now all that money is gone. I don't know how I'll survive."

"I wouldn't be so sure. About the money, I mean." He studied those eyes. "Some still think it's out there yet."

Sabine released his hands. She fell back against the corner of the couch. "Who thinks so? How do you know?"

Baier did not want to tell her about the break-in at his house, or the meetings with the other allies. "Leave that for now. But it seems I'm stuck with this case."

"Do you believe it's still out there?"

"Yes, actually I do." He looked out over his backyard. "I'm not sure how much or where it is. But too much has happened."

Sabine fell against Baier, pressing her lips to his. Then she kissed his cheeks, his forehead, then his lips once again, her hands wrapped around the sides of his head. "Oh, Karl. You don't know how relieved I feel. That's wonderful."

"For you perhaps. But it's turned my life upside down. And I make no promises. That money still does not belong to you or me."

"Karl, please stop that nonsense."

"No, Sabine, I'm going to try to find the gold, or whatever it is that's out there. It's the only way to end all this madness. But I don't know what I'll do with it yet. I'm an American officer, and I have a responsibility to my country and my command. I'm not going to jeopardize that."

Sabine said nothing. She looked at Baier with a mixture of apprehension and anticipation, chewing her lower lip, her eyes unmoving as they glistened behind her tears. Baier couldn't tell

185

if those were tears of joy or sorrow.

"In any case, I'm sure your husband had accomplices. He simply could not have accumulated, hidden, and then moved that hoard all alone."

"But he never mentioned anyone else."

"Think, Sabine. Do you remember the names of any of his comrades, people he served with in Greece, for example?"

Sabine fell back against the cushions again, her eyes on her lap, where her hands sat folded together. "There were a few names, but most have died or disappeared."

"Most, but not all?"

"We'd have to search all over Germany. And beyond. I've heard that some have escaped to South America through a network some in the Vatican have set up."

"Sabine, I can't keep running all over Germany, much less the entire globe . . ."

"But there is one still here in Berlin. I hid for three separate nights at his place. He served with Karl in Greece. Horst Kohler. They were very close, even before the war."

"Where in Berlin?"

"It's a small street off *Potsdamer Strasse*. Not far from Tempelhof."

"At least it's in the American sector."

"Karl, I would never go to the east, not the Russian zone. I can never forget what those bastards did when they came here."

"You need to contact this Kohler and set something up so I can meet him."

"We'll both go. I'll take you there myself. It will be easier."

"Sabine, I'm not sure that's wise. It's best that we don't spend time together in public."

"Karl, he won't talk to you unless I'm there. Don't you see? He doesn't know you. And he doesn't care what your name is."

Baier saw immediately that she was right. "All right, we'll

both go. But at night. And soon."

Sabine slid over next to Baier. Her eyes searched his, then she smiled, softly. She laid her head on his chest. "We can do this, Karl. Just you and me, together. And it will be for us."

Baier noted that she no longer made any mention of her husband, as though he was no longer a player. Perhaps she had discovered something of his fate, or he had gradually passed from her thoughts. But he did not want to ruin the moment by asking. They sat still together for several minutes. Then she sighed and stroked his thigh with her left hand. Baier raised her face to his, kissed her hard on the lips, stood, and drew her to him as he moved toward the stairs.

When Sabine gave Baier the directions to Horst Kohler's hideout, she turned out to have been only partially correct. As Baier drove the jeep he had commandeered the following afternoon from motor pool down *Potsdamer Strasse,* he felt as though the full impact of Berlin's destruction lay stretched and exposed before him. Baier suddenly realized how sheltered one could become in an upper-class, residential part of the city like Dahlem, where the destruction wrought by the bombing and fighting had been relatively isolated. Here it was as though someone had redesigned the city to encompass a series of roads lined with rubble and shattered storefronts. The elevated rail tracks that crossed *Potsdamer* at one point resembled little more than a twisted sculpture of charred metal. When you pulled closer to the buildings themselves, you could see signs of life as the Berliners settled behind those facades that masked some structural integrity still, enough to yield several livable apartments inside.

Kohler's place, however, was not actually located on *Potsdamer Strasse,* or even a side street running off it. Instead, they swung to the left down *Yorck Strasse* in the direction of Tempel-

187

hof until they turned right into *Moeschen Strasse,* a small side street several blocks from the airport. Sabine had gotten the part about the proximity to Tempelhof right, anyway. To their left the ruins of the *Anhalter Bahnhof,* a major point in Berlin's pre-war transportation system, stood in a barren field of broken brick and timber. It had been a source of pride for Berliners. Baier had read that by the start of the war over 30,000 travellers a day passed through the station to points south in Lepizig, Munich, and beyond to Italy and the Balkans. Not anymore. The front of the building stood relatively intact, perhaps two-thirds of it, but it was all alone and forlorn, as if the builders had forgotten to construct the rest of the station and left the building materials lying in the yard. From its front one had almost a direct line of sight over the rubble to the ruins of the old Gestapo headquarters in *Prinz Albrect Strasse,* which, if anything, embodied the criminal insanity that had brought this city, this nation, to its shattered state.

According to Sabine, Kohler lived in a flat at the back on the third floor of a building complex in the middle of the block. Baier pulled the jeep into a covered drive just off the street that opened onto a courtyard surrounded on all sides by a series of apartment blocks that appeared to be in surprisingly good condition. And they were full of families from the look of activity in the courtyard, which ranged from cooking to laundry to bathing. Baier guessed that few apartments in the city offered the full range of amenities and utilities. Most Berliners would be happy with a roof and four walls.

Baier and Sabine climbed a set of stairs to their left after Baier parked the jeep off to the side of the driveway. Sabine turned to the left at the third level up from the ground floor, then made a series of turns that took them to the back of the complex. The hallways were dark and lined with paint that had taken on the tone and color of the soot and dust that seemed to lie in the air like a tragic history.

"How did you manage to find him?" Baier asked.

"Horst made contact shortly after the fighting ended to pass along word of Karl's survival but capture by the Red Army. Horst gave me an address where I could meet him to talk about it further, but it was old by the time I tried to find him. He had already moved twice."

"And this time?"

Sabine kept her eyes focused on the hallway. "I found him myself. We have our own networks in this city, of course."

"Who is looking for him?"

"You people for one," Sabine replied. "At least your counter-intelligence people are. I believe the other Allies are as well." She looked at Baier and shrugged. "After all, he was an intelligence officer, even if many in the *Abwehr* were opposed to Hitler."

"How do you know I won't turn him in?"

Sabine laughed. "He won't still be here by the time your people come."

"And did he have any more news of your husband?" Sabine shook her head. "What can you tell me about him? His background, I mean."

Sabine drew in her breath, then exhaled, as though she was trying to lay out all the information on this man in a single effort. "His family comes from Hannover. I think his father worked for the railways. He and Karl first met at the University in Goettingen. Horst had a natural affinity for languages, Karl said. I think that's why he ended up in the *Abwehr*."

She halted and knocked on a heavy, dark door that seemed to be built of solid oak, perhaps the most impressive structural part of the entire building. It was certainly much heavier and more solid than the scratched and dusty brown frame that held it. The door opened just a crack, and Sabine immediately pleaded for entry.

"It's important, Horst. Let us in. We can help you. But we need some information first."

Baier wondered what he could do to help, especially when a man he assumed was Kohler stuck his head in the hallway to see who all was there. Baier noticed the Luger in Koehler's right hand and thought that a man this desperate might well bring more danger than assistance.

"Hurry," Kohler ordered. He studied Baier. "Who is he, and why did you bring him?" Kohler held the door and motioned with his Luger toward the inside of the apartment.

"He's a friend," Sabine answered. "He's with me now, Horst, and he can help us."

"Great," Kohler nearly shouted. "Another goddamn American gangster. Germany is full of them now."

"Where did you get that weapon?" Baier asked. "You're aware, of course, that Germans are not allowed to carry firearms." Baier glanced around the room and noted, thankfully, that they appeared to be alone. He assumed this was probably a safehouse used for men like Kohler who were on the run from Allied authorities.

"Perhaps you should try to take it away from me," Kohler responded.

"Horst, please," Sabine hissed. "This is no good. The war is over."

"Tell his side that."

"Stop it," she repeated. "We all need help. You included."

Kohler studied Baier, the hard set of his chin betraying a mixture of contempt and suspicion. Light brown hair fell over the tops of his ears to frame a pair of blue eyes and a long, straight nose. "What do you want?" he asked. "I don't have much to offer nowadays."

"We were hoping you might have information," Sabine

continued. "About Karl's money."

A smile lit Kohler's face, and he walked over and sat on the edge of a mattress laid out over a simple iron bed frame in the corner of the room. "I should have guessed." He laughed, more to himself than to anyone else in the room. "Yes, I have information, but that's all. I don't have the treasure itself." He spread his arms wide. "It's certainly not here in Berlin. Not from what I knew last anyway."

Sabine approached him. "But do you have any idea what's happened to it, or who else might have helped?"

Kohler's eyes grew wide in disbelief, and he stared at Sabine for what seemed like a full minute. "Of course, I know. I was one of those who helped. And I'm the only one still alive. Or at least I think so."

"Then why did Karl never mention you?"

Kohler's laugh was louder this time, clearly meant for everyone in the room. "What did you expect? That your husband would carry around a play list for everyone to read?"

"Then where is it?" Sabine pressed. "Is it still in Greece?"

Kohler's look of disbelief shifted to Baier. "Of course not. What possible good would it do there? Except to the Greeks, of course." The smile widened. "It's here in Germany."

Sabine rushed at the bed and grabbed Kohler's face in both hands. "Horst, is it true? The money's actually here? But where and how?"

Kohler pulled her hands away from his face. "We often took coins and bullion and currency when we pulled out of a country. Greece was no exception. Karl and I arranged to have it lifted out and transported as part of the *Abwehr*'s funds when we left."

"How was that possible?" Baier asked.

Kohler waved him off. "Oh, Hell, we had plenty of untraceable funds for our use. It was easy to hide any extra. By the time we got it back here, Karl was able to arrange to have it peeled off, and then transferred south with all the other stuff the government was shipping into Bavaria at the end in March."

"But the end wasn't until late April or May," Baier interjected.

Kohler rolled his eyes. "We weren't about to wait for the damn Soviets to arrive, regardless of what the *Fuehrer* and his lackeys were shouting about our *Endsieg*. Your fucking bombers blew the *Reichsbank* apart on one of their raids in February anyway. And that was when the bank's holdings started moving south."

"And where was Karl Baier?"

"At first he was stuck in that mess in Hungary. But after he escaped, he returned to oversee the transfer," Kohler added. His gaze shifted over to Sabine. Kohler was silent for what seemed like a full minute before he spoke. His voice was much softer when he finally did speak. "He had changed, Sabine. He's not the man you knew."

"Changed? How?" she pleaded. "What do you mean?"

"War does things to a man, Sabine. Perhaps you'll have the chance to see for yourself." Kohler motioned with his pistol in Baier's direction. "You can ask him."

Baier did not respond. He returned Kohler's stare, then looked over at Sabine, shaking his head before his gaze fell to the floor. It was Sabine who broke the silence.

"But where down south?" she asked. "Where exactly?"

"In the mountains. Near the Austrian border."

"Can you find the location again?" Sabine pressed.

Kohler looked back at her with puzzlement, his face almost a grimace. "You should have all that."

Sabine's eyes went wide. She stepped in closer. "What do you mean? I have no idea where it is."

Kohler shook his head. "Karl hid the information, but he put some in a letter he sent to you and some on a laundry ticket. I know that much. There's probably more."

Sabine almost wailed. "I never got that letter, Horst. Not a second one." She turned to Baier. "Could it be that ticket you brought to the shop? Do you still have it?"

Baier sighed. "I'm not sure. I can check, but I doubt it." He paused, and his face lit up with a sudden revelation. "Ernst must have known. Remember, he wanted to keep the ticket."

Sabine turned back to Kohler. "That won't help. He's dead. But he may have passed the information along."

"Why haven't you collected the money yourself?" Baier asked. "Why have you left it sitting there if you know where it is?"

Kohler laughed. "You really think it's that easy, *Ami*? With all your soldiers wandering around. It's not like I can just drive down there some weekend."

"But you're sure it's still there?"

"Well, I can't be positive," Kohler shrugged, "but I doubt anyone else knows what's there. Unless someone else has figured something out from that damn laundry ticket."

Baier thought of the break-in at his house. "We'll have to hurry then. They may have that much already." He turned to Kohler. "You never answered Sabine. Do you think you can find it again?"

"Perhaps. But it's very risky right now. Like I said, the area is crawling with Americans, a lot of them looking for the *Reichsbank*'s loot."

"That's where we can help, Horst." Sabine turned and pointed to Baier. "He's an American, Horst. He's an officer, and he has important connections."

Kohler leaned around Sabine and examined Baier once more. "So you think this is your get-rich-quick scheme, eh *ami*? What, aren't all the souvenirs and women like Sabine enough for you?"

Baier strode over to the bed. He momentarily forgot about the Luger. "What I do with the money is my business. Just be happy you're not in prison or on your way there now."

Kohler laughed and shook his head. The gun returned. "That's big talk, *ami*. Just how important are you? Can you get me what I really need?"

"What's that?"

"Papers, my friend. Identity papers that will allow me to travel and get through your damn checkpoints."

"Where do you need to go?" Baier asked.

"Austria, for starters. Then on to either Italy or Switzerland. From there I can get out of Europe."

"But Horst, why?" Sabine had let her hands fall to her side. She raised them now, stretched them toward Kohler, then let them fall. "Why are you so eager to go?"

He looked up at her, and Baier thought that for the first time since their arrival there was a touch of pain or sadness in his eyes.

"Because Germany is finished, Sabine. Our world is gone." He gestured in Baier's direction. "It belongs to them now. I don't think I can stand to live in it any longer."

"But what will you do?" Sabine pressed.

Kohler shrugged. "Start a new life somewhere. I'll just take some of the treasure once we locate it." He held up his free hand. "Don't worry. I won't need much."

"In that case," Baier interrupted, "I'll be happy to help you go. Just tell me one thing."

"What's that, *ami*?"

"How much material is there? How were you able to consolidate all the jewels and currency and gold your comrade stole from those poor Greeks?"

Kohler's jaw dropped, and he stared at Baier for twenty or thirty seconds. Then he fell back on the mattress as a fit of laughter erupted from deep inside him. He must have howled for a full minute, and when he stopped his eyes were red with tears of laughter, overcome by disbelief at the innocence in the room, at how much information and knowledge were missing or misunderstood. He appeared to be overwhelmed by a powerful sense of comic relief, as though all the pain and suffering of the last months—no, the last few years—had been swept away.

"You . . . you actually believed that story?" He sat up and turned to Sabine. "Karl told that to you as well? And you believed him?" Kohler wiped his eyes on his sleeve. "Well, he was nothing if not thorough. And I have to admit that it was pretty convincing, and I guess it did make a good cover story to keep all those pricks from the SS and the Gestapo at bay."

"Apparently, it didn't keep them all at bay," Karl said. "Someone from the SS was sniffing around down in Greece when I was there."

Sabine stepped over and grabbed Baier's arm. She nearly shrieked. "The SS? Karl, why didn't you say something?"

"I didn't want to alarm you needlessly. I didn't think there was anything you knew that could help."

Kohler stared at Baier. "The SS? That's not good. Do you know any more about him?"

"Only that our Greek guide said he was tall and blond. And that he did not find anything."

"Oh, hell, *ami*, that's no help." Kohler glanced at the floor, as though trying to collect his thoughts. "Whoever he is, I wonder how he escaped the Allies. Most of those guys were summarily shot or tossed in prison." He looked up at Baier. "They're easy to identify, you know. They all have their blood types tattooed on their arms."

Sabine dropped Baier's wrist and turned back toward Kohler. "Horst, if it wasn't the payments Karl collected in Greece, then where did the money come from?" she asked. "Please, tell me. Where did it all come from?"

Kohler waited a moment, still trying to catch his breath.

195

Then he looked at them both, shaking his head. When Kohler stopped he waited another several seconds to let the news settle in. It's as though he's playing to an audience, Baier thought.

"We robbed the National Bank of Greece."

CHAPTER SEVENTEEN

"What do you mean you robbed the Greek National Bank? Who did? You and Karl Baier? Like Bonnie and Clyde? Were there others?"

Horst Kohler rolled over to the edge of the bed, then stood up. His eyes glistened, and his gasps echoed through the room as he worked to catch his breath. After a moment, he shook his head. "Well, it wasn't that exciting. And we didn't take everything. We weren't that greedy." His smile faded. "And of course it was not just Karl and me. We had help from a few others."

"Then how can you say you robbed the Bank. It was more like a requisition, which ended up in Berlin and should then have gone over to the Allies."

Kohler rocked his head back and laughed some more. The Luger swept the air at his front. "You *Amis* are so naive. How accurate do you think the accounting and oversight were by that time?" His head rolled straight, and the hand with the Luger dropped to his side. "Oh, sure, we Germans are fanatics for record keeping. When we want to be. But Karl and I stayed one step ahead."

"How so?" Baier inquired.

Kohler peered at his American visitor. "Do you think the Greek records were complete and well organized? Really?" He glanced over at Sabine with a look of disbelief and wonder. She stood silent and still, a shrunken figure backed against the wall ever since Kohler had broken his news about the real source of the treasure.

"Let me explain something to you, my dear *ami*," Kohler continued. "In 1923, when the Turks expelled the Greeks from Smyrna—now it's called Izmir—the Greeks were not about to let all the money stored in that prosperous commercial city fall into the hands of the hated Turks. Nope. They closed the *Banc d'Orient* and transferred the gold holdings to Athens."

"How much was it?"

Kohler shrugged. "Millions. I'm not sure how much it was. Like I said, it was not well documented. And we weren't that greedy. We didn't need it all. It wasn't difficult for Karl and me to take enough and place it into a separate holding that we gave our own markings and documents so we could track it back to Berlin."

"But how much did you take?"

Kohler smiled again. "Only about seven million British pounds worth. As best we could figure it, of course."

Sabine's gasp shot across the room.

"And then what," Baier pressed. "You must have needed accomplices back here. I mean, that's a lot of gold to move."

Kohler shrugged again and slipped the pistol into his pants pocket. He held up his right hand, now free, with one finger extended. "Just one, actually. A friend at the *Reichsbank*. He let us know when the gold was being shipped south so we could intercept it."

"And when was that?"

"At the end of March," Kohler answered.

"So, where is this friend now?" Baier asked.

"Dead. Like all the others. Or at least that's what I thought." Kohler's smile evaporated. "This SS man has me worried, though."

"How did they die?"

198

"That was mostly thanks to your bombers, Mister *Ami.*" The finger swiveled and pointed at Baier. "You know, those things are pretty indiscriminate in whom they killed. That precision bombing stuff was a load of shit. So don't get all self-righteous with me."

"I wouldn't waste my time, especially not after what your side did to cities like Warsaw and Rotterdam, not to mention London," Baier responded. "Where was Karl Baier during all this?"

Kohler grinned and shook his head before continuing. "On his way back from Budapest. My unit broke up after the Soviet offensive on the Oder, but I was able to get through to the south, and we met up in Austria, just outside Vienna. Then we traveled together to Bavaria."

"But what about all the other material back in Greece?" Sabine Baier interrupted. "The gold and jewels and money Karl collected to help Jews and others escape. Did he ever have that?"

"Oh, Sabine, yes, of course." Kohler's head tilted to the side, and his eyes went suddenly sad. "Yes, Karl had that, but it wasn't that much. It was more like seed money. He used that to buy off the Wehrmacht and SS commands, to keep their eyes away from the real prize." He turned back to Baier. "It wasn't that difficult, really. They were all so greedy, especially at the end. Funny how that works, isn't it?"

Baier ignored the question. "So where is it now?"

Kohler turned and walked back to the bed. He set himself gently on the edge of the mattress again, as though suddenly spent and exhausted, his eyes focused on the floor. "Down south, near Fuessen." He looked up at Baier. "You know, the town near that fairy-tale castle Mad Ludwig built. It's buried in the mountains. We knew there'd be a lot of Americans there, but we were sure they'd all be so obsessed with that stupid castle." He shook his head. "That's all those Bavarians are good for."

Sabine stepped forward. "Can you take us there?"

Kohler looked at her but pointed at Baier. "If he gets me the papers I need." He considered Baier. "Do you think you can do that?"

Baier glanced down at his feet and studied the floor. "I think so. But I'll need something else, something I can sell to my people."

"And that would be?" Kohler continued.

Baier looked up. "Information on your smuggling network." He held up a hand when Kohler began to protest. "I need something on the network you have for getting former regime officials out of Berlin. Otherwise, my superiors won't buy it."

Kohler shrugged and looked over at Sabine. She nodded. "We can do that." He smiled at Baier. "Then it's all yours. Well, the bulk of it. I'll need a little starter money, as I said. You can have the rest. And good luck with it."

In the end, Baier turned once more to Dick Savage. He knew he would have to tell Savage more, certainly more than he had divulged at the dinner, but at least he would keep the circle of those in the know as narrow as possible.

"You know you can get those kinds of papers on the black market, don't you?" Savage inquired. "It's probably safer for you, at least professionally."

"I doubt those would be reliable enough. I can't take the chance this guy will get stopped."

"Why not?" Savage pressed.

"He knows too much. Also, I don't want him to set off alarm bells in the underground among the Nazis still in hiding. If he can just disappear on his own, it will make my job, not to mention my life, so much easier."

"Why me?" Savage continued. He was clearly not going to make this easy. "Why not go through the proper channels. I'm sure Younger would vouch for you."

Baier paused. This was the moment of truth. He glanced at the window, where a heavy set of charcoal gray clouds sat on the edge of the Berlin sky. Savage had a look of curiosity that did not match the pressed, woolen, pinstriped suit that gave him an air of authority and infallibility.

"Because I need another favor. It's an extra set of papers to match the others. They're for a woman."

A hint of a smile broke the pale, thin line that marked Savage's lips. "Good Lord, Karl. Not you, too? What have you been up to? She isn't pregnant, I hope. Or worse, married."

Baier shook his head. "No, no, nothing like that." He smiled in turn. "I'll explain it someday, Dick, I promise. But right now I need to do what I can to get her away. I'm going with them as far as the Austrian border."

"Does Younger know?"

"Yes and no." Savage looked puzzled, even if he was still smiling. Baier continued. "He knows I've been working on a special case." Savage's eyebrows arched. "He doesn't have all the details, though. I've tried to spare him some of this. And he knows I've been involved with someone."

"So, is it the same woman? The one you're trying to move?"

Baier nodded. "Yes, I'm afraid so. And I've decided to help her leave. She has to get out of Berlin, and Germany as well." He studied Savage's face. "I really do promise to tell you everything when I get back."

Savage studied the slip of paper Baier had passed to him when he first entered Savage's office. "Do I dare run these names by C.I.D.?"

"If you think you must. But we need to leave as soon as possible."

201

"Are they in danger?"

"Possibly."

"From which side?"

"Several, I'm afraid."

"Give me a couple of days. And screw the C.I.D. Those bastards are useless anyway."

After he returned from Greece, Baier had never thought he would encounter a more difficult and trying hike than the one on Delos, but he realized now how flat the island had actually been, relatively speaking. The Bavarian Alps were impressive, without a doubt, and they were also high and steep. And the south German sky was lit by a sun he had seen only rarely of late in Berlin, lending a raw beauty to the extended, rocky peaks covered in evergreen and capped with snow. None of the snow had fallen yet at the altitude they were hiking, which brought some comfort to Baier. At least the ground was firm and dry. But as the sweat broke across his forehead and occasionally dripped down his cheeks, Baier wished that he had dressed lighter, at least without the woolen sweater Sabine had insisted he bring along. Or perhaps he should not have talked Younger into allowing this one last excursion. That was how Baier had sold it anyway.

"You've got one week tops, Karl. Then I want you back here. And you'd damn well better check in with the Third Army when you're down there."

"I promise, sir. As soon as I get these people delivered and they pass me the information they've promised."

"Which is? Tell me again," Younger ordered.

"Some insights and information into the underground networks in Berlin that are being used to sneak Nazis and others associated with the regime out of here and down south."

"And that's your business in what way?"

"Scientists and others we need to find are using these routes as well."

"And why south?"

"There's supposedly a channel running from Rome that is getting these people false documents and arranging passage out of Europe," Baier explained.

"Rome? That sounds far-fetched."

"Maybe it is. But there certainly seems to be a lot of movement down to and through Austria."

"And you know this how?" Younger's eyes narrowed, and his brow wrinkled. Baier could tell he was unconvinced.

"This Kohler fellow. The one I met through the woman at the laundry shop," Baier went on.

"So there was some benefit that came from your ill-starred love affair." A smile cracked Younger's frown. "So what's the story with this Kohler fellow?"

Baier glanced out the window, then back at his boss. "He's a former intelligence officer who's been acting as a facilitator for his colleagues and compatriots. But he wants out now himself, and I think we can close off an important channel if he's gone. Plus, I can get some information on the ones still here or in transit."

"And the woman?"

"I'm going to see that she moves on as well. I don't think it will be safe to have her back here anymore."

"And why do you need to go south with them? Why not just send them on their way?"

"Because they won't give me the information until they're well away from here and safe." He paused. "I'd feel better about that, too."

"Then something good might come of this, whatever you discover down there. But remember, you've got one week. Then you damned well better be back here."

One thing that confused Baier on the mountain, though, was his inability to locate *Neuschwanstein*, the marvelous white castle on a cliff that the Bavarian King Ludwig II had built as a testament to his fantasy and folly. From the pictures he had seen, Baier expected something resembling a cross between a fortress and a dream, but all he saw were miles of stone and evergreens.

"That's about ten kilometers away," Kohler said. He waved his hand in the general direction of the sun. "To the southwest. You didn't think we'd be stupid enough to hide the stuff close to that place, did you?"

"I don't really know how stupid you are." Baier had a lot more confidence dealing with Kohler once he had surrendered his Luger, which Baier felt in his pocket as it banged against his thigh throughout the hike.

"Well, there would be too many people near that thing, too great a chance of discovery."

He led Baier and Sabine around the side of the mountain and along a path that kept mostly in the shade as it crept through a forest of pines. Periodically, Sabine would find a boulder to rest on, insisting that her strength had been depleted by the poor diet of the war years and its aftermath. Baier believed her. He had been stunned by the drive south through a desolate German landscape that seemed at times to spring from a tortured medieval painting, like the ones from Bruegel or even Bosch. Refugees lined the roads, and packs of displaced and homeless people from all over Europe roamed the countryside in search of food, shelter, and money. Bombed out cities and villages lurked around every turn in the road. Baier took surprisingly little comfort in the recognition that the sins of the Third Reich had come home to roost, as he wondered how many innocents continued to suffer and how many of those he saw were among the truly guilty. There were plenty of stories circulating about how the Nazi elite had been sure to take care of themselves and their escape as the end closed in.

"Not much farther," Kohler shouted. He had run about a hundred yards ahead of the others. When he reached a small glen of spruce trees, their branches bare, next to a rocky outcropping, Kohler stopped and began to poke at some rocks piled next to a steep incline of gray stone. "Down here," he shouted, even louder as his excitement built.

Baier and Sabine ran to his side. Sabine stood just off to the side, hesitant, watching Kohler, who paid no attention to either of them. Then she walked over, fell to her knees, and clawed at the stones and dirt.

Baier pulled the trenching tool from his pack and dug where Kohler pointed. "*Da. Dort,*" he gesticulated, his eyes wide and his breath coming in gulps.

Baier and Kohler traded off every five minutes or so, and after about an hour they had cleared a small trench several feet deep and about five feet wide. Kohler's breath now came in short gasps, and he thrust his hands into the loose dirt and twigs and gravel. Sabine pushed her way forward and stood over Kohler. His fingers fumbled for something that Baier could not see, his view blocked by Sabine.

Suddenly, Kohler jumped up, a small leather satchel in his dirty right hand. "He's been here already. He got here before us."

"Who?" Sabine asked. She looked as though she was about to weep.

Kohler looked at her and smiled. "Karl, of course. And he's gone to Lisbon."

"Lisbon?" It was Baier's turn to shout. "Why in the hell Lisbon, and how the hell do you know that?"

Kohler pulled a gold coin from the purse. "Because of this. We had arranged for a set of signals for cases just as this one. This means he's secured our gold and taken it to Lisbon."

"How and why?" Baier pressed.

Kohler slid over to one of the boulders next to a tree and set himself on the top of it. "About a year ago a group of financiers and industrialists met in Strassburg and agreed that they would set up a conduit to smuggle money and contraband materials out of Europe in the event of Germany's collapse."

Baier thought for a second. "I guess I can understand their choice of Lisbon." He remembered the city's role as a passageway for people, goods, and intelligence throughout the war. "But what was their purpose? And how do you and your gold fit into it?"

Kohler shrugged and smiled. "Search me. Maybe to finance the next *Reich,* or perhaps just to get rich. I don't really care. And I can assure you that we are not a part of any plans to rebuild our glorious thousand-year Reich, even if we do still have about nine hundred and eighty years to go."

"Then how can you use their network? And who moved the gold there in the first place?"

Kohler shook his head, and the smile widened. "Sometimes I really wonder about you Americans. The network exists for whomever wants to use it, especially now. It doesn't belong to those fat cats. And you'll have to ask Karl how he did it." He slid off the rock. "My guess he had to use a bit of it for some bribes and to secure transportation, like another set of papers and a lorry. In any case, if you really want to find Karl and the gold, that's where you'll have to go."

"How can you be so sure we'll find him and the money in Lisbon? That's a whole new city," Baier said.

Kohler stared at the sky for a moment, his smile widening, then he waved at Baier. "Do you think that Lisbon was just a playground for the Allies and their movie stars like that Leslie Howard, or the Prince of Wales and his whore wife?" Kohler thrust a finger at his own chest. "We were there, too, *Ami.* We even used it to try to get Allied help for the plot to kill Hitler, but you refused. You said it was unconditional surrender or nothing. Just think of the lives that would have been saved, *Ami.*" Kohler's voice grew louder, his face more animated. "We had safehouses and connections there as well. And we still do."

"What about the underground network in Berlin?"

Kohler stood up straight, then pointed at Sabine. "Ask her. She's the one in the middle of it. I only benefited."

"What do you mean?" Baier stepped toward Kohler. "The middle of what?"

Kohler shook his head some more, then let out a deep sigh before looking over at Sabine. "Have you told him nothing? Was it really all for love?"

Baier examined his trenching spade while the heat rose in his skull. He threw it against the side of the cliff and turned on Sabine. "Just what have you been playing at Sabine? Just how much have you been hiding from me?"

"No, Karl. I never exploited you or your position. Not for that. I knew what that would do to you and to us if I did. I only wanted your help with the gold, the money." She stepped toward Baier. "I did it for us."

Kohler laughed. "She's good, isn't she? I can see how the two Karls fell for her." He held out his hands. "My papers, please."

Baier pushed back and swung around to face Kohler. "Just a minute. You haven't given me a damn thing beyond a hiking tour." He twisted his head to look at Sabine again. "Although you have opened my eyes a bit about her." Baier completed his turn and walked over to her. He held out the papers he had brought for her, his mind swirling with anger and confusion. "Here. This is where you get off as well. I can't believe how easy I've made all this for you, how little I know about you after all this."

"Karl, please. I love you. I want to be with you. This is for

207

the both of us." She left the papers in his outstretched hands. Baier was stunned to see tears in her eyes.

He turned and walked back to Kohler, holding up an extra set of papers. "And you've got to come up with a lot more if you want these documents."

"How about an address and contact instructions in Lisbon?"

"Those would only be of use if I was actually going there."

Sabine walked over calmly, her eyes dry now and hard. She took the papers from Baier's outstretched hands. "Oh, you're going to Lisbon, darling, and you're going with me."

"Give me one good reason," Baier shot back. "Why the hell should I go AWOL to continue chasing this chimera? And with you, of all people?"

She moved in close enough so that their bodies touched. Her hands grabbed his and squeezed, while her eyes locked on his and her tongue moistened her lips. "I'll give you more than one. Because we're closer to this treasure than we've ever been before, and because it's the only way I'll tell you what I know about the underground network in Berlin." She paused long enough to free her right hand, reach up and stroke his face. "But mostly you'll come with me because we love each other."

Baier stared at this woman. The touch of her hand across his face, the look and the promise in the depth of those cloudy, hazel eyes softened his resolve with every moment that passed. Shit, he thought, we've already used seventy-two hours in the week that Younger gave me.

CHAPTER EIGHTEEN

The journey to Lisbon took another three days out of Baier's week. He had innocently assumed they could take a semi-straight train ride from Munich, but just getting out of Germany was hard enough, given the amount of rail destruction and the swarm of refugees and displaced persons at every stop. And then there had been the challenge of changing trains at the Spanish border and the seemingly endless delays as their documentation was inspected first by the Spanish and then by the Portuguese authorities. Baier had also assumed that with the war over, the Spanish and Portuguese concern over their countries being used as transit stations for all kinds of refugees, exiles, spies, and profiteers would have eased somewhat. He had been mistaken. With the explosion of human traffic that the end of the war and all its destruction had set off, the border police and local security officials were more suspicious and wary than ever. And Baier had kept thinking of the time ticking away on Younger's clock. Baier realized even before they arrived in Lisbon that he would never make it back in time, so he'd have to improvise, make contact with Younger, and come up with a plausible explanation for the change in plans. It would also be nice, he recognized, to be able to bring back some sort of intelligence coup. Younger had never stated what he intended to do if Baier returned late, but being declared AWOL was not out of the question. Baier realized that he would not miss the loss of any prospects for a military career. He had quickly recognized his basic incompatibility with the military life, but he did want to avoid a dishonorable discharge. To do that—and stay out of the brig—Baier knew that he had better return with something to show for his efforts.

That's when he hit upon the idea of not trying to hide his presence in the city, probably a lost cause in any event. As soon as they arrived in Lisbon, Baier bought some clothes, then set Sabine up in a café with a bowl of fish stew, a bottle of a heavy red Portuguese wine from up near Sintra, and a crème caramel while he swung by the United States Embassy.

"Do you realize how wonderful this all looks after years of rationing?"

"I thought you Germans got to live off the fat of Europe," he replied.

Sabine snorted. "Hardly. Once in a while we received a load of food from France perhaps, or a soldier might bring some back. But mostly we lived off a pretty thin diet with lots of gristle and sawdust."

Sabine's eyes were aglow with the prospect of such an unusual treat spread on the table before her, and she waved with the distraction of someone fully engaged as Baier swung out into the street and grabbed a taxi.

Baier returned an hour later to find Sabine slumped in her chair, dozing, and apparently unaware that her head was rolling periodically from side to side and her dress was bunched in her hands where they had settled between her knees. He lifted her slowly and carried her to the waiting taxi.

By the time they had reached the hotel, Sabine was still groggy but alert enough to let a gasp escape when she caught site of the hotel. Baier had imposed on the military attaché for a number of favors, one of which had been for assistance to secure a two-room suite at the famous Palacio Hotel in Estoril, several miles outside Lisbon and right on the ocean. The Palacio had been the playground for movie stars and royalty, as well as for the less famous and often shady characters that populated Lisbon during the war, when Portugal and its neutrality and location had attracted perhaps the largest assembly in Europe of spies, diplomats, journalists, refugees, exiles, businessmen, and the entire entourage those people bring in a continent at war. It had been a veritable circus on the edge of destruction. And the lifestyle and festive atmosphere had reflected that. Baier and his colleagues had often joked and bet with one another over who just might be lucky enough to win a posting in the fabulous and infamous capital.

Once at the hotel, he could barely believe his luck. Baier stood at the window of his sixth-floor suite, one that had a balcony that looked out over a smooth green sea of grass and a long rectangular pool of smooth blue water bordered by palm trees. Despite the season being late autumn, the air was still pretty warm, at least compared to Berlin, and a handful of visitors and guests sat at poolside, although most were well covered in slacks and sweaters. Sabine relaxed in the bath, a rare luxury for her, she claimed.

"Shall we get something to eat a little later in the restaurant downstairs?" she asked. Baier's bag lay unpacked on the bed. Since they had traveled straight from Bavaria, they had brought little with them. Sabine claimed that she had little to bring in any case. Baier looked at his own soiled slacks and shirts left from their trek up the mountain and across southern Europe. Until his stop here, he had been down to one clean shirt and a single pair of socks. "Then perhaps tomorrow we can buy some more clothes," Sabine yelled. When Baier didn't answer, she continued. "And you don't have to worry, Karl. I have the money for it."

"Yes, I am well aware of that," he said softly enough for her not to hear. "Now, that is." He walked over to the bathroom

211

and studied Sabine as she lay back in the tub, covered in suds, and her head resting on the back rim away from the spout. "Yes, something to eat will be fine," he said. "But we also have business to conduct tomorrow. And then I need to get back to Berlin as soon as possible."

"Of course," Sabine replied. The bath water sloshed in small waves as she stood. Baier watched her body move from the tub to the floor, thin streams of soap running from her neck, her breasts, and legs in an erotic tableau that had him rooted to his post by the door. She strolled up to him and placed both hands on his shoulders, then grazed his cheeks with her lips before she kissed him on the mouth. Her wet body pressed hard against his. "As soon as I get dressed we can go downstairs. If you want to, of course. We can also wait up here a moment or two longer." She slid her hands along his sides. "After we both eat some seafood, we will return to our room." She pulled at his belt. "Unless you cannot wait."

At that moment, Baier forgot all about dinner, his dirty clothes, and rushing back to Berlin as he let Sabine lead him to the bed. They fell upon the mattress together, his hands roaming across her wet back and buttocks while she rocked against him, pulling at his belt buckle and tugging on his pants, her eyes locked against his as the sheets piled around them in a nest of cotton, linen, and wool.

An hour later, they sat at a table downstairs. The restaurant possessed all the old world elegance Baier had expected. Low-hanging chandeliers lined the center of the ceiling, and long, thin windows set between thick, brown panelling opened onto the courtyard and pool. In the distance, Baier could hear the ocean, and he imagined the salt from the sea breeze hanging in the air around him. He grew suddenly weary of the war, the ruins, and Germany. They were all one in his mind at the moment, a mélange of fury, revenge, and destruction that he wanted to keep as distant as possible, at least for one night.

True to her word, Sabine had dined on baked cod and a plate of fried octopus. Baier had opted instead for a dish of pork loin covered in a green pepper sauce. They shared a bottle of a light, fruity Portuguese white wine that Baier acknowledged would have gone better with a hot Iberian summer, but whose sour edge had provided a welcome complement to their food. And it had reinforced their sense of escape to a warm, sunny, almost exotic climate.

When they finished, Sabine suggested they go to the bar for a brandy. Baier reminded her of her previous proposal to retire to the room as early as possible after dinner, and Sabine quickly confessed that she had several goals on this trip. One of them was to spoil herself and Baier as much as possible before they returned to Berlin, and this was simply one more step in the process.

As he ordered their drinks at the padded oak bar, Baier felt a hand on his shoulder. He turned and saw the sleeve of the British uniform and jumped around in shock. Colonel Thompkins stood next to him, his backside angled against a bar stool, one foot on the lower rung and a drink in his left hand. It looked to be a gin and tonic, the lime wedge submerged in a silo of transparent bubbles.

"Karl, old boy. Let me buy you a drink." Thompkins waved the bartender over.

"No, thank you. I've already ordered." Baier stood stiffly, his right hand on the bar and his left in his pants pocket.

Thompkins glanced at the table where Sabine sat. "I see you're not alone. I can't say it surprises me." He winked. "I knew you two would find each other again."

"I doubt there's much here or about me that surprises you at all. In fact, I wouldn't be surprised if you had planned to see

213

me here all along."

Thompkins smiled and raised his glass. "Touché. You do have a point. And I do suspect we are here for a similar reason, in fact, both of us on a similar quest."

"Similar? Do you really need to be so coy?" Baier asked.

Thompkins set his glass down and gave Baier a crooked smile. Baier wondered how many gins Thompkins had consumed. "Yes, you're right, of course."

"How did you know I'd be here?"

"The Palacio? Well, this is where everyone goes." His free hand swept the air around them. "If they can get a room, of course. So it's the first place I checked, naturally." He took another sip. "And next time you should use a fake name. It's things like that you Yanks will need to learn if you're going to stay in this game."

It was at this point that Baier realized how much he was beginning to dislike this man. His initial attraction, the hope for friendship with a kindred spirit that had bubbled forth in their talk of European history that first day, was fading fast. In its place, Baier saw a condecension, almost an arrogance, toward the colonial cousin. He realized now how much Thompkins had been using him. Baier also recognized for the first time that he would not return or even share a single gold coin from Karl Baier's war chest with this man, not if he could help it. Should he find anything, that is. He might still try to get the money back to the Greeks, but he would not do it through this man. Not if he could help it.

"I'll keep that in mind," Baier responded. "But now that you're here, will you tell me how you even knew to look for me? Perhaps I can learn some more from a true professional."

Thompkins clapped him on the shoulder, then raised his glass to the bartender for a refill. "Of course, old boy. If you really must know, you left a trail a mile wide. Traveling under your true name meant we could check your passage, and since you took a fairly direct route, it was easy to guess where you'd cross." His arm swept the room again. "And, of course, the authorities here were more than happy to oblige."

"Why is that?"

"Well, Karl, old boy, you Yanks may have all the money and the flashy cars right now, but we've got the history and the knowledge that comes with it. Our alliance with the Portuguese goes back to the fourteenth century, you know."

"Yes, as a matter of fact, I do know. The year was 1371. It was why they allowed you to use the Azores as a base during the war despite Portugal's neutrality. Or so they said."

"That's right. So you see, we won't be displaced as easily as all that."

"But how did you know I was even under way?"

"Simple. Your fine Major Younger told me. And when you didn't turn up in Bavaria with your pockets full of pixie dust, I knew you were hot on another trail. So I tracked it." The bartender brought over their drinks. "And here we are." He sipped from his new glass. "Does he know you're here in Lisbon, by the way?"

Baier nodded. "He does now. I contacted my office earlier today."

Thompkins raised his glass. "Smart move, Captain. I'm sure he would have found out in any case. What story did you give him?"

Baier ignored the question. "So what do you propose we do now?"

Thompkins seemed to consider this for a moment. Baier suspected he was really suppressing a desire to burp. "That we join forces. Together we'll track down your namesake for sure."

"And then?"

"And then we'll split the haul 70–30."

"Say what? 70–30? I thought you intended to return the money to Greece."

"Well, I do, old boy. Or most of it, anyway. But I believe we both need some recompense for our troubles."

"Won't your superiors be suspicious?"

Thompkins explored the ice and wedge of citrus in his glass. "I also have a confession to make. I'm afraid, you see, that I've been a bit ahead of you all along." He looked up at Baier. "That journey to Greece, for example, was arranged by me for a purpose."

"Which was?"

"To make sure nothing was found. I knew there was no treasure there, or we would have found it long ago. True, I wanted to make sure there was no other hiding place you might try to locate, but mostly I wanted to throw my own compatriots off the track."

"That sounds pretty unpatriotic, something I'd expect from a real bastard, not someone with your record."

"Welcome to the game, Captain." He glanced over at Sabine, who sat at a table against the wall staring at them both with a barely disguised scowl. "She doesn't look too happy, especially since we shut down her livelihood. I'm sure she'll be happy for the new infusion." Thompkins's face turned deadly serious, as a frown and wrinkles replaced the smile and easy, relaxed manner that had occupied it before. "And you're not to worry about Major Younger. I'll vouch for your work here completely. You're helping to cement the special relationship."

"Yes, of course." Baier picked up his two brandies and turned to go. "But what made you change your mind? Or had you planned this all along?"

"Change my mind? About what?"

"About what you'd do with the money."

Thompkins's gaze sank into his glass, now only two-thirds

full. "I suppose that's a fair question." His focus rose to Baier's face. Thompkins almost looked pained as he spoke. "Do you remember my mention of the work I did in Greece? With the SOE, I mean." Baier nodded. "Well, I have to admit to a fair amount of disillusion from my time there," Thompkins continued. "I told you about all those bastards in ELAS, the communist partisans. Well, I also told those bastards in London that we needed to prepare for the coming storm. They as much as told me to sod off, that our priority was fighting the Germans and that my job was to maintain partisan unity. So I tried to do just that, and I lost a lot of good people in the process." He sighed. "Well, the storm is here, Captain, and I'll be damned if I'm going to just hand everything over to those idiots." Thompkins drained about half of his remaining gin. "No, I'm going to make sure I get some of what is coming to me as well."

Baier wasn't sure how to respond. "I . . . I think I understand." He stood. "Until tomorrow, then."

Baier returned to the table and passed one of the drinks to Sabine. He sat and stared into the dark caramel colored liquid in his snifter. "We'll need to drink these fast," he said. "We can't dally."

"Not that I have any intention of doing so, but why not?" She glanced at the bar. "Is that British clown over there that Thompkins fellow? And if so, what's he doing here?"

"Tracking us. That's why we need to be under way early. I doubt he's getting out of bed at the break of dawn, and we'll need to steal a march on the limey."

"We'll be fine," Sabine confided. "I have a few tricks of my own we can play."

Baier glanced quickly at the entrance to bar, where he noticed the attaché from the Embassy. "So do I, Sabine. So do I."

CHAPTER NINETEEN

They were indeed up at dawn to make an early drive into the city. Baier had also secured the use of a car during his afternoon at the Embassy for the convenience of time and transportation, not wanting to have to rely on someone else. Kohler's contact, one of the hundreds of Germans adrift in Lisbon, had agreed to meet them at the safehouse at ten o'clock, so Baier and Sabine ate a breakfast of rolls, coffee, and fruit in a small café in the warren of streets underneath the huge fortress that watched over Lisbon and its harbor, a chaperone of stone and iron. It seemed to have done a pretty decent job of it throughout the war, Baier thought, seeing as how the country's dictator, Professor Salazar, had navigated the tricky waters of neutrality while making a sizeable profit for his countrymen, thanks in no small part to the extensive wolfram, or tungsten, deposits, and a leisurely lifestyle that was the envy of much of Europe. Baier watched Sabine as she peeled an orange and set it beside the apple she had carved into separate wedges moments before. She had been a veritable eating machine ever since their arrival, admonishing Baier that she had not been able to enjoy fresh fruit and vegetables like these for years. And she had smuggled enough currency across the border to pay for the food and the hotel.

"Who knows what might have happened to it if I had left it back in Berlin," she explained. Baier's eyes had bulged at the sight of the bundle of bank notes she had revealed inside her purse. Human smuggling and black market sales in a city occupied by four competing powers and stuck in the middle of a dreaded Soviet zone of occupation obviously paid well. But that had ended, or at least Baier understood that it had, and he intended to ensure that it remained the case. So he wondered if it was fair to deny her even a small portion of the gold her husband had lifted in Athens. Then again, that was no more than an academic question at this point.

Kohler had claimed that their German contact had been living in Lisbon for years as an *Abwehr* agent, and that he had spent the last six months of the war dodging the Gestapo instead of running intelligence operations for Berlin. After the failed attempt on Hitler's life, the Gestapo had gradually assumed control of *Abwehr* operations in Portugal, most of which appeared to have been little more than vehicles for British and American double agents, often with the knowledge of their anti-Nazi *Abwehr* handlers. This particular *Abwehr* officer, Wolfgang Meyer, had worked with Karl Baier during the early years of Germany's occupation of Greece before his transfer to Lisbon.

"Does he know where the gold is?" Baier had asked.

"I doubt it. But he should be able to put you on the trail of Karl, or at least help you get started."

That was as good as anything, Baier had to concede. And after they had finished their coffee and paid a visit to a dress shop for Sabine, the two of them walked slowly and carefully through the Alfama district up the winding narrow streets toward the hilltop citadel, the Castle of Saint George. The address Kohler had provided was just about halfway up the hill and along the narrow cobblestoned streets that were more like alleyways and footpaths, all of them running uphill. Baier marveled at the quaint houses of white stucco and stone with red tiled roofs, despite the aching in his leg muscles as he sucked in as much oxygen as his out-of-shape lungs would allow. This was even more of a trek than their hike through the Alps, he thought, which at least had been along a more gradual slope. He kept reminding himself that once he had gone uphill, he would eventually get to walk down again. And most of it gratefully took place in the shade thrown by the buildings that seemed at times to tilt over the narrow streets.

After the cobbled street took a dogleg to the left and continued further up, Baier stopped to catch his breath and peeked in on a small café-style restaurant at the corner of the turn. With relief he noticed that the number they were looking for stood above a doorway just to the left of the restaurant. The owner was bringing out an assortment of fresh fish, vegetables, and pastas to a counter packed with ice, obviously preparing for the onset of the lunch hour, or hours, as the Portuguese handled the time. He smiled at Baier, pointed to some fish, and waved for him to enter and inspect his wares. Baier shook his head, and the proprietor turned quickly, disappearing into what Baier assumed was either the kitchen or a storage space.

The door to the building next door stood open and led to a narrow stairway. There were no apartments or rooms on the ground floor, the space probably belonging to the restaurant next door. Baier glanced at the street in both directions to see if they were alone. He had passed a message to the Embassy watch officer once Sabine was asleep, but he had seen no sign of his American colleagues.

He followed Sabine upstairs. Their destination was a flat on the second floor. The door stood open, and when Baier reached the doorway he could see that Sabine stood unmoving just inside the entrance. Her body was rigid, the back and shoulders stiff and erect, as though poised for an attack or preparing for defense. When Baier touched her arm, he could feel the muscles stiffen further, a reaction he instantly associated with fear.

It was then that he saw the reason for her stiff, awkward

posture. The first face he saw was Horst Kohler's.

"Greetings, *Ami.*" The same supercilious smile he had worn in the Alps had accompanied him to Lisbon. Unfortunately. "You didn't think I'd really forego the chance to collect on some of the treasure, did you? I told you I needed my starter money."

"Why even keep us in the picture? Why do you need us here?"

Kohler sat on the back edge of a faded brown sofa that looked out over a sea as blue as a tourist brochure. He stood and walked toward them. "Two reasons. There are plenty of Americans here looking for all the gold we bad, bad Germans have been trying to smuggle out of Europe. And you could be of some assistance in helping us avoid them. Your people actually believe we might use the money to refinance another grab for world power. Can you believe such nonsense?"

"Is it really?"

"Oh, come now. Have you found a single werewolf? You Americans are much like us in that respect. You convince yourselves to believe your own myths."

"Why, though, should I help you enrich yourselves, especially if it involves betraying my countrymen?"

Kohler paced in front of them. "That brings me to reason number two. You can have her." He pointed at Sabine who had still not moved since she entered the apartment. Her eyes had glazed over with a vacuous stare that seemed to focus on some distant point on the Iberian Peninsula. "That is, if you co-operate." He paused, studying Sabine. "And you still want her."

"How does this help you if she stays with me?"

"Because with her at your side and a share of the loot, you'll delay your people long enough for us to make our getaway."

"And what makes you think she's yours to give?"

"Oh," Kohler laughed, "she isn't mine to give. Which means there is still one little hitch." He turned toward a chair set back

221

in the shadows of a corner away from the window. "She's his to give."

Baier struggled to see through the darkness that enveloped that part of the room. After about ten seconds a human shape took form. Baier saw then what had captivated Sabine. He took several steps closer. What he saw shook and repelled him at first, but he could not resist the urge to move in even closer yet to study the face before him. Or half a face. The rest was covered in a mixture of red and blackened skin and twisted, charred flesh surrounding a vacant eye that could no longer see but only stare into a dark space from the middle of worn and useless muscle.

"Karl." The word escaped from Sabine in a hoarse whisper that sounded like a blend of a plea and a sigh. Then she fainted.

"It happened on the escape from Budapest." Baier could not help but stare at his German namesake, whose words seemed to tumble out from the good side of his mouth in a Herculean effort to find shape and coherence. "Have you ever been in a real war, Captain? I mean actual combat and seen what modern weapons can do to the human body?"

"No, I've been fortunate," Baier answered. "At least in that regard." He stood transfixed in front of the sofa where Sabine Baier lay on her back, one arm thrown over her forehead and the other across her stomach. She stared at the ceiling with vacant eyes. Baier could hear her quick, shallow breathing. He watched, fascinated, as his German alter ego dabbed at the tears that trickled from the corner of his wounded, marbleized eye and at the saliva that pooled in the corner of the scar tissue where the left side of his lips had once been.

"This is one of the things they'll do to a man." He motioned toward his face with a hand that looked as though it had been burned as well. Only the thumb and index finger remained. "I had been lucky, avoiding harm serving in a place like Greece for so long, but even luckier with two brief stints on the eastern front." A sound that resembled a cross between a laugh and a gurgle fled from the shadow surrounding the chair. "But I guess that luck ran out. It's funny, the explosion ripped through us just as we thought we had made it to freedom. There had been a Red Army detachment on our right flank as we approached some woods, so we swung around and were able to outflank them. We shot them up pretty good and thought that they had been our last obstacle." He paused, and Baier could see his good eye focus on the sofa. "I thought I was on my way home to you, Sabine. But the Reds had already called in an artillery strike. Unfortunately, their field medical teams were not very good."

Baier heard the mild echoes of muffled weeping behind him. "So where did you go after you escaped from Chernov and the Soviets?" he asked.

"I contacted Horst, and we met outside Vienna, then traveled to Fuessen. That's when we took delivery of the gold bullion from the Riechsbank detachment and reburied it." He held up his wounded hand again. "I'm afraid I wasn't much help. So you can understand why Horst was unwilling to give up his share so easily."

"What happened to your colleague here in Lisbon, your former *Abwehr* friend?" Baier asked.

"Oh, he's around," Kohler responded. "It's hard to get rid of someone once they've caught a scent of gold. Your papers, Captain, came in very handy again. It was easy to transfer his photograph for mine. It helped us buy his cooperation for a cheaper price."

"Do you think you can trust him?" Baier asked.

"Oh, he has been well rewarded, relatively speaking." Kohler gave Baier a look of disdain. "And I always considered him a true comrade, Captain. I guess you never know whom you can truly trust when your world collapses," Kohler explained. "I hope I'm doing a better job of that with you."

"And just what do you expect from me now?"

"You've delivered one part of your package," Kohler said. He nodded toward the sofa. "Karl wanted to see his wife again, appeal to her better interests. Perhaps Sabine will decide to remain with him." Kohler's smile returned. "Sorry, *Ami.*"

"Then why would I help delay the pursuit?"

"Oh, you'll have other rewards. We'll compensate you."

Baier finally broke free of the floorboards and took a step toward Kohler but halted when he saw the new pistol in Kohler's hand. Surprisingly, he had a Browning now. "Oh, please, Captain, no false heroics at this point. You've been so peaceful and helpful until now."

"The gold will give us a chance for a new life, Sabine," the German Baier proclaimed. "I can afford medical treatment in Argentina, from a German doctor even."

"I'm not going, Karl." Sabine Baier was sitting upright now, her eyes staring straight into the shadows that encased her husband. "I . . . I can't go with you."

"But Sabine, I will get better. I promise it won't always be like this."

"No, Karl, it isn't that. I don't want to leave Germany. I realize it won't be the same, not ever again, but it's all I know. It's all I've ever known."

"Is it because of him, the American? He will go home eventually, you know. And he will depart alone after knowing what he does about you."

"Oh, Karl, I don't know how I feel about him, or about you anymore. This has all been so much, and so sudden. Can you imagine what I've been through the last few years? I know you've suffered, and I'm sorry for that. But we both have. I just

224

want to stop for a while."

"You can't, you know," Kohler interrupted. "The Americans will come after you when they find out about the *Ami*'s driver."

"Perkins?" Baier shouted. "Are you talking about the killing of my driver?" He marched toward Kohler, the pistol forgotten. Then he turned on Sabine Baier. "Just what do you know about that?"

"Karl, I told you, I had nothing to do with that."

"Well, not directly," Kohler interjected.

"Just what do you mean?" The fingers of both Baier's fists balled together, and the muscles in his arms tightened. He stood ready to rush Kohler and beat the information out of him if necessary, especially if that silly, goddamn smile crept back over his goddamn face. His leg muscles stiffened, and his temples pounded. He edged forward on the balls of his feet. "Tell me, you son of a bitch."

"Perkins worked for her," Kohler continued. "Oh, not alone, of course. But he helped with some of the human smuggling out of the Soviet Zone. It was so useful to have an Allied soldier, who could drive back and forth. And he was one enterprising capitalist. It's too bad he never made it back to the States. Unfortunately, it got him on the Soviet shit list. One of their boys pulled the trigger that night."

Baier swung his body around in a rage. Before he knew it, he found himself standing directly in front of Sabine Baier. He grabbed her wrists and pulled her up. He found it difficult to form the words he wanted to say as they tumbled forth. "Did you know? Did . . . did you have anything to do with this?"

"Karl, please. I only found out a short while ago. Horst told me before we left for Lisbon. He warned me he would tell you about your driver's death if I didn't cooperate and that it would ruin what you and I had in Berlin. Then I would never be able to go back, that it was for my own good." She looked at her husband, tears pooling in her eyes. "He thought it would convince me to stay with you and keep you quiet."

Baier dropped her arms and wheeled on Kohler. He, in turn, raised the pistol again. "Not so fast, *Ami*. Let's not ruin things. You still come out of this with some good information on the underground in Berlin. And I'm sure you've picked up some other valuable material on all the bad Germans passing through during your visits to the American Embassy here." He examined Baier's face, as though looking for an opening. "And there is the prospect of sudden wealth."

"And how is it you know so much about Perkins's death?" Baier pressed. "Why should I believe you?"

"Let's just say I picked up a lot of information on my own. Remember, I was a professional as well, and I worked as part of Sabine's network, too."

"Do you know who pulled the trigger, who exactly was responsible for the shooting?"

Kohler's smile returned. "You can ask Chernov. He's waiting for us now."

"Chernov?" Baier's mouth moved, but it was several seconds before any sound escaped. "He's here? In Lisbon?"

"Let's go," the German Baier ordered. "We've lost enough time here."

He struggled to stand, and Sabine Baier rushed to his side to help. He leaned heavily on her shoulder from his wounded side, wincing in pain as he settled his weight on her body. "Thank you, Sabine. It's good to feel you at my side again."

"I'm so sorry, Karl. I truly am."

"Let's leave that for now. There's always later," he responded.

"I'm not so sure, Karl," Sabine said. "Not anymore."

CHAPTER TWENTY

The drive to Sotubal took a little over an hour, closer to an hour-and-a-half. The road was a narrow strip of concrete, cracked and potholed intermittently, which dictated cautious and slow progress. Despite the brisk November air, the burst of sun that followed the car from Lisbon allowed them to drive with the windows rolled halfway down. Baier sat in the front of the Mercedes with Kohler at the wheel, while Sabine sat in the back with her husband.

Baier studied the two Germans behind him in the rearview mirror. They struck him as an unlikely pair, perhaps because neither one looked at the other. Sabine stared through the windshield for most of the trip, her eyes periodically searching for Baier's as though pleading for understanding, with her arms wrapped tightly around the handbag in her lap. Only then did Baier remember the clothes they had purchased, which rested on the seat between her and her husband.

"So why are we heading south?" Baier asked, as he glanced at the road behind them. He had agreed to let Kohler drive since he knew the way.

"There's a perfect little cove and beach just off Sotubal, to its west," Kohler answered.

"I would have thought you guys would just as soon have left from Lisbon or up near Estoril, say maybe Cascais."

Kohler frowned and shook his head. "Too many people, too much possible attention."

"But wouldn't all the people provide some good cover? Wouldn't you blend in?"

Another shake came from Kohler's head, and his right hand left the steering wheel to wave at the windshield. "But not the right kind of people. We would have stood out, especially with Karl." Kohler's head gestured toward the back seat. "There are people looking for us, you know."

"Like who?" Baier pressed.

"Like that bastard Thompkins," Kohler replied. "He's like one of those English bulldogs, you know. He picks up a scent and wraps those jowls around the bait and just won't let go." Kohler gazed out the windshield for a minute, frowning, as though reflecting on something distasteful. "And there's that damn SS ghost."

Baier glanced over at the driver and guide. "Have you found out who he is?"

A smile broke through on Kohler's face. "Actually, yes. And it was an unpleasant surprise."

"Well?" Baier pressed.

Kohler waited a moment longer before looking over at the American. "He was our old friend and colleague, the one here in Lisbon. It seems he betrayed us twice. Once, by lining up with the SS while he was assigned here in Lisbon, and then by learning of our treasure from our big-mouthed friend in the Reichsbank."

"How did that happen?"

"Which? Joining the SS or learning about our gold?"

Baier leaned forward. "Both, but more the latter. I thought he was cooperating with you. You said you had paid him off."

Kohler shook his head. "Only when we had to. He threatened to blow the whole operation. Use it as a bargaining chip with you people to erase the records of his complicity with the SS."

"That would never happen."

Kohler laughed out loud. "Your people are already making just those kinds of compromises. They want to learn more about your Soviet allies." Kohler laughed again, as though to put an exclamation point on his claim.

The Mercedes left the main road and followed a dirt track for several miles that eventually broke through a pine forest and some marshland where a smooth, pristine beach of white sand opened before them. A range of small hills shielded the area from the wind and, Baier presumed, wider views and attention from the distance. Halfway up the slope a medieval fortress of gray stone and a square, defensive wall of imposing balustrades set a historical marker and timeline for the visitors. Baier wondered if it was occupied by anyone.

The German Baier noticed where his American counterpart's gaze was focused. Kohler had parked the car at the edge of the forest road and short of the sand. The two Baiers stood next to the front, shielding their eyes from the glare of a midday sun.

"This was a major area of contention with the Moors." The words seemed to bubble from the broken and scarred lips. "That's been over for years now, and the region has lived mostly off fishing and some agriculture. It's known now mostly for its sardines, but there are also several very good wines made here, especially the muscatel. I've had plenty of time to sample a variety of local foodstuffs." He glanced at the American, who was studying his German namesake with a look of skepticism. "Oh yes, it isn't as hopeless as all that. I can still enjoy life, despite the pain and discomfort."

"How long have you been in Portugal?" Baier asked.

"Oh, about five months now. There was a good deal of work to be done to arrange our shipment and escape."

"I thought your *Abwehr* comrade took care of all that."

The German laughed and coughed at the same time. "Do you really think we'd leave everything to him? Especially after

229

what we've learned about him?" The German's one good eye twinkled with a tinge of mischief.

"Did you use this Vatican network I've been hearing about?"

The German's good arm rose and fell. "*Ach nein.* Wolfgang and Horst were not able to make those arrangements so soon, and we decided not to wait." He paused again to glance over at the American. "Gold has a tendency to make one impatient."

"Greedy, too," Baier responded.

"Perhaps. But I don't think we've been all that greedy. We've lost a lot because of this war. We're just trying to recover some of it."

"That's a convenient justification, especially coming from the side that started it."

Baier heard a grunt that resembled a laugh. "I don't have to argue with you. I really don't care if you approve or not," the German explained.

They turned together and followed Kohler and Sabine toward another small castle about one hundred yards down the beach, sitting on a rocky outcropping that extended toward the water like a dark arm of stone and moss. This one appeared to be a smaller version of the one on the hill but without the balustrades. Chernov stood just outside the gate to their side, a broad smile on his face, and a Russian Makharov pistol in his left hand. He was dressed in a civilian suit of dark brown and a long beige raincoat. A fedora rested on his head, tilted toward the back of his skull. He looked like a man out of his element.

"Surprised, Captain?" Chernov shouted.

"There's little that can surprise me anymore," Baier replied. "How did you find us?"

Chernov leaned against the stone wall. The castle itself appeared to be boarded up and deserted. The Makharov slid past his pocket and along his pants leg. "It isn't hard when your colleagues tell you where to go beforehand."

Baier surveyed the beach and the edge of the woods and realized that Chernov was alone. "Colleagues?" It was then that
Kohler's comment about Chernov waiting for them came back
to him. He had been too angry to notice the lack of concern in
Kohler's remarks.

Kohler stepped up beside Baier. "You see, Captain, Colonel
Chernov has been working for the *Abwehr* for years. We had
leverage, and he had motives."

"His family?" Baier remembered the siblings living in Europe
after the Revolution swept Russia.

"That, and a disillusion with the Revolution, or what Stalin
has done with it," Chernov explained. "You see, during my
tours in Europe before the war I not only had to recruit among
the counter-revolutionaries, but I also had to spread stories and
lies about how successful our revolution was. Can you realize
how painful that was, seeing the prosperity all around me and
knowing what a horrible mess our rulers were making of things
back home?" He paused, considering the sand at his feet. Then
he smiled when he looked up again at Baier. "And I must admit
to a certain miscalculation early in the war. I thought the
Germans would win."

"So Herr Baier's escape after Budapest was your doing?"
Baier asked.

Chernov nodded and stepped forward. "In part. Yes, I helped
by removing his Ukrainian guards at the right moment. But as
I'm sure you've noticed, your German alter ego is quite
resourceful. And then I lost track of him as well. That was wor-
risome, as I'm sure you realized, and I wasn't sure how much to
trust my German friends here."

"And your family? Are they still alive?"

Chernov turned his head to give a sideways glance at the
ocean. "Yes, as far as I've heard. My last communication with
them was two months ago. They fled to Brazil early in the war,

and I plan to join them there." He turned again and nodded at his German companions. "After they've found their way to Argentina, of course."

"And the gold will help in establishing a new life, of course," Baier added.

Chernov smiled again and nodded. "Gold always helps, Captain." His face turned solemn all of a sudden as he studied Baier's face. Baier felt as though Chernov's eyes were probing his for a degree of understanding, sympathy even. "But I do regret the deaths that came of all this, Captain."

"Which deaths do you mean?" Baier asked.

"Well, Ernst Hoffmann had to die, but that was not such a great loss. He was a man of little principle."

"None, actually," Sabine Baier broke in. Baier noticed that she had crept up behind him. She was not close enough to touch, but Baier had the sense that she was looking for protection. Or that she was nearing a decision.

Chernov glanced at her. "That is probably true. But alas, as you well know, he discovered my second vocation, working as closely as he did with you, my dear, and I could not allow him to threaten me."

"So it was you who searched my house and left him there?"

Chernov nodded. "Yes, I didn't expect to find anything."

"Not even a laundry ticket?"

Chernov frowned. "A what? Don't be ridiculous. It was the message I intended to deliver. That was the real reason for the visit. I had to be sure you realized how serious this business was and that there was someone involved desperate enough to take such extreme measures."

"So I thought. But how did you know I wouldn't just spill it all to my superiors?" Chernov tipped the Makharov in Sabine's direction. "Sabine?" Baier continued. "What did she have to do with that?" Baier stepped away from her. He wanted distance for himself from all the others to help him think through everything.

"Captain, any fool could see that she had you hooked. Moreover, she served as my principal point of contact after the fall of Berlin. I had lost touch with her husband, of course, so she acted as my go-between with Herr Kohler." Chernov spread his arms. "You see, Captain, they had promised to get me out of the eastern zone if necessary. And knowing what I did, I still had some leverage."

"We all have to make a living, *Ami*," Kohler stated.

Baier turned on Sabine. "This is the man you referred to so disparagingly as 'that fucking Russian'?"

Sabine Baier looked at Chernov with a gaze of cold, hard hatred. "He's still a fucking Russian."

"Who else did you work for?" Baier pressed.

She just shook her head. The look of pleading he had noticed in the car had turned to one of anguish. In spite of himself, of all that he had learned over the past twenty-four hours, Baier felt for her, and he had to fight the urge to walk over and take her in his arms.

Instead, he turned back to Chernov. "You mentioned deaths, in the plural. Who else?"

Chernov grimaced, then shifted his shoulder. The pistol rose to his waist. "I'm afraid your driver, Corporal Perkins, found out as well. I believe he learned it from Ernst. You see, Perkins was making quite a lot of money working for Sabine. Just ask her."

"Leave me out of this. I had nothing to do with it." Her words seemed to drift in from the hills behind them.

Baier just stood there, his face hot and temples throbbing. His gaze caught the pistol, and his feet stayed stuck in the sand as though he had grown roots. The sound of the ocean swept around him, along with the smell of a salt-infused breeze. A chill crept up his spine as the wind ruffled his hair. It was as though a shock had paralyzed him and was preventing him from reacting as he knew he should.

"You're very calm, Captain," Chernov said. "Perhaps that is wise. You are at a distinct disadvantage here. But I assure you, it was not an easy act on my part, and it is certainly regrettable. I had no desire to harm your driver or any other American. But I had no choice. I was desperate. You see, once I no longer worked in counter-intelligence, I could never be sure that I would remain undetected. I was really quite worried, and I'm afraid it affected my judgment. Certainly you understand that."

It took several seconds before Baier could find the words and several more before he could speak them. "Not really."

"Please, Captain." Then the Soviet officer shrugged. "Then again, there isn't much you can do about it at this point."

"I'm confident that justice will be done eventually," Baier replied. "I'll see to that."

"Perhaps we should be off," Kohler interjected. "Meyer could show at any minute."

"Let him," the German Baier said. "If the bastard shows, he's a dead man. And he probably knows it." He spat on the sand at his feet. "He's gotten all that he can hope for at this point. I'm sure he's taken his papers and disappeared."

Baier turned to watch Kohler as he strolled to the water's edge. A single rowboat approached, propelled by a middle-aged man in a ragged sweater and a knit woolen cap. A cigarette dangled from his lips. It looked almost like a picture from an old tourist brochure. On the horizon Baier saw what appeared to be a fair-sized fishing trawler, about twice as large as the one that had carried him to Delos and back, a journey that now seemed almost ancient after all that had passed. "You're not sailing to South America in that I hope."

Kohler laughed. "No, of course not, *Ami*. That's just for the first leg." He walked over and laid a hand on Baier's shoulder. "You'll understand if we don't lay out our entire itinerary for you."

Baier saw that the sailor had pulled the boat up on the shore and stood in the ankle-high surf waiting for his passengers. The cigarette was gone. Kohler and Chernov started their march through the ankle-high surf, but Karl and Sabine Baier hesitated standing on the beach.

Kohler turned to face them, his arms spread wide. "Karl, what are you waiting for? We need to be under way by nightfall."

"You go, Horst. I'm staying."

"No, Karl, go," Sabine said. "Don't stay for me. It's over." She moved closer to her husband and took his hand. He did not let go. The German turned to her and spoke in a low voice. "It isn't just for you, Sabine."

Kohler waded back, strode up to his German friend, and embraced him. "Are you certain?" The German Baier nodded. "Then here we must part, *Kamerade*. It is hard to believe that it's truly over for us. It has been an honor to serve with you and fight at your side for the Fatherland. I wish you all the best, and perhaps we shall meet on the other side of this ocean someday."

The German Baier winced with pain, or perhaps remorse, at the embrace. He slid his good hand up Kohler's arm and rested it on the back of his head. "*Kamerade*, you know I feel the same. Live well over there. I shall never forget you."

Baier wanted to sympathize with these men, but the images of the destruction and suffering their Fatherland had wrought would not go away. Even if they were not personally responsible for individual acts of terror, their service had helped perpetuate the criminal acts of their leaders and fellow soldiers. There was such a thing as collective guilt. Baier had come to Germany convinced of this, and he believed it still. And yet he admired these two men for their courage and their friendship, and even

235

for their dedication to a national ideal that had been so badly perverted. He had the distinct feeling that a chapter was closing. He wished he knew what new one was opening for him.

Kohler pivoted in a sharp military maneuver in the sand, then joined the other two as they climbed into the rowboat.

CHAPTER TWENTY-ONE

"The gold isn't on the boat, is it?" Baier had replaced Kohler at the wheel of the Mercedes for the return trip to Lisbon and on to Estoril, and he tried to keep his eyes on the road for potholes and bumps. He remembered several from the trip down. Nonetheless, he chanced a quick glance at the back seat, where the German Baiers sat, again apart and staring straight ahead.

"Why do you suspect that?" his German counterpart responded.

"Because you gave up so easily," Baier explained. "After all that effort taking the gold out of Greece, getting it to Bavaria, and then on to Portugal, it's hard for me to imagine someone just walking away."

"Perhaps he realized how futile it all is. How unlikely these dreams are," Sabine suggested.

"Perhaps, but unlikely," her husband replied.

"Are you going to give me an answer?" Baier asked.

"Yes." The German sighed. "About half of what is left is on the ship. All that was brought to Lisbon."

"And the remainder," Baier pressed. "Where is that now?"

"I had it transferred to Austria, also somewhere in the Alps, when Horst returned to Berlin. You'll understand, of course, if I don't give you the exact location."

"So you planned to stay all along?"

"Not really," the German said. "But I did not want to risk everything on one voyage, and I suspected I would return

237

someday, once you people had left."

"I wouldn't count on that anytime soon. You've left quite a mess behind."

"There was also the insurance of leaving Sabine well supported in case she decided to stay."

When he glanced in the mirror Baier noticed his German counterpart had slid his good hand across the seat and placed it on the knee of his wife. There were tears in her eyes. Baier thought for a moment while he studied the road about all that had passed since their arrival in Lisbon. They had passed the pine forests and marshlands, and now vineyards and fruit orchards spread toward the surrounding hills as the dusk of early evening threw its shadow over the slopes that had been sprayed with sunshine on the trip down. Baier suddenly felt like a drink, perhaps a glass of one of the deep red wines that Portugal produced. That would be wonderful after all he had been through over the last twenty-four hours. Then he suddenly realized he had not eaten since breakfast. That would be the first order of business when they reached the hotel, gold treasure be damned. "Do the others know, or even suspect?"

"Horst knows, I'm sure. He never asked, and I never had to say as much. But I'm sure he understood. The crates were too light for their number to contain it all. That's why he accepted my staying behind so easily, I believe."

"And the others?" Baier continued.

"They are not my concern," the German stated, matter of factly. "Horst will know how to deal with them. Chernov was probably relieved to discover I was not coming, thinking there would be more treasure for him."

Baier could hear the German resettle himself in the back. When he glanced in the mirror, Baier saw his namesake leaning on the door, his gaze turned to the passing countryside. "Fuck the Russian, anyway," the German said. "Horst can dispose of him as he chooses." Those words came out with more force and clarity than any he had spoken the entire day.

"Harsh words for someone who worked with you throughout the war," Baier said.

A sound something like a grunt but mixed with a spate of coughing erupted from the backseat. "I can assure you, Chernov worked for himself and no one else."

"And you're not worried about your former *Abwehr* friend? The SS traitor?"

"Not really." The German Baier stared off into space.

Baier thought for a moment. "He's already dead, isn't he?"

His German namesake did not speak for a full minute. It was as though he found it difficult to let the words escape. "Yes." In the end it was all he would say.

In the mirror Baier could see Sabine staring at the back of her husband's head. "What about the British?" she asked.

"I'm sure we'll find Thompkins waiting for us when we return to the Palacio," Baier answered. He let a slight chuckle escape. "I wouldn't be surprised if he's waiting for us in our room."

"What will we do?" Sabine pressed. "The man is far more dangerous than Chernov."

Baier nodded. "Yes, I know. But I think I can take care of him."

In the end, the return trip took twice as long. The only route to Estoril that Baier knew took them back through Lisbon. And just as he had expected, Thompkins was waiting for them at their room in the Palacio.

"Hail the conquering hero, ol' boy." Thompkins lifted the drink in his right hand in a salute to Baier as he walked through the door. Thompkins was wearing civilian clothes, a light gabardine suit and light-blue shirt, but no tie. Either the Iberian atmosphere or the gin had loosened the colonel further, although Baier noticed that Thompkins kept his suit jacket buttoned. His smile disappeared when he saw the Germans follow Baier into the room. "What the hell are they doing here?"

Baier nodded at them before answering Thompkins's question. "They decided to stay. I guess they want to help build the new Germany. I'm taking them back with me."

"And what, dear boy, do you plan to tell your superiors about your little adventure here? And what, more importantly, about our agreement?"

"Well, Colonel, I don't recall any agreement. I do remember an offer and a threat of some sort, but ones that I chose to ignore."

"Oh, really?"

"Yes. As for my superiors, they'll be very happy with the information I'll bring with me on specific German industrialists and scientists we've discovered using Lisbon for their escape route. One, in fact, was engaged in the development and production of Zyklon-B. It seems communication between our people in Lisbon and Berlin has not been as close as it should have been. Bureaucracies can be difficult things to manage." Baier paused, not to gather his thoughts but only for the dramatic effect. "They'll also be very happy when our destroyer intercepts the trawler with the gold."

"What?" Baier's German namesake shouted. "A destroyer? From where?" He moved further into the room and stopped just behind Baier.

Baier turned to the German. "That's right. I set it up during my visit to the Embassy and a follow-up meeting in the bar here. We've been shadowed our entire trip, and a trailing car passed us as we turned onto the path leading to the beach. With any luck, the Embassy and Navy have been alerted and are looking for the boat now."

"And if they don't find it?" Sabine asked.

Baier shrugged. "Fortunes of war, I guess. But, with your co-operation, of course, I will have done all that I could."

"Just a damn minute," Thompkins barked. "That's Britain's gold. That's my gold." He rose from the settee, a pistol in his hand.

"No, Colonel, it's Greece's money. And they'll get the bulk of it back, thanks to the United States."

"The bulk of it?" Thompkins stammered. "Does that mean what I hope it means?"

"I'm afraid not, Colonel. Naturally, some of it has been lost in transit, and there were, unfortunately, bribes paid along the way during its transportation. But records being what they are, and with the turmoil of the war's final months, it's difficult to determine just how much was taken." Baier nodded at the gun. "Is that really necessary? I thought we were all on the same side now."

Thompkins took a step forward. "You know damn well why it's necessary." He waved the pistol at the Germans. "If you think I'm going to let my share of that loot just slip away because she's been a good fuck for you on those lonely nights in Berlin, you've got another thing coming." The gun swerved and centered on the German Baier. "That one won't be missed. There's not much left anyway."

The first shot caught Thompkins in his midsection, the second one punctured his chest. A look of surprise spread across his face as he dropped his own gun and groped at the growing patches of red on his shirt. His head shot up, pain and curiosity in his eyes. "You bloody Krauts," he murmured. "What have you done?"

His knees buckled, and Thompkins collapsed on the floor. Baier was too shocked to move at first. Then he pivoted toward the sound of the shots and saw Sabine Baier holding the Luger that Horst Kohler had brandished when Baier first met him at the safehouse in Berlin.

It was moments before he could catch his breath. When he became aware of his own heartbeat it was pounding inside his chest like a kettledrum. "Why, Sabine? What have you done?"

The Luger fell to the floor, and her hands opened to Baier as though she was pleading for forgiveness and understanding. "I had to do it, Karl. He would have ruined us. He would have ruined everything."

Baier couldn't be sure if she was speaking to him or her husband. Nor was he sure if it really mattered at this point, whether she could even distinguish between the two of them right now. He stepped carefully over to Thompkins and felt for a pulse. Cloudy, tearful eyes looked back at him, then Thompkins shuddered and fell into spasms that convulsed his entire body. The pulse disappeared.

Baier rose and turned to Sabine. "Where did you get that?" He pointed to the pistol.

"I took it from your suitcase this morning. I've been hiding it in my purse." She swallowed. "I didn't know what to expect. I wanted some protection."

Silence covered the room like a shroud. It was the German Baier who spoke first.

"I know a police captain and a doctor who will take care of this for us. The doctor will certify the death however and for whatever time we want." Baier looked up to see the German standing over him. He was wearing his first smile of the day. "I suggest we blame it on Chernov. The Russian killed him to make good his escape before he fled to Sotubal." He paused to let the story complete itself in his head. "There's also the matter of Meyer's body." He motioned towards Thompkins. "The body should be in his room."

"Meyer's body?" the American Baier asked.

The German nodded. "That's correct. That was a form of

insurance in case we needed to keep the Englishman occupied." He thought for a moment. "Yes, we'll blame both Meyer and Chernov. There was shoot-out, and only the Russian escaped. That will preserve the reputation of this man and give you Americans another prize if they catch the trawler. No one will want to ask many questions then."

Baier looked back at Thompkins and thought of Perkins. He remembered first that awful night under the tree by the park, then his first day in Berlin and the drive to his house on *Im Dol* from the airport at Tempelhof. Then the image of the *Trummerfrauen* returned, working quietly and steadily to disassemble the ruins so the city could be rebuilt. They had been the constant in all this, the reassurance that something sane and safe would re-emerge eventually. It was time to step back, to put a period to this whole affair. "Yes, let's blame this on Chernov and Meyer," he whispered. "We'll give them the Russian and the SS man." Baier looked up at his namesake. "Make your calls, Karl. Then we'll leave for Germany."

Sabine Baier kicked the Luger aside as she stumbled to the door, then out into the hallway. Her husband limped over to the telephone and dialed. Baier walked into the hallway and called after Sabine. She hesitated, turned, then walked back to Baier. She stopped at his front, her eyes focused on his chest. "I'm sorry, Karl. I couldn't think of another way. I'm so confused right now." She sighed as she looked into his eyes. "I don't even care about the money anymore."

Baier placed his hands on her shoulders. "I think I understand. I wish you hadn't, Sabine. The man did not deserve to die. But I think I understand what's happened to you here and over the last few months."

She looked into his eyes. Baier saw the tears pooling. "Do you really, Karl? Do you understand how everything has changed in just a day? That I no longer comprehend where I

243

belong and where I'll go."

"Yes, Sabine, I do. Or as much as I can. So much has happened to us, both of us, I mean, in the last few months. I'm unsure about a great deal myself. But in the end, we'll need to do something to make this right when we get back to Berlin. The money, the deaths, and now Thompkins. We have a lot to think and talk about. All of us."

Sabine Baier turned away and started for the hotel room. "I'll pack what little we have." She brushed Baier's hand, letting it linger there for a moment. "When we get back perhaps I'll join the *Trummerfrauen* for a bit."

Baier gripped her fingers, then let her hand fall. "Yes, that would be a good thing to do."

They walked together back to the room to wait for the police and the doctor.

EPILOGUE

Sitting in his office in the Berlin Operations Base, known affectionately or not as BOB, in *Foehrenweg* in Dahlem, Baier could hear the steady drone of airplane propellers overhead. He assumed they were American, as did most in Berlin, part of the massive airlift that had been shipping life's essentials to the people of this city for about eleven months now, ever since the Soviets had imposed their blockade on the western sectors of Berlin back in May of the previous year. But Moscow had miscalculated. Not only were the Western Allies holding firm in their part of the city, but the currency reform in the west, which the Soviets alleged had forced them to act against the Allied presence in Berlin, had taken hold and was beginning to revive economic life in those parts of Germany administered by the three Western powers. There was even movement toward a new constitution to establish a West German state, to be named the Federal Republic. The Americans and British had already been administering their respective zones together for months now, and Baier smiled at the thought of how much closer the two nations had become in their efforts to put this country on its economic feet again, establish a democratic government, and face the challenges posed by the Soviet Union against realizing those goals.

The smile evaporated when he wondered what Colonel Thompkins would have thought of this, if his disappointment with Britain's wartime policies in Greece and the emerging

245

American pre-eminence would have persisted. Baier found himself thinking of Thompkins often, as events in Greece played out through the civil war that Thompkins had been among the first to foresee, at least to Baier's knowledge. He had had no surviving family, never having married, and his parents had died in the Blitz. Thompkins had been decorated posthumously for his work in Germany and the events in Lisbon after Baier had passed his story to the British command. Thompkins probably would not have been pleased that Washington had to step in down in Greece as well and assume the leading role for the West, as London's precarious financial situation forced it to retrench in the eastern Mediterranean and elsewhere. Still, they did have Cyprus. Perhaps Thompkins would have enjoyed a posting there.

Baier glanced from his desk to the windows that overlooked the deep gray, flagstone courtyard just past the back door and then out across the border of tall green shrubbery that marked the edge of the property. The sun dropped lower in the sky, reminding Baier that his day was nearly done and that he would find a dinner guest at home tonight. Shadows cast by the stand of oaks in the yard that housed his agency's office pranced across the lawn, pushed by a stiff wind from the east in rings of confusion, like dancers lost on a stage. He was thankful that he had only blocks to walk to reach his home on *Im Dol,* just the other side of *Koenigin Louise Strasse,* a route he could walk in his sleep by now.

Dick Savage was in Berlin on one of his frequent visits to the city. As the deputy chief of the State Department's European bureau, he often complained to Baier that he had little time for matters other than Germany, or even Berlin. Baier knew the complaints were not all that serious, not in view of Savage's longstanding involvement in German affairs and their shared experiences in this city. He had told Savage on numerous occa-

246

sions that he should have joined Baier at the Central Intelligence Agency when it had been created two years ago; he would have found many opportunities to apply his professional skills in corners of the globe where no German was spoken.

"Too many Ivy Leaguers and Catholics in your organization," Savage had claimed. "I keep wondering when you guys will go to war with each other."

"But at least half of us would have appreciated those fine tailored suits you prefer," Baier had responded.

"Yeah, but which half?"

"You would have figured it out. Eventually."

Savage claimed that he always enjoyed the chance to eat one of Sabine's home-cooked meals, especially the liver dumplings and smoked pork. That's what he was getting this evening, along with a heaping portion of red cabbage, or *Rotkohl.*

As he walked home Baier recalled Savage's lack of surprise when Baier had told him that he was marrying Sabine Baier. They had waited for a decent interval after her husband Karl's death that first winter after the war, his body weakened by his extensive wartime injuries. Baier had done what he could to provide additional nutrition and medical care, but it had not been enough. His namesake had appreciated the effort, however, promising Baier an ever increasing share of his treasure hoard, still hidden safely away in the Alps for all Baier knew. More important in his eyes had been the gratitude and new affection he had won from Sabine for trying to help her husband in his final months. If anything, that had solidified and strengthened their emotional bond, even after all they had gone through in those first months after Baier's arrival.

And Baier knew he had Sabine to thank for his professional success in Berlin. Her old smuggling network had provided the foundation for an asset stable in the eastern zone that had grown over the last year, inspired even more by the heavy-handed and clumsy efforts by the Soviets to force the Western allies out of Berlin and consolidate Moscow's control over their sector of Germany. He had practically had to turn assets away after the forced merger of the KPD and SPD in the Soviet zone and the undermining of the local Christian Democratic opposition. In fact, his biggest problem, he already knew, would be keeping enough of those people in place once the economy in the western areas took off. But for now he was able to pass General Clay and the policymakers in Washington a steady stream of information on the economic travails and popular mood in the east, as well as Soviet military planning. Or lack thereof, which was more often the case.

He smiled inwardly once more at the memory of how quickly he and Sabine had forgotten about the treasure hunt that had brought them together. She had indeed worked as one of the "rubble women" until her husband's death, a sort of penance and cleansing experience for her. She claimed she had even enjoyed the work, as it helped her regain some of the innocence lost during the years living under the Nazis and in the immediate postwar period.

There had been no word of what became of Horst Kohler and the treasure he had snuck out of Europe. The US destroyer had found no trace of them in the Atlantic, and Kohler might now be resting at the bottom of that ocean, for all Baier knew. More likely, he was living the life of a Latin entrepreneur. Chernov had definitely made it to South America, where he had disappeared after a gunfight while resisting his arrest for the murder of Thompkins. All the while he had shouted that this was nothing more than an NKVD revenge attack for his years of espionage on behalf of the Germans and subsequent escape. Justice, in a way, had been only partially served, since he had failed to find his family. One rumor had placed him in Turkey, and Baier hoped he was depressed and despondent. And broke.

Baier found Sabine waiting for him at the door of their *Im Dol* residence, the same one in which she had lived with another Karl Baier, now a distant part of both their pasts. Or so Baier hoped. She wore a white apron smudged with red and brown spots over her bright green dress. Her hair was pulled back in a bun, a style she said she preferred when she cooked. Tonight, though, her cheeks were fused with a red glow, and her hazel eyes sparkled with light and excitement.

"Karl, I have wonderful news." She threw her arms around his neck and kissed him full on the lips.

"It certainly sounds like it." Baier squeezed her as he slid his arms around her waist, savoring the feel of her body against his, much as he did the first night she had appeared to him in this house. "Does this call for champagne at dinner tonight?"

"Yes, but let's wait until after, when we're alone. I want you to hear it first, when there's just the two of us."

"Sure," Baier replied. "If that's what you prefer."

She squeezed his fingers almost enough to hurt. He let her lead him by the hand to the kitchen to finish the dinner preparations before Dick Savage arrived. "I wonder what news she has now," Baier mused. Treasure can take many forms, he reminded himself, and he did not want anything to disturb the idyll he had found in this corner of Berlin, a city that had brought so much turmoil to the lives of so many.

ABOUT THE AUTHOR

Bill Rapp began his professional life as an academic, earning his BA from the University of Notre Dame, his MA from the University of Toronto, and his PhD in European History from Vanderbilt University. After teaching for a year at Iowa State University, Bill left for Washington, D.C., and has spent the last three decades as a foreign affairs analyst for the US government. In addition to *Tears of Innocence,* he has another novel set in Berlin during the fall of the Berlin Wall, which he experienced personally while working at the US Mission in West Berlin. He also has a three-part private detective series set in his hometown outside Chicago. Bill currently lives with his wife, two daughters, and two schnauzers in northern Virginia.